RUNEMAKER

ALEX R. KAHLER

RUNEMAKER

ink
yard
press

ISBN-13: 978-1-335-46226-8

Runemaker

InkyardPress.com

Printed in U.S.A.

for those who wish to write a better future

"If we are to wait
for the gods to answer
we will die with our hands
cupped to our ears.
We must act.
We must speak as gods.
We must make Creation kneel."

—Elizabeth's Diary
(no date found)

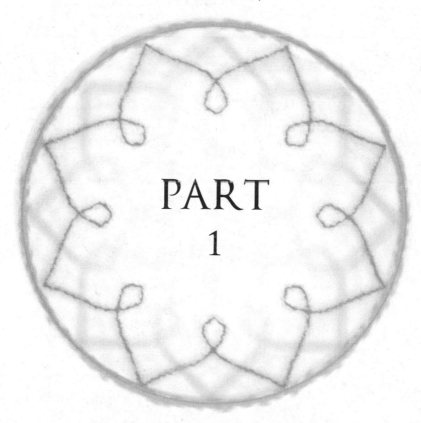

PART
1

THE HEARTS OF MEN

CHAPTER ONE

TENN THOUGHT HE KNEW HELL.

He'd seen cities ravaged—men and women and children torn apart or devoured alive while their homes burned around them. He had watched his friends die because of his own mistakes. But as he stood surrounded by the flaming ruins of some unknown city, listening to the manic laughter of the guy he had traveled so far to find, he knew those visions had only been precursors. This was the start of something different. Something worse.

It wasn't just the breadth of destruction that chilled him. Everything was smoke and charred buildings and melted glass, the sky itself a roiling mass of red clouds as if it, too, had been burned in the attack. No—sheer destruction was something he was used to.

It was the smell.

It settled deep within his nostrils, seeped through his blood. A great deal of magic had been channeled to level the city. More magic than even he had used, or—as the case had often been—had used *him*. But this wasn't the same power. This felt tainted. Stained. This magic smelled like decay.

It reminded him of how the necromancer Matthias's magic had felt: otherworldly in its power, a shadow to Tenn's light. The same elements as those he himself harnessed, but pulled from a different place. A darker place. One stained with blood and grave dust.

And somehow, this boy, this naked, tattooed, laughing boy, was the one who had wielded it. He couldn't have been much older than Tenn. Maybe nineteen or twenty, tops. And somehow, he had leveled what might have ben the largest city in Britain.

The spirits had said that the guy before him would help Tenn end the Dark Lady. So why was he wielding a power that seemed to be pulled right from her breast?

Tenn knelt at the boy's side. He wanted to blush, to look away, but his gaze was snared. He'd seen his face in the visions, in the dreams that had followed, but he was more real, more beautiful, than Tenn had ever let himself imagine. He was naked as day, seemingly every inch of his dark skin covered in tattoos and wounds, and his body was as carved as the incubus Tomás's. His sleek abs, his chiseled arms, the sharp planes of his hips and fuzzy abdomen… Tenn coughed and looked back to the guy's face, to the slight scruff, the pierced lip, the sharp eyebrows and Fire-flecked eyes.

He was beautiful in a way that even Tomás and Jarrett could never emulate. Wild. Ferocious. Perhaps it was a gift of Fire— a physique to rouse passion in anyone looking. At least, that's what Tenn tried to convince himself, what with Jarrett standing only a foot away.

The guy was stunning.

He was also clearly unhinged.

Tenn had already tried asking him who he was, where they were, what had happened here. Every time, he'd gotten a similar response—a laugh, a curse, a shiver. Every time, Tenn doubted the wisdom of the spirits more. They had told him to come here, to find his "other half," and had given him the tools to do it. So why did it seem like everything had gone off course?

Tenn's only certainty was that this was most definitely the one he was meant to find, and not because of the magic that had leveled the landscape, and not just because Water seemed to quiver in the guy's presence, agitated like tides pulled toward another moon.

He knew, because no matter how hard he tried, he couldn't heal the boy with Earth.

Blood smeared his flesh. Blood and hundreds of wounds that made no sense for the scene—small serrations, bruises, brands, abrasions. Burns across his palm. The first digits of his pinkie and ring finger freshly snipped off. As if he had been tortured. Not as if he'd just fought a huge battle.

Tenn's eyes shifted to the boy's Hunter's mark, the tattoo that bonded him to the Spheres, all concentric circles and runes. Another brand—larger and fresh, a crooked pink cross—raised a welt over the tattoo, nearly obscuring it.

For some reason, the brand made Tenn's gut clench and Water tremble in fear. He couldn't stare at it for long.

Even though it repulsed him, he placed his hands gently over the mark, trying not to squirm when the boy groaned, his eyes fluttering without seeing. This was clearly the cause of whatever kept Tenn's magic at bay. Maybe, if he tried healing *this*...

Tenn opened to the Sphere of Earth, that magical, heavy energy center deep within his pelvis, and spread that power up through his arms, into his fingertips. Into the boy.

And felt nothing.

Normally, there was a snap. A connection as power met flesh, as purpose met need. As wounds closed and bones mended and flesh smoothed.

But this...this was something he'd never experienced before. He could *sense* the boy's body under his fingertips. Could sense the wounds with blinding, burning clarity—the boy was in *so. Much. Pain.* But no matter how much Tenn pressed, no matter how firmly he willed his magic into the wounds, his powers skirted over and around the boy's cuts like fog on ice.

The boy was here. The boy was *here.*

Yet he was even farther away than when Tenn had been in America.

"What happened to you?" Tenn whispered.

"We need to get out of here," Jarrett said. He knelt down at Tenn's side, examining the boy with a strange look in his eyes. Jealousy? Fear? Tenn couldn't place it. All he knew was, in the days leading up to this journey, Jarrett had grown distant. Moody. A trait Tenn knew all too well. "If this was a battle, we don't want to be here when whoever did this returns."

Tenn's thoughts were slow.

"I don't think this was a battle." Tenn looked at his lover. "I think he was the one who did this."

"Him?" Dreya said. She was perfectly poised even now, on the other side of the world, on a battlefield that was not a battlefield, by a savior who was not a savior. The Sphere of Air burned pale blue in her throat, keeping the smoke and embers away and—judging by the slight furrow of her eyebrows—scanning the surrounding area. Her twin brother, Devon, stood at her side, dark and unreadable as ever, his chin tilted back as though admiring the fire-rimmed sky.

"That is impossible," she continued. "The destruction spreads for miles. No one could do that, not even—"

"Not even you." The boy coughed. Giggled. "I'm more powerful than you, Tenn. Just like she promised."

Instantly, the group quieted, focusing back on the boy. Tenn's heart leaped—the boy's voice lilted with the hint of a Scottish accent, but there was something familiar in it. Something almost comforting.

"You know my name," Tenn whispered.

"I know everything about you." His eyes rolled around, unfocused. "Everything. I know you're here to kill me."

"We're not," Tenn said. Gods, this felt like putting a puzzle together face-side down. He knew what this was supposed to look like, this meeting of the *chosen ones*, and yet no matter what he tried, he couldn't make the pieces fit. Doubt seethed in his stomach, roiling with Water's own depression. "We're here to help you." *Somehow.*

The boy laughed even louder.

At least, he started laughing. Then his laughter broke into a sob. For a brief moment, Tenn thought the guy was going to have a breakdown. Then he clenched his teeth and hissed in a breath.

"You can't help me. No one can." He closed his eyes and was lost once more.

Jarrett sighed.

"We aren't getting anywhere. Come on. We need to get him somewhere safe."

"How?" Tenn asked, snippier than he meant. He wasn't angry at Jarrett—he was angry at *this*.

This didn't feel right. Not at all. A strange magic hung thick in the air and this nameless guy was barely coherent and *this was not how everything was supposed to go.*

Then Water simmered in the back of his mind—of course this wasn't how it was supposed to go. Since when had anything in his life gone *right*?

"The runes—" Jarrett began, but Tenn cut him off.

"They don't work like that. Only someone channeling magic through them gets transported."

The runes that had allowed them to travel might have been more powerful than the world had seen—potentially ever— but that didn't mean they were perfect. In order to use the runes he'd learned for travel, the traveler had to be attuned to Earth or Air. Judging from the destruction around them, Tenn doubted the boy was anything but a Fire mage.

"So we get him to snap out of it."

"What do you think I'm trying to do?" Tenn bit.

It was Devon who saved them from further discussion.

He stalked over to the boy's other side and knelt down. Stared at the chuckling boy with narrowed, pale blue eyes, his expression serious behind the folds of his burgundy scarf. Then, without preamble, he reached across the boy's body and grabbed the wounded Hunter's mark. Hard.

Instantly, the boy's laughter broke into a scream.

"Devon, what the—" Tenn said, but Devon's eyes cut him off. As did the naked boy's words.

"Stop! Stop!"

Devon released the boy's arm and rocked back on his heels.

"Who are you?" he asked, words muffled by his ever-present burgundy scarf. "And where are we?"

"I'm Aidan, you arsehole!" the boy yelled. "And this is London. *Was* London." He giggled again. "Was, *was*…"

"Fixed him," Devon said. He stood and walked back over to his twin sister, who watched it all with absolutely no expression on her pale face. "Somewhat."

"What do you mean, London?" Tenn asked.

Aidan. The boy's name is Aidan. The name rolled through his thoughts, somehow right. Even if everything else seemed so wrong. Tenn looked around at the desolate landscape. This place was nothing like the London he'd imagined. Where was the Thames? The Eye? Parliament? Everything around them was flat and glassy, smoking and charred. "Did you…did you do this?"

Aidan nodded. The smile on his face, streaked with blood, was positively demonic.

"And I'll burn the whole world down if I have to," he whispered. "Just you to try to—"

But whatever he was about to say was lost to the violent shudder that tore through his body, his teeth clamping so tight Tenn could hear the snap of bone. Aidan convulsed on the ground, grunting hard in the back of his throat, and his whole back arched up in a rictus.

Tenn reached for Aidan, tried to pulse more power through

him. But once more, he couldn't. The power didn't connect.
The boy continued to spasm under Tenn's grip.

"Tenn, do something," Jarrett said. His voice was uneasy.
Jarrett was rarely uneasy—Air allowed for nothing less than
certainty. The only certainty was this: if this boy had leveled
the largest city in Britain, he would have no trouble taking
out a few measly Hunters.

"I'm trying!" Tenn said. "I can't heal him!"

"And you won't."

The voice cut through Tenn's thoughts. At the same moment, the twins and Jarrett snapped to attention. Jarrett drew
his sword, and the twins pulled deep through their Spheres—
Fire flickered around Devon's fists, and Air swirled Dreya's
hair into a halo.

But when Tenn looked to the voice, he didn't see a necromancer or Howl. He didn't see Tomás.

Instead, the woman walking toward them was no older than
himself. Black skin slicked with steaming water. Waterlogged
dreadlocks tinted magenta. Torn pink T-shirt and ragged black
jeans, enormous boots. A broken steel pipe held in one hand.

She stepped up to Aidan's side as though there weren't three
Hunters ready to tear her apart. She looked only at him, and
her face—chiseled from war and bloodshed—was soft.

Tenn looked to his comrades. He hadn't felt her approaching, even though Earth should have alerted him to footfalls
on the soil. Judging from the expression on Dreya's face, she
hadn't felt the woman approaching either.

The only other person Tenn knew who could move like
that was Tomás.

Was she one of the Kin?

"Who are you?" He didn't move from Aidan's side.

She didn't answer at first. Just stared at Aidan. Reached out. Hovered a hand over his forehead.

"What have they done to you, wee man?" she asked.

She pressed down on Aidan's skin. Miraculously, he relaxed immediately. He shuddered again, and kept shivering, as though he were freezing even as sweat dripped down Tenn's skin. She slid off her coat and draped it over Aidan's naked body. It didn't help his shivers, but it was more than Tenn or anyone else had ventured to do. Tenn felt like shit for not doing more.

"I'm Kianna," the stranger said, not looking away from Aidan. Her words were soft, British. "And who the hell are you?"

"He's Tenn," Aidan replied. "He's here to—"

Kianna didn't wait for him to finish. She slid her hands under Aidan and picked him up, standing in one smooth motion. As though she were just picking up a doll. The movement silenced Aidan, save for a hiss of pain. She held Aidan close to her chest, one arm behind his back and the other under his knees. His head lolled against her shoulder.

"What are you doing?" Tenn asked, standing. It was only then that he realized Kianna towered above him. And he'd always considered himself tall.

"Already told you." She turned and started walking away. "Your magic can't help him. So I'm taking him somewhere safe. He needs to rest."

"You're not...you're not taking him anywhere." Tenn's voice shook. Being *demanding* was never his forte. *So why was Jarrett not stepping in and taking command like normal?*

Kianna looked over her shoulder. The glance she cast was positively condescending.

"Oh? Who's stopping me?"

Tenn looked back to the others. Devon shrugged.

"You can't," Tenn said. Tried to firm his words. "We traveled from America to find him. We need...we need..." But he couldn't finish his sentence. Because he had no idea why they needed Aidan. No clue what this broken boy could possibly do for them. But he knew he had to find out. He knew everything depended on it.

Clearly, the desperation in his voice worked. She didn't stop walking away. But she did call out again.

"You can follow if you want," she said. "But I'm taking him out of this hellhole. And if you get in the way, I promise I will kill you."

CHAPTER TWO

THERE WASN'T MUCH TO DELIBERATE.

It didn't matter if Kianna was a Kin or a necromancer or a friend. It didn't matter that she had somehow not only managed to survive, but walk through the destruction without being noticed by any of them. It only mattered that she had Aidan, and she was moving, and Aidan actually seemed calmer in her arms.

Even if he did keep giggling.

Tenn and the others jogged to keep up with her. Dreya kept a constant swirl of Air around them, blowing away the heavy smoke, casting aside the worst of the embers, cooling the molten ground before it could burn through the soles of their boots. If she or Devon minded the soot that blackened their white clothing, they didn't mention it. They walked through the destruction like wraiths. Otherworldly. But then, they were otherworldly all the time.

Jarrett kept pace at Tenn's side, his fingers light on the sword at his waist and Air a flurry in his throat. Tenn wanted to reach out, to take his hand. He wanted to, but something felt off, something he couldn't put his finger on, and after the last few weeks of recovering and rebuilding a future together, the fissure was as unexpected as it was cutting.

Tenn's true focus was the woman walking at his side, stepping over debris and melted pools of glass as though this were a stroll through the park. The only sign of stress was the tightness in her eyes. A knowing. Or, if not a knowing, a concern of what might have been.

"What happened here?" Tenn asked.

Her eyes flicked to him.

Something told him they were never going to be friends.

"You'll have to ask this one," she said.

She gave Aidan a little lift. His head rolled to the side, his eyes closed.

"They're everywhere," Aidan muttered. "She's everywhere."

"Good luck with that," Kianna said. She didn't speak for a moment. When she did, she looked to Tenn—it was about the most attention she'd paid him since she arrived. "How do I know you don't have something to do with this?"

Tenn's heart flipped over. Wondering what she'd seen. And overlaying it with another scene—him, kneeling over Leanna, his hand crushing her throat as Tomás laughed beside him and the world sparked and howled.

Kianna laughed.

"I'm kidding," she said. Looked forward again. "You're too moody for reckless destruction. This has Aidan's name written all over it."

But does it?

Tenn looked around at the ruined expanse of London, a

sick knot growing in his gut. Not just because this wasn't how he'd expected this to go. But because, in truth, he hadn't come here to find Aidan.

He'd come here hunting Tomás.

Ever since he'd burned the tracking runes onto Tomás's heart, he'd been keeping loose tabs on the Kin. Tenn had felt Tomás getting farther and farther away. And then stopping.

For nearly a week, Tenn had felt Tomás out here, barely moving. Tenn knew in his gut that Tomás had found Aidan. Tenn had wanted to leave immediately. But he had stayed. At Jarrett's urging. At the insistence that they all needed to rest. That America's forces needed to be rallied. Back in the Guild in Outer Chicago, back in the safety of his shared room with Jarrett, back in the arms of his lover while the rest of the world burned. Jarrett had said they were needed in Outer Chicago to keep peace and mop up the rest of the necromancers that would be vying for control after the Kin Leanna's death. Instead, Tenn had barely left the compound, had barely been needed.

Now Tenn wondered if that waiting had caused all of this, wondered how many had died because he had chosen comfort and himself over duty.

The Sphere of Water surged in his gut, dredging up his darkest shadows.

If you had been faster. If you had been stronger...

London had been a Guild, once. A Hunter-controlled haven for civilians to hide away from the monstrous hordes. The last vestige of civilization.

Now, even the bones of those who once lived here were glass.

This is your fault, too. He didn't need to know exactly how many people had died in this city. He could feel their deaths hanging above him. Specters. Thick and cloying as the smoke that curled outside their shield's edge, the world beyond a hell he couldn't place.

Something had happened here. Something involving a great deal of Fire magic. Had Aidan and Tomás fought? Was Tomás...

Tenn brought the tracking runes to mind. And there, distantly, miles away, he could feel the Howl's heartbeat. Still alive, then.

Tenn wouldn't be so lucky.

Although a small part of him was relieved that Tomás *was* alive. If only so he could be the one to kill the incubus that had toyed with him for far too long.

At least, that's what he tried to convince himself.

A deeper, darker voice wasn't entirely convinced that Tenn didn't enjoy being toyed with.

"Where are we going?" Jarrett asked. His words snapped Tenn from his thoughts. Which was definitely for the best. He didn't need to be thinking about Tomás and his lascivious nature now.

"Not sure," Kianna replied. She looked to the flames around them. "Away from here. Unless you happen to enjoy inhaling the smoke of the dead?"

Tenn looked at Jarrett, saw the telltale crease of Jarrett's forehead. Kianna was pushing him too far. And with Air blowing away Jarrett's softer emotions, that was an easy line to cross.

"Why couldn't we sense you?" Jarrett asked. Paused. Air flared brighter in his throat. "Why *can't* I sense you?"

Kianna gave him a wry smile.

"Your magic is flawed." She looked back to where she was going. "Or I'm just good at being sneaky."

Jarrett wasn't having it.

In a heartbeat, with a pulse of Air, he was in front of her, sword out and pointed at her throat. Another step, and she would have impaled herself. But she paused. Stared down the length of the sword and into Jarrett's eyes. Looking as indifferent as possible with a blade bared at her throat.

"Jarrett —" Tenn began.

Kianna took a half step forward. Pressed her throat to the tip of the blade. In her arms, Aidan was blissfully unaware—passed out, the sword inches away from his own face.

"I heard once that the samurai only drew their blades if they were prepared to draw blood," Kianna said calmly. "And yet, I don't think you're going to hurt me. I don't see it in your eyes."

"You'd be surprised."

Kianna smiled.

"It would be the last thing you did, wanker. I only injure to kill."

"So do I," Jarrett replied. He leaned in, seemed more than ready to slice open her throat.

"Jarrett!" Tenn yelped. He jumped over. Placed his hand on Jarrett's arm. His lover's muscles were taut and unyielding, and Tenn didn't try to force his hand. Not when there was a chance it would make things worse. "That's enough. We're on the same side."

Jarrett looked over at Tenn, and that glare made Tenn's skin grow cold. Tenn knew Air users could become emotionless, knew Air could sweep aside anything beyond thought and action. But up until now, that was a side Jarrett had never shown. His pale eyes were cold.

"Are we?" he asked.

But he didn't press it. He stepped back, lowered his sword. He didn't sheathe it.

"This is ridiculous." He looked to Tenn, Air still a pale fire in his throat. "We never should have come here. This is what we get for following your damn 'spirits.'"

The words stung. So did the tears that tried to poke their way up, blurring Tenn's vision.

"If you are going to be angry," Dreya said, stepping up beside them, "at least do something useful with it. Fighting amongst ourselves will lead nowhere."

Jarrett turned his glare to her. Tenn expected him to soften. He didn't. What the hell was going on with him?

"Fine," Jarrett said. "If we're stuck here, I'm going to find a Guild. No use walking around blindly."

Before any of them could agree or argue, Air swirled bright in Jarrett's throat and wind billowed his black trench coat out like a raven's wings. He was airborne before Tenn could open his mouth, shooting up to the horizon like a star. Tenn wanted to call out.

Though what he was going to say—*be safe? come back?*—was beyond him. All he knew was that this was *not* how this was supposed to go.

"You two together?" Kianna asked when Jarrett had disappeared from view.

Tenn swallowed hard. *Are we?* He nodded.

She chuckled.

"Lucky you. He's a real treat."

She kept walking.

Tenn didn't try talking to her again.

CHAPTER THREE

THEY WALKED IN SILENCE FOR WHAT FELT LIKE HOURS.

It might have only been minutes. Maybe days. It was impossible to tell, with the sky roiling red and angry above them and everything around them smoking and engulfed in flame. It didn't help that Tenn was surrounded by people who refused to talk. Normally, he hated chitchat, but right now he would have killed for a little bit of banter. Anything to lighten the mood that lay heavy across them. Anything to distract him from the questions that raced through his brain. The uncertainty. The fear.

Jarrett didn't return.

Dreya, Devon and Kianna said nothing. And Aidan just slept in Kianna's arms, giggling to himself occasionally.

It wasn't just the silence that grated on Tenn's nerves, though—it was the fact that everything looked exactly the same. Time didn't seem to pass and neither did the landscape. Tenn had imagined that eventually, the destruction would have to give way. That the intensity of the blast would lessen farther from the source, and they would find something left of London—a flat, a fish and chips shop, an Underground entrance. *Anything* to show that this place had once been a thriving metropolis.

But the city had been leveled as if by a knife, everything sharp and hot. Tenn could feel the rain above, coalescing in the burning clouds. He felt the rain, and he almost reached out to it, almost brought it down to cool the angry earth, to douse the flames and bring this all to an end.

He also knew that playing with weather rarely yielded the results you wanted. With his luck, the ensuing steam would choke them out, or a flash flood would threaten to wipe them away. But maybe just a light drizzle. To feel like he was doing something, at the very least.

Right now, with no mission or clue what they were doing or what was happening, he felt absolutely useless. He couldn't even ask anyone and expect to get a real answer.

There was nothing to do in the silence but think. They needed to reach a Guild. Needed to heal Aidan. Because Tenn knew destruction such as this wouldn't go unnoticed. The entire *world* had turned upside down since he killed Leanna. America, without its ruling undead matriarch, had been thrown into chaos. Necromancers had declared an all-out war. Not just against the humans they'd normally stalked, but against each other. Tenn wondered if something similar had happened here. Maybe, once he got Aidan safe, he could go back and try to do another journey or whatever it was with the Witches. Try to figure out *why* exactly he'd been sent to find Aidan.

Aidan was the key.

The trouble was, Tenn had no clue what that key was for. Right now, judging from the pure expanse of destruction Aidan had caused, Tenn doubted it was a door he wanted to open, anyway.

What if you weren't sent to save him? a voice whispered. *What if you were sent to prevent this? And you failed. What if it's up to you to keep this from happening again?* He looked over to Aidan nestled in Kianna's arms. Killing him was the last thing he wanted to do. He needed to save Aidan, whatever the cost. They couldn't risk losing a power like his.

Then, after what felt like days of walking through hell, they reached the end.

It came as a shock. Their shield pressed through fog, and suddenly the fog billowed against brick. A large, long brick building that pushed three stories through the heat, its facade burning red and orange. Still smoking. Still hot.

Dreya pressed through her powers and the shield expanded, heavy smoke billowing to the sides like a drawn curtain. Rows upon rows of houses solidified through the smoke, all of them smoldering, arched windows shattered and wooden doors flecked red with embers.

The destruction cut off like a knife.

All of it, like a knife. As if the fire had spread, and then been sucked back.

Tenn had never seen power like this.

Even with the heat rising around them, a shudder crept through his body.

Everything about this felt wrong, and every time he thought that, his eyes snared on Aidan.

How could he have channeled so much power without burning up? Even at the height of Tenn's unintentional magic, he'd not been able to level a city the size of London. He'd done the impossible by bringing Jarrett back from the brink of death, yes, and he'd channeled more Water than anyone before him. But so much of that had been outside of his control. Or through the runes.

The gods speak to you through Water. So what gods spoke to Aidan through all of this Fire?

Tenn glanced at Aidan's tattoos. They crossed all over his body, from knuckles to ankles. Some of them were designs—swirls and faces, even a sexy merman on his pec—and others appeared to be runes or sigils. How much was decorative, and how much had a more esoteric meaning? Had the boy learned how to read runes himself? Were these markings special, for strength or extra magic? Who had taught him?

Once more, he glanced at the brand covering Aidan's Hunter's mark. The symbol burned in Tenn's mind, sucking his thoughts in like a black hole. It was more than a brand. More than a welt. More than a symbol. It didn't speak to him, not like the runes of the Witches. Instead, it was a great silence in his mind. In that emptiness, there was no magic, no light, no hope. And that void scared Tenn more than the eyes of the Dark Lady herself.

The runes were the language of the gods, divine and pure.

This brand, he knew, was of human making, and there was nothing sacred or pure in its intention.

Kianna coughed, and Tenn realized he'd been staring at Aidan's scantily covered body for far too long. He blushed and looked away, his thoughts sloshing with questions. Chief amongst them, guilty though he felt for not focusing on the crisis at hand, he wondered where Jarrett was, and why he was acting this way. They kept walking.

The night deepened—Tenn had left Outer Chicago in the early afternoon, and the sudden darkness was disconcerting, especially without hours of travel to get here—and the cold crept in. With every step, Aidan's shivers got worse.

"We need to stop soon," Kianna eventually said. She glanced down to Aidan, her face scrunching in concern. "He's about to freeze to death."

Tenn placed his hand on Aidan's brow, considered taking off his coat to help. After attuning to Water, the wet cold never bothered him—it felt like home. Tenn hissed the moment their skin touched.

One, from the shock of energy that pulsed between them. And two...

"He's burning up," Tenn muttered.

"Really?" Kianna said. "I hadn't noticed." She sighed. Heavily. "He's cold-blooded. And after what they did to him..."

"Who did what to him?"

This was the most talkative Kianna had been since they met. He wasn't about to pass it up.

"The Church," she said. She cast him a dark look. "Whatever this is—" she nodded at his forearm "—cuts him off from Fire. And the boy is addicted to it during the best of times. At least they got what was coming to them." She paused, then muttered, "Too fast, if you ask me."

"The Church?" Dreya asked. She stepped closer to the two of them, her pale eyes troubled. "The Church did *that*?"

Kianna looked at her. Nodded.

"They've gone militant. Captured us a few days ago. Tortured us. We'd come down here after an envoy of ours went missing. They'd overtaken London's Guild in the wake of Calum's death."

"Who's Calum?" Tenn asked.

Kianna glared daggers at him. Clearly, she didn't like being interrupted.

"Americans. Still so up their own arses that they don't know what's happening in the bigger world. Calum was the Kin who ruled Scotland. Until this one killed him."

She looked down to Aidan.

"For all intents and purposes, *he's* the king, now." Her eyes grew soft. Almost sad. "Long may he reign."

Dreya scouted out a flat that was mostly intact, and they made their way up to the second floor. Even with Dreya and Devon clearing out the dust with Air, the place still smelled musty as hell, and Tenn tried not to notice the dead roaches and rats that were swept out with the debris. Still, it was relatively dry, and the moment Devon opened to Fire and created a glimmering ball of flame in the middle of the room, tendrils of fire smoothly licking up like water falling in reverse, it was even a little warm.

Kianna laid Aidan by the fire and wrapped him in moth-eaten blankets. Devon nudged the fire closer to the boy until sweat broke out over Aidan's skin.

He didn't stop shivering.

"Do you know what's wrong with him?" Kianna asked.

Tenn shook his head.

"I've never seen anything like it," he whispered. "Magic

doesn't affect him. It doesn't even touch him. I don't know what's wrong, let alone how to heal it."

Kianna bit her lip and watched Aidan's restless sleep. Dreya settled down beside her as Devon spread out their scant meal—bread and cheese and a few carrots—but it sat untouched.

Tenn's gut twisted in knots. Eating was the last thing he wanted.

He wished the spirits would have given him more of a clue on what to do next. He wished the Witches were around so he could speak to the spirits again.

He wished he could convince himself the spirits were real, and actually knew what they were doing.

So many wishes, and not one of them changed a damn thing.

"I don't think it's the brand," Kianna finally said, her words a low rumble in the silence.

"Oh?" Dreya asked. She reached over and trailed a finger over the wound on Aidan's arm; Tenn expected Kianna to break Dreya's hand, but she just watched Dreya's ghostly fingertips as they outlined the jagged cross on Aidan's mark.

"No. The Church gave him that. Gave it to everyone who used magic. But Aidan wasn't like this after. They tried breaking him, but he stayed strong. No. Something happened to him after he went back in."

"What do you mean?" Dreya asked. "He went back in?"

Kianna nodded. "I got him out. Him and this dude Lukas who cut and run the moment we were out of the Guild. But Aidan said there was something he had to do. I know him. I knew he wouldn't leave without doing whatever it was. I just figured he wanted to kill Brother Jeremiah for doing all this to him. I kept running. And then…bang."

"But how did you survive?" Dreya asked. Her eyes hadn't left Kianna for the entirety of her story.

"I jumped in the Thames when I heard the explosion," Kianna said. "When you spend your days around a Fire mage, you learn to keep water close at hand." She paused, gently running her fingers through Aidan's short hair. "And I had this."

With her free hand, she pulled a thin gold chain out from under her shirt. On it was a medallion of the same symbol branded on Aidan's mark.

"Where did you get that?" Tenn asked.

"Nabbed it from one of the guards after snapping his neck," she said. "Had a feeling it would come in handy."

Dreya reached out and gingerly took the pendant.

"It is cold," she whispered. Her voice was distant.

Tenn had a feeling that if he'd tried touching the pendant, he'd be missing a hand. Instead, Kianna just looked at Dreya a little warily, firelight dancing in her dark eyes. The Sphere of Fire opened in Dreya's chest.

"I cannot melt it," Dreya said, her eyes transfixed on the amulet. "Like the brand, it is immune to magic."

"I assume it's how they took the Guild over," Kianna said. "They must all wear that symbol. Makes them immune to magic. Just as it makes those branded with it unable to use it."

Dreya let the pendant fall back to Kianna's chest.

"So that is how the Septs remain safe," Dreya said. "If all members of the Church carry this ward, necromancers would be unable to attack them. Magic would have no effect."

Great, Tenn thought. *More enemies to deal with.* If the necromancers *and* the Church had declared all-out war, they needed to find answers on how to end it all. Fast.

Devon shrugged. "Doesn't explain the Howls staying clear."

"It also doesn't matter right now," Kianna replied. "You three say you came here to find him. What for? What's the plan? The wee man used so much magic they'll have felt it clear over in Berlin. And now that we have *two* Hunters with the blood of the Kin on their hands, the rest of them won't be content to just sit around and wait for you to knock at their doors. I say we have a day, tops, before every surviving Kin is stalking your bedsides."

An image of Tomás wearing nothing but jeans and a smile, perched at the foot of Tenn's bed, crossed his mind, but it burned out in the truth of her words. He'd relied on the element of surprise when hunting Leanna. That was a luxury he could no longer afford.

"We don't have a plan," Tenn admitted. He had a feeling lying to Kianna would be the last thing he ever did. "We just knew we had to find you. We hoped…" He swallowed. "I hoped that maybe you two would know how to end this."

As if on cue, Aidan started giggling.

CHAPTER FOUR

"AREN'T YOU WORRIED ABOUT YOUR LOVER-BOY FINDING HIS way back to you?" Kianna asked.

It was late. The twins had gone to a bedroom to pass out, while Tenn and Kianna stayed in the living room, propped against a sofa and staring at the flames. Aidan half slept, half ranted between them.

Tenn's heart flipped at the phrase. *Lover-boy.* Once, it would have made him feel amazing. Now, he just wondered if it was still true. *Where the hell is he?*

He shook his head and drew back his sleeve, revealing the darkened pigment of the tracking rune he'd seared with Earth onto his wrist, just above the arcs and runes of his Hunter's mark. He could have sworn he saw Aidan's eyes open, just briefly, and flicker to the runes.

"What is it?" Kianna asked.

"A rune. Lets us find each other, wherever we are."

"Convenient."

Silence stretched between them.

"Why don't you like me?" Tenn finally asked.

"I don't like anyone. Least of all other Hunters."

"You like *him*." He nodded to Aidan.

"He's different."

"How?"

Kianna didn't say anything, just stared at Aidan with an unreadable expression in her eyes.

"He isn't like the rest of the Hunters I've met. He doesn't do this because he's trying to save anyone or create a better future. No, he isn't delusional like that. He fights because he burns. Because he knows the truth of this new world."

Tenn felt something lodge in his gut. *I'm trying to create a better future.*

"What is this truth?" he asked.

Kianna looked him dead in the eyes.

"It's not going to get better," she said. "Point-blank. No matter how many kravens we kill, no matter how many necromancers we destroy, there will always be evil in men's hearts. Often parading as righteousness. And now that you lot have magic, that evil will always have a way to destroy more effectively than ever before. You can blot out the Dark Lady, but a new god will come and take her place. You can't kill evil, Tenn. The best you can do is enjoy the little things in life until you hit an early grave."

Tenn swallowed hard. In a matter of seconds, she'd confirmed every fear he'd been holding inside of him since the Resurrection. She also destroyed the shred of hope he'd been holding—that they would find Aidan, and together, they would save the world. Somehow.

He had to convince himself that she was wrong. The world

could be saved. There *was* good. The Dark Lady *could* be destroyed, and once her mark was cleansed from the world, they could return to something better. Otherwise, why had he been sent here? What was the point?

Kianna chuckled.

"I know that look," she said. "You think I'm full of shite. Or rather, you *want* to believe I am. But let me tell you, love. I've seen the hatred and vileness of humanity even before the Resurrection. No matter how much magic you have or how many pretty little runes you've scratched into your skin, you can't change the world. Not really. All you can do is prolong humanity's time on it. And if you ask me, our time ran out years ago."

"Why are you fighting, then?"

She shrugged and looked back down to Aidan.

"At first, because I wanted to survive. But this one taught me the finer things in life. The joys of bloodshed, or a good victory shag. There are things worth killing for. Not many, but a few. And frankly, I enjoy the killing as much as I do the reward."

"That's—"

"Sick? Twisted? I've heard it all, Tenn, if that really is your name. And frankly, I don't give a fuck if you care about my reasoning. All I care about is getting this one healed up so we can do what we do best—kill."

He could sense it then, the slightest waver in her voice. A hitch in her resolve.

"You're scared for him," Tenn whispered. "You're worried that he isn't going to make it."

Her eyes narrowed, and whatever companionship or banter they'd created was snuffed out like a light.

"The only thing that scares me is becoming a twat like you," she said flatly. And then, without another word, she lay down at Aidan's side and closed her eyes.

Tenn couldn't sleep.

He didn't *want* to sleep. Everything seemed to be going wrong—Jarrett was mad and gone, the twins were unhelpful, Kianna hated him again, and Aidan… Aidan was still a mystery, but the more Tenn learned about him, the less he expected the mystery to yield something good.

He had to believe he'd been sent here for a reason. That he was supposed to somehow help, because that was what he *did*. He'd fixed the runes that would have turned Jarrett into a Howl and brought him back to life. He could fix this. He could fix everything—*had* to fix everything. He had to believe that was why he'd come here. Otherwise, what else was left?

After a few minutes of staring at Devon's magical flames— was the guy staying awake, or had he somehow managed to learn how to channel magic even while asleep?—he pushed himself up to standing and slid into his coat and boots. He wasn't going to pass out. Not anytime soon. Water churned in his gut, begging for him to tap in. Begging for him to sink in the misery of defeat. It whispered to him, oceanic and end-less: *You have failed. You will never succeed.* And even darker, in the shadow of the waves, was a voice he didn't want to place. Feminine. Eternal. *Succumb to me. Give in. There is nothing left to fight for.*

He knew that voice too well; he wasn't about to listen to it now.

So, his clothes still wet, he left the flat and opened to Earth, rooting himself down through the concrete and sandstone, the map of the flats opening in his mind like a blueprint. He followed it down, through the darkness, down the concrete steps and out into the sodden night beyond. He didn't know where he was going, just that he couldn't stay inside. He needed to move. To feel like he was doing something. Even as Water churned inside him, trying to drag him under, he fought to keep his head above the tide.

He made it a block. Rain pattering around him. The Guild and half of London glowing to his left. He made it a block, and then he couldn't fight anymore.

He dropped to his knees. Fire burned in the back of his throat, behind his eyes, even as water seeped through his clothes.

And as he let himself weep for all the pain and confusion, the Sphere of Water pulled him down with icy fingers.

"What do you think it will look like?" Tenn asks.

He lays curled against Jarrett's chest, tracing the planes of his lover's collarbone with a finger. The night is heavy and dark, and although the room is cold as ice, sweat trickles down their skin, slick and sweet.

"What do I think what will look like?" Jarrett asks, his words slurred. Tenn can already feel Jarrett's breathing slow and deepen as sleep claims him.

"Our future," Tenn says.

It's the conversation he always circles back to. The light that ever guides him forward.

Jarrett doesn't answer, not at first, and Tenn wonders if perhaps he's fallen asleep. Then Jarrett shifts and faces Tenn, their foreheads touching.

"I don't know what the future will look like," Jarrett admits. "But I do know what I want it to look like. A house somewhere in the country. A big backyard and garden. We'll grow our own food, and with your magic our garden will be like an edible jungle. We'll get you attuned to Air, and together we'll fly all over the world, and everything will be a new discovery. Every inch of the Earth has changed, and we will see it. Together."

Then he leans in and kisses Tenn on the lips.

"But if you do not hurry," came a voice from beyond the vision, "there will be no futures left."

Tenn jolted. Tears still streamed down from his eyes, mixing with the rain, and his heart pounded in his head. He clutched for his staff, but it was back in the flat. So he opened through Earth and Water and tried to peer through the gloom, to see who spoke in the burnt-umber twilight.

No one stirred in the rain. No one came forward.

Except for a fox.

Silver-white and glittering in the distant embers, it perched on a nearby car and watched him. Silently. Stoically. Its pale eyes seemed more human than not.

Dreya's voice filtered through his thoughts. A conversation from days or weeks ago. How foxes were the eyes of the Violet Sage, the elusive woman who'd learned how to channel all four Spheres at once. She was watching him.

How long had she been watching? And did she approve of what she saw?

"Was that...was that you?" Tenn whispered. With no one around to make fun of him for speaking to an animal, the potential that it might speak back felt even more likely. He'd believe anything was possible anymore.

The fox bowed its head.

"What do you mean, there won't be any futures left?" Tenn asked. The more he talked, the more ridiculous he felt. This should have been impossible. But it was rumored that the Violet Sage also guarded the keys to attuning to Maya. Perhaps, for her, anything was possible.

If that's the case, he thought, *why isn't she doing anything to help?*

"*He teeters on the brink. Either he will serve life, or he will serve death. Only you can help sway his hand.*"

Tenn swallowed.

"But how?"

"*Help him. Make him trust you.*"

Easier said than done. The guy already thought Tenn was here to kill him.

"He hates me."

"*He fears you. Just as your lover fears what you might become.*"

Then its gaze darted to the sky. It stared up into the roiling, red-stained storm for a moment, then leaped from the car and vanished into the night.

Tenn's nerves tightened. And when he felt the prick of Air magic in the distance, rocketing straight toward him, he didn't know if he felt relief over Jarrett's return, or a different sort of fear.

"There's a Guild a few miles east of here," Jarrett said. "Farther down the river."

No *hello*, no apology. Just him arriving in a whirl of wind and rain, his blue eyes searing into Tenn the moment he landed.

"Okay. Good."

Tenn's mind reeled. Here was the man he'd made love to only hours before, and now it felt like Jarrett was someone else entirely. "I guess, um… I guess we can go tell the others."

What he wanted to say was *why are you acting like this?* but those were the only words he could force out.

"No. Not yet. Not until we know what we're doing with him."

Tenn took a step back.

"What do you mean, *doing with him?*"

"We can't trust him, Tenn. Either of them. Don't you see? They did *that.*" He gestured to the burning horizon.

"But he's the one we were sent to find."

"But *why?*" Jarrett asked. The question Tenn had whispered to himself countless times. "He's clearly unhinged, Tenn. He's clearly *dangerous.* Not just to us or himself, but to the rest of the world. Who knows if what happened here was the extent of his power or the tip of the iceberg?"

"You think I can't see the danger?"

"I think you don't care," Jarrett said. His eyes narrowed. "I think you enjoy it. He's wounded. You know he'll hurt you. And for some sick, twisted reason, that makes you want him."

Want him?

"What the hell are you talking about?" Tenn asked. He was used to dealing with his own sadness, with loss, with depression. He couldn't remember the last time someone had pissed him off.

"You know exactly what I'm talking about," Jarrett said. "The problem is, you're too naive to care."

"But the spirits—"

"To hell with the spirits, Tenn!" Jarrett roared. Air billowed around him, spraying Tenn with biting rain. "How do you know the spirits are on our side? How do you know they're even *real*? Do you have any clue how many people have driven themselves to death because they thought they heard God? How many people died thinking they were protected, that because they were doing God's work they couldn't be harmed? I'm not going to be one of those people. I'm not going to be another nameless zealot killed way before his time."

"The spirits are the only reason you're alive," Tenn growled.

"No. The reason I'm alive is you. Because *you* read the runes and *you* changed them. No spirits. No divine intervention. Just you and magic."

There wasn't the slightest hint of softness in Jarrett's voice. Every previous time Jarrett had mentioned what had happened in Leanna's chamber, it had been with gratitude, with disbelief. Now, he sounded upset that Tenn had saved his life. Would he feel this way if he knew Tenn had been speaking with the Violet Sage? Or would he take that as another clue that Tenn had lost his mind.

Jarrett took a step closer.

Tenn took a step back.

"If the spirits or gods were real, why won't they tell you how to end this? Why send you to the ends of the earth to meet a guy with no wits and a shit-ton of dangerous magic? What if it's because they don't know? Or they're not real? Or because they aren't actually on your side? Why do you always assume the good in people, when everything in life shows you the opposite?"

Tenn couldn't keep his thoughts together. He could barely keep up with Jarrett's barrage.

He also couldn't imagine anyone ever saying that he always assumed the best in people.

"Look at the facts, Tenn. We were sent to the middle of an inferno to meet a boy who could burn down the world. We have no clue what we're supposed to do and clearly neither does he. Meanwhile, there are real people fighting and dying in America. Real people we could really be saving."

"If you want to go back so much, why don't you just leave?"

The muscles in Jarrett's jaw corded out. For a moment, Tenn thought he would call his bluff.

"Because you can't be trusted around broken birds," Jarrett finally said. "And too much rests on your shoulders."

"I'm not leaving him." He tried to make his voice steady. Tried, and like so many other things in his life, failed in doing so.

Jarrett swallowed. Looked away. Tenn figured that was the end of the conversation, but Jarrett's next words stilled his heart.

"How did you get me out?"

"What?"

Jarrett didn't look at him. His jaw was set and his eyes fixed on something far away. Something he definitely didn't like.

"From Leanna's compound. How did you get me out?"

Tenn's thoughts short-circuited. *He* hadn't gotten Jarrett out. Tomás had.

It was the one thing he hadn't been able to explain to anyone—the twins or Jarrett. It felt like treason. It *was* treason. Admitting that he had not only been helped by, but had helped in return, one of the Kin… There was no way he could admit that. Especially not when Jarrett was like this.

Thankfully, there hadn't been much talk about that night since it happened. Too much time spent recovering or planning or defending. Too much time focused on everything but Tenn's betrayal.

Tenn looked to his feet. He could feel Jarrett's eyes boring into him.

"Secrets will be the death of us," Jarrett said.

Tomás's words flickered through Tenn's mind—*Jarrett still hasn't admitted why he was sent to find you. Convenient...*

"Then you first," Tenn said. He didn't know where the resolve came from, but he was tired of being shit on. He'd sacrificed everything to save Jarrett. Had done what no one else could. And yes, he'd worked with the enemy, but he hadn't given anything to Tomás, hadn't promised any help. He'd killed a Kin and saved his partner—what did the rest matter? "Why did you come find me? I know it wasn't to protect me. So why?"

He didn't expect Jarrett to answer. He looked back to his partner and saw the waver in Jarrett's eyes, the brief flick of uncertainty.

"There's a war going on, Tenn," he finally said. He raised his arms to the sides, taking in the expanse of London, the burn on the horizon. "And there are two sides. Those of the living, and those of the undead. The Prophets told us you had power. Great power. And I was personally sent to find you and ensure that you would use it for the right side. They knew we had a history before even I did. They knew I could bring you to our side and use that power to fight the Dark Lady."

Tenn felt the unspoken words hanging in the air between them. A guillotine.

He had to hear them. *Had* to know once and for all if Jarrett coming back into his life had been romantic destiny or something...darker.

"Or else—"

"Or else I was to do to you exactly what I will do to the boy if he goes bad. The same thing I once thought you would do." Jarrett's eyes were hard once more. "Eliminate the threat."

CHAPTER FIVE

"DID I KILL THEM?"

Aidan's voice echoed through the emptiness, giddy despite the encroaching dark. He knew he wasn't alone. He could feel it in the hottest recesses of his smoldering heart.

"You did," Tomás responded.

And just like that, they stood together, a cathedral arching up around them, Gothic and imposing, stained glass flickering across the tiles from the burning hellfire outside.

Faintly, he could hear the screams.

If anything, it made him smile wider.

Tomás was his usual stunning self, even in the blur of the dream. Light caressed his olive skin, kissing the ripples of his stomach, the lines of his chest, hiding in the folds of his sheer button-down shirt and tight black jeans. He stared at Aidan, but not with the hunger of before. Not with the purpose. No, Tomás's head cocked to the side, tousled hair brushing his shoulder, and he studied Aidan in a way that made him feel less sexy and more scrutinized.

Aidan's smile dropped.

"What?" he asked.

"Can't you remember?"

He reached out, took Aidan's hands gently in his, turning them over and over, examining the crossing lines of his Hunter's mark, the dark glint of his tattooed flesh.

"Remember?"

"My dear prince," Tomás said. "You're dying."

Windows shattered around them. Fire roared into the cathedral, eating at the rafters and raining ash and molten glass to the bone-layered floor, but Aidan couldn't feel it. He was falling, suffocating in a cold void that swallowed every spark within him.

He looked down to his arms. To the welts and burns and bruises of torture that pockmarked his skin. To the two missing fingers on his left hand. To the pink, angry welt that cursed his Hunter's mark.

The moment he saw that, the world around him roared back into blistering focus.

Brother Jeremiah's torture chamber, the bastard kneeling before him, garden sheers in one hand and Aidan's bloody digit on the floor as he readied himself for the next snip. Jeremiah, holding out the shard of crystal the Dark Lady had used to bring Calum back from the dead, the crystal he'd been sent to London to find. Kianna, bound to the chair, bruised but not broken as Jeremiah tried to levy the two against each other. Kianna, rescuing Aidan from the cell. Aidan, running back in.

And then.

The crystal in Aidan's hand. Burning and melting as

Calum's stolen power flooded him. As Jeremiah admitted working for the Dark Lady.

As Jeremiah screamed.

As everyone screamed.

Including Aidan.

Including Aidan.

Aidan's screams cut through the roar and the fire, sound and fury bursting off in a tidal wave, until they were back, back in the blackened cathedral, and Aidan cowered on the ground before Tomás, his bloodied hand clutched to his cold and powerless heart.

"What…what happened?"

"You failed me," Tomás said. His words were as cold as the ice inside Aidan's chest. "You lost the stone. You lost Her words. And now you are dying for your folly. I can't imagine you have much time left, my prince."

Aidan swallowed. Tried to find a semblance of pride. Of heat. He couldn't.

"I thought I was your king," he said, looking up at the Kin.

"Apparently we both thought incorrectly," Tomas replied. "You are broken. And I have no use for broken things."

He shook his head sadly. Then his face changed, pity turning to rage.

With a snarl like a wolf, he kicked Aidan in the chest.

Aidan woke with a scream as pain exploded through his ribs. Pain, and a cold worse than anything he'd ever known.

A hand pressed down on his forehead in an instant. He fought it off. Tried to fight it off. He couldn't move. Couldn't even lift an arm.

"Shh," came Kianna's voice. Soothing, for the first time in her life. "Hush, wee man. You're okay. You're okay."

But even through the haze of agony, he knew she was lying.

Another twist of pain in his chest; he turned his head to the side and coughed, blood splattering across the moldy white carpet.

White carpet.

Flickering.

He turned his head to the other side. To the ball of white and pale blue flame that billowed up like a waterfall. Magic. Someone was using magic. But he couldn't feel it. His chest constricted at the sight, at the need.

Who…?

Apparently, he'd spoken the word.

"We have company," Kianna said bitterly. "And you're drool-ing."

Aidan blinked. Tried to focus his vision past the flame to the shapes lumped on the other side. A few duffel bags. A plate of bread and cheese.

A boy with dark hair and sunken eyes, wearing the black trench coat of a Hunter.

Aidan jolted back. Or tried to. It was more of a spasm that amounted to nothing. Distantly, he knew Kianna would say that was the story of his sex life, but the humor was lost to him.

He knew the face from his dreams.

Tenn.

The one who had been sent to kill him. The one who had already killed one of the Kin.

The one who wanted to steal Aidan's immortality.

"What…is he doing here?"

He could barely speak. Not through the pain and blood in his throat, not through the cold that lanced through his chest. Even though he was so close to the fire it should burn him, even though he was pooled in sweat, he'd never been colder in his life.

Pain shot through him again, a punch to the chest, and he seized into himself, trying to curl into a ball. And failing miserably.

"He's here to save the world," Kianna said. Barely audible through his pain. "And apparently to find you."

"To...to kill me."

"Doubtful," she replied. "Seems like he wants to help. Fat lot of good it's done you."

Help.

Tenn couldn't help him. No one could help him. Tenn wanted to kill him. To keep him from gaining power.

Kianna reached over, placed a tentative hand on his shoulder.

"How you feeling, Aidan?" She actually sounded like she meant it, like she was concerned, and that—even more than the pain, even more than the cold that burned where the Sphere of Fire should be—told him he was screwed.

Like oil, his dream spilled through his consciousness, sticky and black.

Tomás's disdain. Tomás's curse.

"I'm dying," Aidan whispered.

He couldn't help it. The moment the words left his lips, he started to cry.

Tears dripped from his eyes like the blood he'd shed. He was dying. He was dying.

Faintly, he remembered the power he'd wielded. Remembered burning through Jeremiah like tissue paper, remembered burning through London like a spark in the brush.

He remembered the power, and with that memory came another twist of pain, making him shake and cry even harder.

He'd leveled London. Channeled all the power Calum's Sphere had held, and it had burned through him like a wildfire, searing through his insides and leaving him a shell of ash and ice.

"We're all dying," Kianna said. "The lucky ones are already dead."

He hated that he heard the waver in her voice. Hated that he could feel her fear. Not *of* him, but *for* him. It wasn't a switch he was okay with.

"You don't understand—"

"I know that you leveled most of London. I may not use magic, but I know that's enough to make anyone feel like shit. I also know you spent the last few days getting tortured, which probably doesn't help any. You need to rest, Aidan. You'll be fighting again soon."

"I can't—"

"You're awake."

The words made Aidan's chest even colder.

He stared past the fire, to the boy who should have been sleeping on the other side.

Their eyes met, and despite everything, Aidan felt it.

An ember, sparked.

CHAPTER SIX

SPARKS FLARED IN TENN'S CHEST THE MOMENT THEIR EYES MET. He'd heard the two of them talking. He'd tried to fall back asleep. But something kept him close to consciousness. An awareness of the boy's presence.

A need.

And with Jarrett sleeping in the other room, that need was not something Tenn had anticipated.

He watched the way Aidan's lips moved, the way light glinted off his piercing. Watched the sweat bead and drip on his forehead. He even kept quiet when Aidan started to sob, shaking in the blankets as if in the depths of a snowstorm.

The Sphere of Water echoed Aidan's pain, churning in Tenn's gut with an agony he couldn't quite place. Loss. But something even deeper than that.

Like holding food in your hands while starving, but being too close to death to eat.

The pain twisted through Tenn's veins, but he forced it down. He'd had years to learn how to handle Water's dangerous undercurrent. Or, try to handle. He wanted nothing more than to walk over and soothe Aidan. To open to Earth and heal the cuts, the brands. To make him better. The fact that he couldn't do any of those things made the need stronger.

You can't be trusted around broken birds.

Jarrett's words stilled any movement, cut Tenn off at the ankles.

So he stayed there, eyes half-shut, trying not to eavesdrop while Kianna soothed her friend and Aidan fell apart only a few feet away.

It was its own unique agony.

When he realized they were talking about him, however, he couldn't keep up the charade.

"You're awake," he said, as if it was the first thing he wanted to say to the boy he'd spent the last two weeks waiting to find.

Aidan jolted, his eyes going wide—a rabbit staring down a gun's barrel—before narrowing with anger. No, not anger—something darker. A long-standing hatred. The kind born of fear. The Violet Sage was right. Aidan was scared of him.

How was the boy already terrified of him, when they had only just met?

The moment the thought crossed his mind, another, more sinister image arose: Tomás. Had the incubus been poisoning Aidan's mind, turning Aidan against him? What hope did Tenn have of convincing Aidan to trust him? Tomás was far more persuasive than Tenn could ever be.

Aidan didn't speak for the longest time. He stared across the flames, and for the briefest moment, with the flicker of fire across his face, he looked monstrous. Sharp eyes, a cold sneer, as bitter as any bloodling. *He will serve life, or he will serve death.* Then the light shifted, and Aidan looked himself again.

Water lurched in Tenn's stomach: the pain in Aidan was nearly tangible, and it ached within Tenn like a bruise.

Tenn pushed himself up to sitting. Slowly. Like he was trying to calm a cornered cat.

"I'm Tenn."

"I know," Aidan replied. Again, the narrowing of the eyes. The timbre in his voice that expected the worst.

There were a thousand questions Tenn wanted to ask in that moment, but for some reason he couldn't speak. None of them seemed right. Especially not with Aidan like this.

"Are you feeling okay?" he asked instead.

Aidan grunted. "The fuck does it look like?"

Despite the bravado in his voice, Aidan shuddered and squeezed his eyes tight. Took a deep, shaking breath. It sounded like a wheeze.

"Why are you here?" Aidan asked.

"To find you."

"Why?"

"I don't know."

The truth of the words hung heavy in the air. Jarrett's warning from earlier ran through Tenn's mind, along with that of the Violet Sage. He was supposed to help Aidan. But if he didn't work fast, Aidan would become his enemy. Either that, or he could do what Jarrett wanted and kill the boy while he was down.

Tenn would much rather try to save him. He *had* to. Murder wasn't in his nature. Trouble was, that still didn't answer why Aidan was important. Just as Tenn didn't know why *he* was important to all of this.

Aidan broke the silence with an angry chuckle.

"Great," he muttered. "Just great."

He rolled over, his back to Tenn.

"At least get me another blanket," he said. "I'm bloody well freezing."

CHAPTER SEVEN

AIDAN AWOKE SHIVERING.

The fire still burned before him and Kianna still sat guard at his side, but even their combined heat wasn't enough to curb the chill in his bones. He'd barely slept, and whatever dreams he'd had were nightmarish at best. Thankfully, he couldn't remember a single one.

He couldn't remember much anymore. All he knew was the room was empty save for the two of them and the sky outside was dark and dripping. His thoughts were finally congealing enough to make sense. A sort of sense, at least.

"How you feeling?" Kianna asked.

"Like my insides are a freezer," Aidan muttered. He curled in tighter to himself, inched closer to the heat. He couldn't feel it. "Can't you make it any warmer in here?"

"It's already an oven, love."

He looked at her, then—really looked—and saw that she was in a T-shirt and jeans. Fresh bandages covered her arms, hiding whatever scars the Inquisition had left her with. Memories sparked in his brain.

Jeremiah.

The Dark Lady.

The shard. The shard.

"He was working for Her," Aidan whispered.

"Hmm?"

"Brother Jeremiah. He was working for the Dark Lady."

"I knew I hated organized religion for a reason." She paused. "What happened in there, Aidan?"

Aidan closed his eyes. Not out of shame, but from the wave of pain that ricocheted through his body, the shuddering cold.

He told her.

He kept out the incriminating details. Told her he'd gone back in for vengeance, and not for a shard both the Dark Lady and one of the Kin demanded he retrieve for them. He told her Brother Jeremiah had kept it, had said it held great power, that it was the stone used to drain Calum and turn him into an incubus. Aidan said he stole it, used it to kill Jeremiah and level London.

He didn't tell her the shard spoke to him. Didn't tell her he'd read the runes in the Dark Lady's tongue. He didn't tell her he wasn't certain which side he was on anymore—the living, or the undead. He knew she would kill him for any of those things.

After being so close to death, he found he quite liked being alive, even if it sucked.

Frankly, he was impressed that he was able to string a sentence together, let alone lie through his teeth. His remaining teeth.

The thought made him look down to his hand, to the nubs

of his ring and pinkie fingers. The wounds had been cauterized. Was that his doing, or Jeremiah's? Jeremiah had left the knuckle tattoos. How generous.

"Where are they?" he asked.

Kianna shrugged. "Still sleeping."

"And Tenn?"

Another shrug. "Left a few minutes ago. I try not to ask. The less they think I'm a friend, the less drama I have to put up with. I heard them talking, though. There's a Guild nearby. They want us to go. Think maybe it will help you."

Aidan laughed.

"They can't."

"I know. But it's the only shot we have."

The way she said it—it was a hammer to the final nail in his coffin. If *she* thought he was hopeless, he was.

"What *is* wrong with you?" she asked.

Aidan shook his head. "I don't know. I channeled Calum's power. And I think it burned me up. I'm dying."

"You keep on saying that and I'm going to force you to wear heavy eyeliner and write some poems about it."

He tried to push himself to sitting. He still shook when he was upright, but at least he didn't fall over.

"How did *you* survive?" he asked.

"Takes more than a bit of fireworks to kill me, love. I bolted the moment you went back inside. When the bomb went off, I jumped in the Thames and held my breath until the fire stopped. Probably helped that I had this."

She pulled a gold chain from her neck, revealing an amulet in the shape of the cross branded on Aidan's arm. Aidan hissed an inhale as the welt on his wrist throbbed angrily.

"Why do you have that?"

"Figured it couldn't hurt. Everyone in the Church wore one, and it cut you off from burning the place down, so I did the math—how else were they surviving against necromancers and Hunters if they could be killed with magic? I figured this was the key." She slid the necklace back under her shirt. "Don't think your friend was so lucky."

"Friend?"

"Lukas. Your cell mate. He took off in the other direction the moment you went inside. Doubt he survived the blaze."

Aidan grunted. Lukas was unimportant. Everything but saving himself was unimportant. He shivered. Moved closer to the fire.

"Any closer and you're going to catch," Kianna warned.

"Better that than freeze."

Another shudder broke through him. He just needed to ride this out. Ride this out and he would get better, and everything would go back to normal. Ride this out, and get Tenn out of the way. Before Tenn could kill him. Before he could try to steal Aidan's thunder.

"We can't trust them," Aidan said.

"No shit. A group of Hunters shows up right after you blow up London, saying they're here to help? Please. I don't buy it. Whatever they're doing here, it has nothing to do with helping. Probably spies or something from a Guild, here to see how you did it. We'll shake them soon. After we get you fixed up, we'll sneak out and head to the mainland. Just like we'd planned."

Aidan wasn't about to correct her. Not about to tell her that he'd been dreaming about Tenn for weeks. So long as she viewed them as the enemy, it didn't really matter why.

He nodded, staring into the fire. Even this close to the heat, he couldn't feel a lick of warmth. Not only from the Church's brand, but from the sudden numbness spreading through his veins.

"They're going to come after me." He didn't say whom. It didn't matter. Word would spread. He had killed Calum. He had destroyed London and the Church's hold here. If that didn't paint a target on his back, nothing would. The Kin would want to kill him, and without Tomás's help or Fire's strength, he didn't stand a chance. It wasn't the thought of dying that scared him—it was the thought that Tenn would kill the Kin instead and steal Aidan's victory. Aidan's immortality. "We're going to be hunted."

"I know. Saves us the hassle."

"I don't have any magic. Not anymore."

He looked down at his arm. At the cauterized wounds, at the throbbing welt. At the runes he couldn't understand. If only they were like the runes on the shard. Maybe then he could change them. Maybe he could *fix* them. He could almost hear the Dark Lady's whispers, the language that would alter the runes, the way to make them whole. Almost, but not quite within his grasp...

"I won't kick you while you're down," Kianna said, pulling him from his thoughts. "But if I was the type, this would be the perfect time to say *I told you so.*"

"I hate you."

She smiled.

"Good. There's hope for you yet."

CHAPTER EIGHT

TENN HADN'T SLEPT, AND HE DIDN'T FEEL LIKE LYING AROUND waiting for the rest to wake. So he'd left. And wandered. Up and down the abandoned streets, the rain now a faint mist around him, the sky gray and tinged with pink from the rising sun and burning Guild. He kept his eyes open for the fox, though now he wasn't so certain it wasn't just a figment of his imagination.

He never saw a trace of it.

Years ago, way before the Resurrection, he'd dreamed of visiting the UK. Doing all the touristy things in London like riding the Eye or getting afternoon tea. Now, here he was, and even though the city had been ruined, it still held on to its old-world charm—the long tenement flats stretching along winding roads, the bitter tang of stone and moss, the dreary sky. His gut twisted at the posters still hanging in shop windows, at seeing pound signs and British verbiage. It wasn't just Water resonating with the pain of this place, but the hurt of knowing an entire city—no, an entire *culture*—was lost to him. Forever.

If he'd been fast enough, if he'd come here before the Res-urrection, he might have had a chance to know what this city was like. But this was just another future denied to him. Which made him wonder... Aidan's dialect hinted at Scottish, but he was definitely American. What was he doing here?

Just that thought made a dozen other questions about Aidan's shrouded past whirl through his mind. Maybe, someday, he'd be able to ask. If Aidan ever trusted him.

If they made it out alive.

After a few hours, Tenn couldn't delay the inevitable any longer. It was time to face the team. To look Jarrett in the eye. It was time to move out, before the army moved in.

He turned to go and froze.

Tomás lounged on the hood of a car, one leg bent and the other draped over the grille, elbows propping his torso up. Rain slicked across his olive chest, made his tight jeans cling and his hair twine over his chiseled, scruffy jaw.

Despite the cold and the anger and the fear, the sight of him made Tenn's chest burn.

"What are you doing here? And what have you done to Aidan?"

Tomás grinned.

"And here I thought you were the one following me?"

Tenn blinked, and Tomás was behind him, pressed tight to his back, one hand on Tenn's neck and the other pressed on his chest. "Do you fear the boy has come between us? Or perhaps you wish to be between me and the boy?" He leaned in, his breath hot against Tenn's ear. "I know what lies within that throbbing heart of yours, Tenn. I know you want him, just as you wonder if you should destroy him. Just as you wonder if it is *right* for you to desire, when you already have. Even though that little hungry voice within you tells you to desire *everything.*"

Tenn struggled, but Tomás's grip was tight. He couldn't move even if he wanted to.

And Tomás was right—Tenn didn't want to. There was something about being in Tomás's orbit, in his radiant heat, that he found he'd actually...missed.

What the hell did that make him?

He felt Tomás smile against the back of his neck, as if the Kin knew every secret in Tenn's dark mind.

A moment later, Tomás was once more a few feet in front of him, the barest tinge of Air magic in the ether between them. Tenn struggled not to collapse.

"As for the boy, and what I've done to him..." Tomás shook his head and smiled. "Sadly, I have done not near enough. He is willful. As I'm sure you will find out."

"He's dying. Because of this." Tenn pointed to the smoldering horizon. "Because of *you.*"

"I am honored," Tomás said, bowing deep. "But I am afraid it was all the boy and his own—to quote the British—*cock-up* that brought this devastation about." Tomás's mocking smile turned serious. "Trust me, I had no hand in this. The boy failed me. Unlike you."

"What are you talking about?" Tenn asked. "No riddles. I followed you over here and found him instead."

"I thought he would prove useful. I was wrong."

"But why? You abandoned me. For him."

The moment the words left his mouth, he hated himself. Not because it sounded needy, but because it was true.

He hated that Tomás had left him alone the last few weeks. And he hated himself more for wanting the enemy more than he wanted his own partner.

"He is jealous," Tomás purred. "He thinks I have found another."

"I'm not..."

But Tomás just shook his head, dismissing the lie before it fell from Tenn's lips.

"Don't worry, my prince," he whispered. "I will always have a dark spot in my heart for you."

Tenn wondered if Tomás was alluding to the brand he'd placed on his heart, or some deeper desire. He also knew it was a lie—Howls didn't love. This was all just another incubus ruse, a way to snare his heart and cloud his judgment.

The trouble was, it worked.

"What have you been doing?" Tenn asked, trying to remain on the offensive. "Why did you go after Aidan?"

"I was helping. As I always do. Aidan wanted glory. I told him how to get it. I helped him defeat my brother Calum, just as I directed him to an object of immeasurable power that I demanded in exchange for my assistance. And rather than bring it to me, he used it. He did *that*." A gesture to the horizon, a hint of rage in his otherwise-calm features. "The boy betrayed me, and I do not take kindly to betrayal."

"What was it? What was the object?"

"The shard that completed Calum's turning. Calum was not like the rest of us. We, who were born of living hosts. My mistress prepared Calum's body before his death. And when he died, she used special runes and stones to bring him back to life. To the well-trained eye, the shard I sought contained the secrets to his resurrection."

Tenn swallowed.

He'd heard stories of the Dark Lady's abilities. But he'd always assumed they were just that—stories. To have Tomás confirm the darkest one to be true, that she had learned how to raise the dead...

"Why did you want it?" Tenn asked. "You can't use runes. No Howl can. So why did you need it? Who did you want to bring back?"

"You will find out soon enough. If you live until then."

Another blink, and he was so close, Tenn could see nothing but the copper flecks in the Kin's hazel eyes. Tenn wanted to burn in the incubus's heat, to rip off Tomás's remaining clothes and do to him what he could never do to Jarrett.

"My siblings know the two of you are here. Together. They know what you both have done. They will be here soon. I suggest you leave the boy and flee. Let him burn on his own pyre, or risk dying in his flame."

"How would they know?" Tenn asked, his breath raspy with want. "How would they know I'm here?"

Tomás smiled.

"You've learned, little mouse. They know you are here because I have told them. I cannot pretend to have forgiven you for this." He reached out and caressed Tenn's heart with a burning, frozen finger. "And I look forward to seeing the coming game. It will be glorious."

The way he said the last word made Tenn shiver and swell at the same time.

"Run while you can," Tomás said, his lips brushing Tenn's.

"I would hate for our game to end so early. You have proven you can read the language of the dead gods. Perhaps you will still be useful to us."

"Us?"

Tomás leaned in and pressed his lips to Tenn's. Fire exploded in Tenn's vision. Fire, and a passion he had never felt before. He could see it, in Tomás's kiss—the flames of the world, the crowds of screaming fans knelt in homage, and Tomás's perfect body twined against his. Above it all, with burning red eyes, the shadow of the Dark Lady stretched and devoured.

When Tomás pulled away, Tenn wondered if he would ever feel so warm, so divine, again.

"She still waits," Tomás whispered. "But she will not wait long, my prince. Her voice grows louder, and soon, it will remake the world."

Then, with a breath of magic, Tomás was gone.

CHAPTER NINE

AIDAN NEEDED TO GET THE FUCK OUT OF HERE.

It felt like his bones were itching even as they burned and froze. Kianna sat beside him, idly talking to some pasty girl named Dreya. Vaguely, Aidan wondered if they were going to shag before this mission was through—Kianna only talked to two types of people: him, and the select few she wanted to see naked. It made his gut burn. Not because he was jealous, not because he didn't want her to have her fun, but because he was dying, and no one in this godforsaken room seemed to care.

Not Kianna.

Not Dreya.

Not the silent dark-skinned boy brooding in the corner.

And definitely not the stuck-up blond prick pacing back and forth with his sword unsheathed like he was showing off his goddamned dick.

The door opened, and in stepped Tenn.

"Fucking great," Aidan muttered to himself. Loud enough for the room to hear, sure. But screw them.

Tenn paused in the doorway and looked him over. Aidan watched his expression like a hawk. He knew Tenn's secret. Tenn pretended to be all altruistic and caring but he was a murderer, just like Aidan. Tenn killed Leanna. He'd been shagging Tomás. And maybe that was why Aidan was pissed that Kianna was flirting with a girl and everyone else was content to be about their own business.

He felt abandoned.

And he didn't have any sort of flame to burn that weakness away.

"About time," the blond dude said. Jarrett. Dreya had tried introducing everyone. Blondie was Jarrett and the other dude was her brother, Devon, apparently twins, though how the hell they were related when they were night and day was beyond him. Too much meddling with magic, probably.

Aidan snorted. If only Kianna knew he was blaming someone else for using too much magic.

Tenn looked between Jarrett and Aidan and oh, Aidan knew that look. Tenn and Jarrett were lovers, and they were having a fight. He knew that look because that was the look he and Trevor had shared more often than not. Well, before he burned Trevor to the ground.

His snort became a laugh, and before he knew it he had fallen back on the ground and pain was lancing up his side and he didn't know if he was laughing or crying or if it made a difference in the cold. Everything was so. Damn. Cold.

"Is he okay?" Aidan heard Tenn ask.

"The feck does it look like?" Kianna replied.

Aidan felt her hand on his shoulder. Trying to calm him down. Her grip was like ice. Like crushing ice.

He squeezed his eyes shut and tried to stop falling apart. Tried to take deep breaths because that's what you were supposed to do. Tried to find calm. Instead, in the darkness behind his eyes, in the shadows between the icebergs of his blood, he heard his mother, screaming out for help. Just as another voice promised he still could help her, if only he spoke the right words, if only he gave in...

His eyes snapped open.

Apparently a few moments had passed, because Tenn was now on the opposite side of the room conferring with blondie and the not-twins were huddled together, looking at each other as though they had telepathy. They were probably just unhinged. Kianna stood beside Tenn and blondie, growling something under her breath, and for a brief moment Aidan wondered if they were about to leave him. Then Kianna shook her head, turned back to him, and began gathering the few things she'd managed to scavenge from the flat: a cricket bat, a few kitchen knives, some new clothes.

"What's going on?" He tried to whisper but his voice was too rough.

"We're leaving," Kianna said.

"All of us?" Aidan looked to Tenn, whose head was down. Defeated. That was the look. He glanced at Aidan once, and Aidan felt the same spark as he had the first time their eyes locked. Not passion. Something darker. Something covered in blood.

"There's a Guild east of here," she mumbled, sliding a knife into her boot sheath. "They want to take you there."

"I'm not going anywhere with *him*," he spat, looking straight at Tenn. Hell no. He would rather die than put up with that miserable wretch.

"Oh? Planning on walking somewhere on your own?" Kianna nudged him with her foot. "You're coming with us. Even if I have to knock you out to get you to cooperate."

He knew she'd do it, too.

"Then what?" he asked.

"We get you better."

There was no mistaking it—the way she didn't look at him, the particular tilt to her words. She was lying.

"You don't think I can get better," Aidan said.

"I don't think you were ever right in the first place." She tried to grin and failed. "Once you get healed they want to assemble an army. Try to bring over troops from America. Then we're going to take down the rest of the Kin. All of us."

Aidan held back the words that burned in his throat. He looked at Tenn again, who seemed sad beyond belief. And he looked at Kianna, who still refused to meet his gaze.

They expected him to die. She was already readying herself for it. She was already figuring out what she would do after.

That inner acid turned to fire, the first warmth he'd felt since the Inquisition had branded it out of him. They weren't going to the Guild to save him. They were going to drop him off. To let him die. They were going to abandon him. After everything he'd done for them. Everything he'd sacrificed. They were just going to let him go.

Screw that.

He wasn't about to go gently.

They thought they could just leave him in some sickbed and go off for glory themselves?

He closed his eyes and felt the shadows whispering in the back of his mind. The words he'd spoken to activate the shard. And the ones hidden in the corners, words for powers beyond his wildest dreams.

Runes to make everything right again.

Absently, he pressed his fingers to the brand on his wrist.

The Dark Lady smiled with his lips.

His story wasn't over. Not yet.

CHAPTER TEN

THEY NEARED THE NEW GUILD AROUND SUNSET.

Jarrett had gone on ahead, flying off to alert the Guild of their arrival, leaving the rest of them to trek on in silence. Dreya and Devon kept near the back, by Tenn, while Kianna carried Aidan as easily and resolutely as if he were a bag of laundry.

Tenn couldn't get Jarrett's anger out of his mind, nor could he stop reliving the conversation they'd had.

Jarrett hadn't been sent to save Tenn. They hadn't crossed paths because they were star-crossed lovers. The Prophets had known Jarrett and Tenn were connected, that they'd gone to Silveron together and shared a spark.

The Prophets had used that. Turned it into another weapon.

Jarrett had been sent to ensure Tenn didn't become a threat.

One way, or another.

It made Tenn look back on all their shared encounters, all the nights twined in bed together, and wonder if any of it had been real. Had it just been an act to keep Tenn placated? To ensure he wouldn't fight for the wrong side? It made Tenn's gut twist and Water writhe in despair. Had any of that love been real? Any of it?

And the lengths Tenn had gone to, to save Jarrett. The sacrifices he'd made. The deals with the devil. All to save a boy who may be nothing more than an actor in a play. A boy who would happily see Tenn dead if it meant upholding duty.

The worst part was, he was no different. He was doing to Aidan exactly what Jarrett had done to him. Make him trust. Make him malleable. Convince him to fight for the right side.

It made Tenn sick.

"Do not think on it," Dreya said.

Tenn started. They'd barely spoken since Leanna's compound. The twins had been in all the same meetings as Jarrett had. Technically, they'd been sent under the same orders as Jarrett. But for some reason, even though Dreya had covered up her own bloody past, he didn't think she lied. At least, not about her standing with Tenn.

Dangerous as it was, he felt he could trust her. Somewhat.

"Think about what?" Tenn asked. He knew she could read her brother's mind, but did that extend to others, as well? Maybe it was a gift of Air…

"Jarrett. I know it troubles you. But I do not believe it is your fault."

"Sure as hell seems like it," Tenn muttered.

Dreya sighed. Her eyes flickered toward Kianna.

"Do you remember what happened in that house, the night Jarrett was taken?"

How could he forget? He'd *felt* the memories of the house, had seen a Breathless One burst through the window and kill the family having dinner within. *Places hold memories*, Dreya had said.

"Emotional transference," Tenn replied. "What about it?"

She nodded to Aidan.

"We had told you Water was not the only Sphere that resonated with the hurt of a place. Fire does, as well. And Aidan... whatever he did, he damaged his Sphere greatly. It is like a wound, one that screams in anguish and tugs at the hearts of all who are near it. I think that is why Jarrett has been so angry. He senses Fire's anger, even if he is not attuned. We all feel it. Devon especially. It makes us...sensitive."

Tenn looked to Aidan, as well.

"So you're saying, as long as we're around him and he remains broken, we're all going to be unstable?"

Dreya nodded. "It is only a theory. But I think it makes the most sense."

He didn't tell her his own theory.

Jarrett wasn't here to protect him or Aidan. He was here to ensure neither became threats.

And with the secrets hanging heavy between all of them, the threat was growing stronger by the day.

Admittedly, Tenn had hoped the Guild would look more... European. Or at least something other than tall earthen walls with protruding spikes and a great swath of burnt-down space around it. At least a mile all around the Guild was barren field, a heavy mist roiling over the black burn. Even from here, Tenn could tell the place was smaller than Outer Chicago, or even Outpost 31. Hell, it looked like it was no more than a few city blocks. His heart dropped the moment he saw it.

If this was where they were meant to hold out against the Kin, they didn't have a chance.

Once more, he glanced over to Aidan, the advice of both Tomás and Jarrett ringing in his ears. Maybe they should just leave the boy behind. Let him fend for himself. Especially since the more Tenn was around Aidan, the less he thought the Fire-tainted boy could help anyone.

The gates lowered the moment they neared, a small guard appearing in the entrance. Jarrett was at the lead.

"You made it," he said. He didn't seem happy or disappointed. The aloofness was worse.

Tenn nodded. Truth be told, he wasn't really looking at Jarrett anymore. He was looking past his shoulder at the ragtag team of Hunters and the jumbled mess of buildings farther in the Guild. In that moment, he knew they wouldn't stand a chance against a small band of necromancers, let alone the Kin. Not with all the runes in his limited arsenal.

"What's wrong with him?" a girl asked him, nodding to Aidan.

She was a year or two younger than Tenn, wearing a long plaid trench coat with a broadax strapped to her back. She stared openly at Aidan and Kianna. Aidan was laughing to himself and saying the words *not broken* over and over again.

So much for a good first impression.

"The Church," Tenn said. "They tortured him."

The girl grunted. Answer enough. If the Church was anything over here like it was in America, their reputation preceded them.

"Name's Amiina," the girl said. "I'm in charge of Outpost

Hera. Jarrett's told me about your travels. And what happened to London."

Jarrett didn't meet his gaze. *What exactly did he tell her?*

"This Hunter needs our help," Tenn said, trying to keep his voice steady. He didn't like the way Amiina was looking at Aidan. Clearly, Kianna didn't either. She stared daggers at the Guild leader.

"I don't know if we can," Amiina said. She looked to Jarrett. "Tall, pale and handsome over here says a battle is coming. Frankly, I haven't decided if that means I want you on this side of the wall or the other. Especially if the Kin are coming after you. But…it's our duty to fight off the Dark Lady, and that means readying all the fighters we have." She raised an eyebrow at Aidan. "Even if they are…questionable."

She gestured, and two other guards stepped forward.

"Take them to their chambers and get the medic in to see that one."

Kianna growled and squared her shoulders. "*This one* stays with me."

Amiina shrugged and turned away, heading back in to the safety of the Guild.

"Suit yourself. Gates close at sunset. Sounds like this may be our last night on earth. I don't know about you, but I plan on spending it in a bed."

Jarrett looked between all of them, but his gaze lingered on Tenn. As if asking whose side he was on.

Trouble was, Tenn wasn't certain anymore.

Before he could say anything, Jarrett turned and followed Amiina inside.

"I don't trust them," Kianna said, low enough that only Tenn and the twins could hear.

"We don't have a choice," Tenn whispered.

"That's what sheep believe." She glared daggers at the Hunters who helped gather their things. Despite her words, she began walking forward, holding Aidan proudly. "And I don't plan on being led to the slaughter."

CHAPTER ELEVEN

THE GUILD WAS JUST AS DEPRESSING WITHIN THE WALLS AS it was without, and it didn't take Tenn long to feel like a caged animal. Especially because every Hunter here looked at him with the same disdain as Caius and his followers had in Outer Chicago. He'd wandered up and down the narrow streets, past converted shops and flats, through small blocks of hovels that housed the few civilians who couldn't or wouldn't fight. Every single person that could wield magic had been on high alert since Tenn's arrival. Everyone knew what this entailed: one Kin had been killed, and the rest were coming to enact their revenge. Tenn could tell from the looks in their eyes that no Hunter expected to make it another night.

Once more, Tenn wondered if coming here had been the right move, or if these were all just needless casualties he could have avoided. The Kin were after *him*. Well, him and Aidan. But try as he might, he couldn't see another option. Aidan had needed medical attention, and this was the only way to do it.

Unless you weren't sent here to save him, a voice whispered.

It sounded eerily like Jarrett's. *Maybe this wasn't supposed to be a rescue mission, after all.*

But he couldn't let himself believe he'd been sent to massacre someone. The spirits wouldn't do that. Right? The Violet Sage told him he could save Aidan. He had to hold on to that. *But how long until he falls so far into the Dark Lady's clutches, there's no turning back?*

That, like everything else, he had no answer for.

Wandering the Guild in the dark and the rain might have been depressing, but it beat staying within the Guild's headquarters and risking running into Jarrett. He hadn't said a thing to Tenn since they got in, and no matter what Tenn told himself, he couldn't believe it was solely because Aidan's Sphere was fucking with everyone's emotions. Jarrett had never been this distant, though Tenn knew it was a trait Air users often held. When Jarrett looked at him, it wasn't with love or admiration. It was calculating.

And Tenn knew precisely what those calculations were—Jarrett saw him as a threat. And every wrong move Tenn made was another tick in the wrong box. He wanted to tell himself he knew Jarrett better, that his lover would never… eliminate him.

Then he remembered the look in Jarrett's eyes the night before, and his circle of doubt started all over again.

He finally gave up the effort of avoiding everyone around nightfall. But he didn't go back to the room he'd been given—he hadn't had the nerve to ask if he was sharing it with Jarrett. He headed down to the medic's ward, where he found Aidan exactly as he'd left him—comatose in bed, with Kianna sitting guard.

"How's he doing?"

He had to unbutton his coat the moment he stepped inside and closed the door behind him. A fire raged in the hearth, and sweat broke across his skin.

Kianna didn't look to him.

"Not good," she said. "The doctors here are shite. Turns out the NHS hasn't improved much since the Resurrection."

"What did they say?"

She shrugged.

Tenn sat down on a chair on the opposite side of the bed, looking between the two of them.

"They say his life expectancy is shorter than yours and mine," she said. Then she looked down to her hands. "They can't do anything. Magic won't touch him, and medicine won't either. At this rate, they expect him to freeze to death by tomorrow night."

"I'm sorry." It didn't seem like enough, but he couldn't find any better words.

They sat without speaking for a while, the only sound the crackle of flames and Aidan's labored breathing. Tenn wanted so badly to reach over and heal him. The fact that there was absolutely nothing he could do was a torture he knew all too well.

"What's your real name?" Kianna asked.

"What?"

"Tenn. It's not a real name, is it?" The way she said it was not a question.

"Why does it matter?"

"Because we're going to die soon, and talking about your past is better than bemoaning our lack of a future. Plus I figure you owe me, since you came out of nowhere with the Kin on your heels. So. What's your name?"

Tenn didn't want to answer. Answering just opened up too many other questions. But she was right—their chances of a future were slim unless he could somehow magically figure out a way to heal Aidan and defeat the coming Kin. And since that didn't seem to be in the cards...

"Jeremy," he finally said.

"Jeremy," she repeated, as if rolling the word around in her mouth. "Common. Not at all as inspiring as the great and mighty Tenn. I can see why you changed it."

Tenn grunted. He wasn't about to ask if Kianna was her real name—he had a feeling it wouldn't go over well.

"But that's not why you changed it, is it?" Kianna asked. He looked at her, to see her staring at him like a hawk eyeing a mouse. "No. You aren't the type who wants to inspire stories. You'd prefer a common name like Jeremy over something as memorable as Tenn. So why the switch? What were you running from?"

Tenn swallowed and tried to quell the images Water churned in his guts. The bloody hall. The shed. The shed. *The shed.*

"To," he said.

"Pardon?"

"I wasn't running from anything," he continued, his words already coarse with tears. "I was running *to* something. Home."

Kianna just watched him expectantly.

"It's the number of days it took me to get home," he said. "When we learned about the threat. When the Resurrection took place. That's how long it took me to get to my family."

"What did you find?" Her words were oddly gentle.

"Death," he whispered. He blinked, watched tears fall to the stone floor. "Ten days of running and screaming and bloodshed. And I was too late. My family was gone. My past was gone. So I changed my name. As a reminder of what happens when you try to hold on to the past. A reminder that I was too slow, and because of that, their deaths are my fault."

He didn't expect Kianna to answer. Silence stretched between them, and with every breath, he gathered himself up just a little bit more.

"I'm sorry," she finally whispered. "I lost my family, too."

"We all did," he said. Too harsh. Too harsh. He forced himself to sit upright, to look her in the eye. But that gaze was too hard, and he found himself staring at Aidan's sleeping form instead.

"He's the key to ending it," Tenn said. Even though they were his words, he was finding it harder and harder to believe them. "I don't know why, or how, but I was sent here to find him. To end the Dark Lady once and for all. He's the key."

"Then you better hope he lives through the night," Kianna said. "And that he didn't hear any of that. It would go straight to his head."

CHAPTER TWELVE

AIDAN'S EYES FLICKERED OPEN.

He felt like a human ice cube despite the fire burning in the hearth. He'd heard someone talking. A few people. But that had been ages ago. Ages. And now he was alone. The chairs beside him empty. Empty and cold and filled with shadows.

He blinked. No longer as alone as he thought.

"Tomás," Aidan whispered. "You're back."

Tomás didn't move.

"I am always here," he said. "Watching. Waiting. You hate him, don't you?"

"Of course I do," Aidan said. He rolled his head back. Looked at the ceiling; even that movement hurt with cold. Shadows danced in the flames. So many shadows. So little flame. If only he could pretend this was a dream. "He wants my glory."

"Interesting. Still clinging to fame, even now. You will die before you find glory, my broken prince. Long, long before. And he will rise up in your stead. You, I'm afraid, are worthless."

Shadows closed in. Aidan tried to find the fire. Tried to

reach down into the pit in his chest and pull back something.
A spark. A light. Anything.

He found ice. Only ice.

"I'm not worthless," Aidan whispered. Without Fire, he
couldn't fully believe it.

"Really?" And Tomás was there, perched at his bedside, and
even though Aidan could barely keep his eyes open, he could
tell the incubus wasn't looking at him with desire or strategy.
He was looking at him with pity. "I believe you are mistaken.
All men die. All men, that is, save for me."

Tomás smiled, his canines sharp and gleaming.

"Howls aren't immortal," Aidan said. A shock of cold burst
through him, ripping through his intestines, and he curled
over in pain. Tomás clucked his tongue.

"How do you know? We have only been around for a few
years. But I have stopped aging, broken one. The Dark Lady
promised eternity, and she delivers on her promises." Tomás
leaned in. "*All* of her promises."

He pressed his hand to Aidan's chest.

"Perhaps she could heal you, as well. Perhaps she could help
you live forever, as I will. You and your dear, dead mother, re-
united for eternity. And Tenn, mortal and buried while you
live forever in glory."

Aidan's eyes flickered shut. Behind them, the cold shadows
began to warm. His whole body slowly relaxed, heavy heat filling his limbs. Only his chest hurt. His chest, where Tomás's
hand pressed. His chest, where Tomás's hand burned and froze.

"How?" Aidan whispered, the word slurred.

He felt Tomás lean in, his breath hot—so hot—against
his ear.

"My mistress is the ruler of death," Tomás whispered. "To meet her, you must die."

Aidan didn't have the strength to fight. He didn't *want* to fight. The warmth was so beautiful. Like a cocoon of shadows. A womb. And he had been cold for so, so long. He wanted to sink into that warmth. To wrap himself inside and sleep forever.

"I want—" Aidan mumbled. Words tripped on his tongue, stuck in his throat.

"Hush, broken one," Tomás whispered. "My worthless, pitiful failure."

Tomás's hand clenched. Aidan wanted to scream, but he was too deep, the pit he sank through too dark. Eternity clawed at him, an endless, simmering nothingness, and he couldn't fight.

For the first time, he didn't want to fight.

Because there, in the darkness, he saw her face.

She held out her arms.

And as the last bit of heat and life left him, Aidan fell into his mother's embrace.

CHAPTER THIRTEEN

TENN JOLTED AS GUNFIRE ECHOED DOWN THE HALL.

Two quick bursts. A thunderous silence.

The sound came from the nurses' ward. He'd left only minutes ago, promising to grab dinner for the lot of them. He ran down the darkened hallways, past Hunters calling out or standing in shocked confusion, because this was the UK, and who had guns here? Who would ever use guns now?

Tenn knew.

Panting, he reached the room where Aidan had been. He froze the moment he reached the doorway.

Partly from shock. Partly from the gun barrel pointed directly at his face.

"Fuck," Kianna said. She lowered the gun and looked down to Aidan. Aidan, whose dark skin was pallid. Aidan, whose chest didn't move.

"Is he—?" he asked.

"Barely," she replied. She looked over Tenn's shoulder, to

where a few Hunters watched on nervously. "Go grab the nurse!" she barked. She raised the gun at them. "Now!"

The Hunters fled. She pressed her free hand to Aidan's forehead but didn't drop the gun. Tenn looked at the wall behind Aidan, to the spray of red on white paint. Bile rose in his throat. It reminded him all too much of coming back to find the Witches torn apart in their trailers. But there wasn't a body, so who had she shot?

Tenn took a hesitant step into the room.

"What happened?"

Kianna's jaw clenched. They stood there for a long while, watching Aidan struggle to breathe.

"I don't know," she finally replied. "There was a man kneeling beside him." She shook her head. "Not a man. He'd be dead if he was. Vanished the moment I shot him. Hit him in the chest. Twice."

Tenn swallowed hard. Even with a fire blazing in the hearth, he felt chilled to the bone.

"Tomás," he whispered.

Kianna jerked her gaze to him, her eyes narrowed.

"Who?"

Thunderous footsteps behind them derailed the conversation. Amiina and a half dozen guards flooded into the room. Along with Jarrett. Tenn wilted back against the wall and wished he were anywhere but there. Especially since Jarrett was pretending not to see him. One of the guards rushed to Aidan's side, a medical kit open in a heartbeat.

"What happened?" Amiina demanded. Kianna looked like she couldn't tell if she wanted to punch the nurse or not.

"There was an incubus," Tenn said. He had to think fast.

Had to keep the entire Guild from finding out that one of the Kin had been here. He knew that if they had the slightest inkling of what was stalking their corridors—and why he was there—Tenn and his companions would be out on their asses faster than lightning. Or killed. Probably the latter.

"Impossible," Amiina said. "No Howl gets past our defenses."

"Then how d'you explain a damn incubus perched on my mate's chest?" Kianna snarled. "Some bloody fine defenses you've got."

"How do *you* explain no body?" Amiina replied.

"He ran off after Kianna shot him," Tenn said. "She must have gotten it in the arm or something. I got here just as he fled."

Jarrett didn't say anything, but he'd gone from ignoring Tenn to staring at him like he wanted to set Tenn on fire. Kianna, too, glared daggers. Clearly, she didn't like the suggestion that she would miss her target.

Amiina looked at them all, studying them. Then she snapped her fingers.

"Comb the Guild and lock the gates," she said. "No one leaves or enters without my express permission. If anyone tries to flee, kill them."

The guards nodded and ran off, leaving just Amiina and Jarrett in the doorway. At Aidan's bedside, the nurse worked away, checking his vitals and rummaging for nonexpired medication.

When Tenn could no longer hear the Hunters' boots down the hall, Amiina stepped up to him and growled in a hushed voice.

"If we don't find an incubus by nightfall, I'm throwing you lot out." Her eyes narrowed. "I still haven't decided if I'll be throwing out corpses."

Then she turned to Jarrett.

"Take care of this." Without waiting for a reply, she was gone.

Jarrett glowered at Tenn for a moment. "I told you this would get us killed," he said. With a shake of his head, he turned and left.

For a moment, there was nothing but silence. Then the nurse cleared his throat and stood.

"Um, he'll uh, he'll make it," he said. "For now, at least. Keep him warm. I gave him some sedatives to help him rest. I'll, em, I'll have someone bring in some soup."

He was out the door before finishing his sentence.

Kianna watched the nurse go. Then her eyes snared on Tenn. She raised the gun and pointed it at him, right between the eyes.

"Talk."

Tenn opened his mouth. To admit to her about Tomás. To lay all his sins bare.

But before the words could leave his lips, thunder rolled through the hall, shaking the core of the building.

He toppled to the side and she fell on top of the bed; it was a miracle she didn't shoot him in the process. It wasn't the earthquake that stilled his words.

It was the *power*.

He could feel it, even from here. Stronger than Matthias. Stronger than anyone.

They didn't have to wait for the Kin any longer.

"They're here," he whispered.

CHAPTER FOURTEEN

TENN AND KIANNA RACED TO THE TOP OF THE GUILD'S WALL.

"This is bad," Kianna muttered.

They stared out over the burnt expanse of land. Only now, they weren't greeted with darkness. Great flames twisted up to the sky in front of them. Maybe a mile or two away. Tops. Tenn opened to Earth and stretched his senses out through the soil, fearing what he'd find in the field. The army that unfolded under his senses outnumbered any he'd ever seen. Whichever Kin this was, they hadn't come to mess around. Howls swarmed by the thousands, and the sheer amount of magic used by the necromancers was enough to make his skin crawl.

They were here to wipe out Tenn and his comrades. Once and for all.

"I don't suppose you have any fancy runes to kill them all, eh?" Kianna asked.

Tenn shook his head. He couldn't stop staring at the army. They stretched across the entirety of the horizon. How had they *gotten* here so quickly? He'd thought he was the only one possessing runes of travel. But maybe, like Tomás, they had another way.

Shouts raced along the wall as Hunters readied themselves. Tenn watched as their Spheres blinked to life. But they were like candles against the sun. They didn't stand a chance.

"We need to run," Tenn said. It was the only thing he could think of. Get them out of here. Find someplace safe. Figure out how to... What? He still had no clue what to do.

"Like hell," Kianna said. She opened the chamber of her gun and slid in two more bullets, then snapped it into place. "We die tonight. I'm not going to die with my tail between my legs. And neither should you."

She grinned at him. In the light of the coming fires, she actually looked excited.

"Come on, you already killed one Kin. What's one more? Just a shame that Aidan isn't here to see this. He'd have loved it."

Then, before Tenn could tell her she was mad, she turned and darted off along the wall, heading toward the field.

Tenn watched her go, his heart in his throat. He could sense death coming, and Water sang out its siren song. It was time to give over to the power. *Your pain gives you strength. Your pain gives you strength.*

It was almost time to unleash it.

It was almost time to drown.

CHAPTER FIFTEEN

AIDAN FLOATED IN DARKNESS, THE WORLD AROUND HIM A shifting, breathing thing, all warmth and velvet and closeness. It should have been suffocating. Terrifying. Instead, he felt like he was finally home.

The darkness coalesced, and there, hovering before him in a gown of black silk, was the Dark Lady. A smile played on her crimson lips, her long blond hair billowing around her in a halo.

"You are dying, Aidan. Can you not feel it? The coldness of death's doorway? Can you not hear the sound of my voice, singing you home?"

"I'm not going to die," Aidan said, and with every word he felt a bit more solid. A bit more certain. He knew he didn't have much time left. But he also knew he wasn't bluffing. "You need me. You need me alive."

"Do I, now?" she asked, her smile widening.

Aidan nodded.

"I've read the words you've written, just as I've heard the language of the gods you serve. You need me."

"All men are replaceable."

"And yet here I am, still clinging on to life. Because you know as well as I do that no one else can do what I do." He knew, then, that it was true. The reason he'd been singled out. The reason Fire had begun acting so strangely, had connected him to a darkness he once thought he battled against.

He could do what even the Dark Lady could not.

"I read the runes you used on Calum. I know they weren't perfect. I know what you could have done differently."

"You destroyed those runes when you unleashed his power," the Dark Lady said. "And now, that folly is killing you."

"I remember them," Aidan said. "And I know why you wanted me to get it. You didn't need the stone. You needed the runes. You need someone to bring you back from the dead."

For the first time, the Dark Lady didn't look smug. She looked uncertain.

Aidan let his smile widen. Here, close to death, he could finally feel the heat of Fire in his chest. The sparks racing through his veins as victory neared. Victory not over just Tenn and the Howls, but over Death herself.

"I'll do it," he said. "I'll bring you back to life. For a price."

CHAPTER SIXTEEN

TENN WAS HALFWAY TO THE WALL WHEN JARRETT STEPPED out and intercepted him. The last person he wanted to see.

"We have to get you out of here," Jarrett said.

"I'm not going anywhere." He looked up to the blazing red sky. Thought of the boy he was bound to save only a few hundred feet away. He couldn't leave Aidan. He couldn't leave anyone. Not after he'd come so far.

"Please, Tenn," Jarrett said. And his voice softened. Took on the tone that melted Tenn's heart like butter. "Please. I'm sorry about before. About everything. But you have to understand—you are important. So very important. And if you die here, we lose. All of us. We all lose."

Bile rose in the back of his throat. This felt way too much like when he had let his old Guildmates die for him, back at Outpost 37. It seemed like years ago, but even now, even with the true battle looming around him, he could hear Matthias's mocking laughter as he chased Tenn down.

Tenn was done running.

"I can help them," he said. "I have runes—"

"You know they aren't enough. The twins are already rallying Aidan and Kianna. They're going to fly him and the two of them out of here. And we have to be out there, waiting, for when they arrive."

"What?"

"They want you to create a safe spot," Jarrett said. His eyes flickered to the red above them. "Just out of harm's way. Like you did before. For me. They'll bring Aidan and Kianna to us." He looked back to Tenn. "Trust me. Please. This is the only way."

Tenn swallowed.

An explosion shook the Guild, toppling him into Jarrett's arms. Jarrett, who held him strong and secure, warm and loving. Tenn took a deep breath. There was logic in Jarrett's words. He didn't want to leave the others to die, but this was the only way to keep them safe. At least for now.

"Okay," he said into Jarrett's chest.

Jarrett kissed the top of his head.

"Thank you," he whispered. "I know where to go. I just need you to draw the runes."

Tenn nodded and knelt. Quickly scrawled the runes in the dirt.

"Ready," he said.

Jarrett took his hand.

"Ready."

Tenn opened to Earth. Jarrett opened to Air. And as the world around them vanished in a swirl of dust and shadow, Tenn had to convince himself he wasn't running away.

He was helping.

He was helping.

CHAPTER SEVENTEEN

AIDAN COULD BARELY MOVE. COULD BARELY SEE. BUT HE WAS strong enough — just strong enough—to grab the dagger Kianna had left on the nightstand.

Strong enough to bring it to the welt over his Hunter's mark.

He was so cold, he didn't even feel the dagger as it sliced through his flesh.

He was so close to death, he could barely see his own work. Not at first, and not as blood slicked over his skin.

He didn't need to.

The runes he scrawled glowed bright red, streaming out like light, like blood, and maybe he had been through too much pain, maybe he'd become dull from the torture, but he didn't feel a damn thing. Only light. Only light.

And the hiss of the runes that pooled in his blood like poison.

Thunder rolled outside. Dust fell from the ceiling. Distantly, he heard the shouts of this ragtag Guild as they assembled for one final battle.

It sounded like a coronation. A battle hymn.

It sounded like the praise he had never truly been given, but would finally take.

Because he knew, in the back of his mind, the Kin and the rest were coming for him.

They thought he was an easy target. Broken after the Inquisition. Helpless.

He sneered at their faces in the flames of the hearth fire. Scratched deeper into his tender, burning flesh. Over scar tissue. Through tattoos. A different sort of ink pooling and spreading in his veins.

Magic.

He felt it as surely as he'd once felt Fire burning in his chest.

It tingled under his skin, crawling and biting like fire ants.

It burned in his breath, a smoke he would never exhale.

And with every rune he cleaved into his skin, the power grew.

He rewrote the runes that had once given him strength.

He massacred the Church's brand with words far deeper, far more ancient, than any human fear.

He wrote the words of the darkness. The words of that first, impregnating spark.

He wrote a language to shatter the world and bring it back anew.

If he so desired.

And he desired.

The final rune connected. A snap of power. A silence.

He cried out in triumph, in bliss, as the Sphere in his chest once more connected to his senses, as the power that was hidden from him lapped through his limbs like a tiger's tongue. He cried out, and the flames in the hearth burned back, reached out to him, bowed to him.

Fire filled him, burning away the weakness, the disease, the exhaustion.

Fire filled him, burning away every goddamned human frailty.

Fire *willed* him, and he was nothing but the flame.

A fire.

A spark.

A god.

He stood from the bed. Tendrils of smoke curled from his bare feet, the bloodied rug beneath him charring to ash.

The Dark Lady had given him the final runes. Had taught him the secrets hidden in the abyss. He had filled in the rest, the words she would never know, the words spoken only for him.

He had promised to aid her.

But first, he would destroy.

CHAPTER EIGHTEEN

"NO," TENN GASPED.

He'd thought the runes would take them somewhere safe. Somewhere near, but safe. Just out of harm's reach. Somewhere he could leap in or help from afar.

But when the dust cleared and he stared up at the great expanse of wall—brilliantly lit by the afternoon sun—he knew that Jarrett had taken them even farther.

"We have to go back," Tenn said. Panic churned through his veins as comprehension took hold.

They were back in America. In Outer Chicago.

Half the world away, his friends were fighting someone else's fight. *His* fight.

Jarrett stood at his side, stoic and unmoving as ever, his pale eyes fixed on Tenn.

"We can't."

Tenn wanted to scream at him. He'd lied. He'd *lied*. And now the twins and Aidan and everyone else were going to die because of it. He wanted to fly back, but he couldn't. He needed Air. He needed Jarrett. Reality washed over him, cold and numbing, and he found he could do nothing but stare at Jarrett in sad disbelief.

"Why?" It was the only word he could think of. He squeezed his eyes shut. Prayed that when he opened them, he'd be back in England. Back with his friends. His only friends. His dying friends.

Jarrett didn't answer right away. When he did, his words were heavy. Distant.

"I told you that I was sent to ensure that you weren't a threat. To ensure you fought for the right side. But you've kept far too many secrets, Tenn. Secrets that have gotten a great many people killed. I can't risk that anymore."

He raised his hand, and on cue, the gates to Outer Chicago opened and a squadron of guards marched out.

Tenn didn't even fight back when they placed him in hand-cuffs. Even though a flick of Earth would have freed him. Even though he could have escaped.

Where would he have gone?

What would he have done?

It was only when Jarrett pulled something from his coat that Tenn flinched. Only when the cold metal touched his skin that he realized how truly screwed he was.

The sigil from the Church. The same one Kianna had been wearing.

The moment it looped around his neck and settled on his chest, he felt the cold sink through his skin. Felt his Spheres wink out, untethered, floating away in the darkness within.

He couldn't have reached for them if he tried.

He didn't try.

Without Water to pull him down or Earth to steady him, Tenn was numb. His story was over.

For the first time in four years, Tenn gave over to the cold and the silence.

CHAPTER NINETEEN

BLISS.

Pure, unadulterated, screaming bliss.

Aidan walked through the battlefield, flames licking up his sides, dripping from his hands. An offering. A blessing.

He laughed to himself.

The Church had finally done what it intended to do all along.

He was purified.

He was reborn.

Reborn into a new world, clean and pure—both him, and the world.

Around him, the flames purified. Turned broken bodies to ash. Turned soil and blood and sin to steam. There weren't even screams. Not anymore. Not through the all-consuming heat. Not through the purity of his light.

Distantly, he wondered how many Hunters he'd killed. How many had run to the battlefield to meet the enemy head-on, only to die in his fury before ever reaching their charge.

He didn't care.

Fire filled him.

Gods did not care about mortals.

Gods cared only for worship, for respect.

And those that did not respect the gods were damned to feel their wrath.

Aidan strode through the piles of ash, the kravens and necromancers, the bloodlings and even the incubi who couldn't swallow his heat fast enough. All of them ash. All of them traitors to the only god worth serving: Death.

Behind him, around him, within him, he felt the Dark Lady like a light in the dark, a warmth in the endless winter night. She guided him forward. Her gift filled his veins—the words of power, the words that allowed him to tap into a magic greater than his own Sphere, the ability to harness the great spark of creation, the flame that turned the engine of time. And his handiwork—their handiwork—spread around him.

The destruction seemed absolute. Flame everywhere. Blinding.

And yet here, in the midst of the flame, was a patch where the heat was not so great. A space where lesser men might die.

The Kin was far from a lesser man.

Even now, with his skin charred black and his hair burnt to nothing, he lived. He lived, because one could not simply kill a Kin with flame. One needed to do it the old-fashioned way. With muscle and tearing and blood. Aidan delighted in it.

He stood over the burning Kin. The man had been tall,

once. Muscular. Aidan could tell the man was Breathless, from the way his own lungs burned in the Kin's presence. Even now, the Kin held on to life. Tried to turn Aidan's vitality against him.

He had to admire that even now, even facing destruction, the man refused to give in.

"You have spark," Aidan said. His lips twitched in a smile as sparks rained down around them, ashes and embers in the breeze. Then he felt the Dark Lady through the flames, and his mirth turned to anger. "Do you know who I am?"

The man's lips cracked and bled as he opened his mouth. His words were barely more than a rasping hiss. There was no point asking who he was. It didn't matter, not anymore. Aidan would rip this Kin from the fabric of the world, and his legacy would be replaced with Aidan's own.

Gods and mortals.

Aidan knelt at the dying Kin's side. Leaned his ear to his lips.

"What was that?" he asked.

Another rasp.

Aidan grunted and stood.

"My name is Aidan Belmont. I believe I'm the one you were sent here to kill."

Aidan chuckled.

"Looks like there was a change of plans."

He kicked the Kin's side. The Kin grunted. Skin cracked. Blood hissed on the charred ground.

"Personally, I'm grateful that you brought everyone here. Makes me feel special." He held his arms out to the sides, to the flames that surrounded them in a cocoon, an embrace that should have burned Aidan to crisp. He felt nothing but pleasant warmth. He kicked the Kin again, his approval turning to ashen disgust in his mouth. Just like with Calum, this didn't feel like a great victory. This was too easy. Far, far too easy. "This also saves me from chasing down your asses all across the globe. Given the bodies, I'd assume this was your entire army?"

A grunt. Close enough to a yes.

"Good."

Aidan stood straighter, rolled his shoulders back. He glared down at the Kin. "I have a message for you. From your mistress. From the woman you failed to serve."

The Kin's blue eyes widened. Ah, yes. Not at all what he expected to hear. Good.

"The Dark Lady does not forgive treachery. You failed her. Worse than failed. You betrayed her, and then had the nerve to carry on living, to use the gifts She gave you. You've been living on borrowed time, my friend." With every word, the Kin's eyes grew wider, his breath faster. He knew. He knew.

Aidan smiled and knelt back down, his knee crushing the Kin's chest.

"I asked you if you knew who I was. I told you my name. But we both know it is not the truth. Not entirely."

He pressed his hand to the Kin's throat. The man's flesh felt like sandpaper and cracked leather under his palm.

"I am the hand of the Dark Lady. And she has come to take back what you failed to earn. As she will do to all who opposed her."

Aidan squeezed.

The Kin's throat collapsed in. Like paper. Like eggshell. His starved Sphere of Air collapsed, too. And with barely a whimper, the most powerful Howl in Western Europe died beneath Aidan's hand.

Easy.

Far too easy.

"You took far too much enjoyment from that."

Aidan jerked up.

To see Tomás walking through the flames unscathed, his shirt torn and bloodied.

Aidan stood slowly. Memories filtered through his thoughts, but the fear that should have accompanied them was distant. He had just killed one Kin. Killing Tomás, if necessary, would be as simple as swatting a fly.

And yet, the Dark Lady said nothing about killing Tomás. So far.

"You're one to talk. You seemed pretty content when you were trying to kill me."

"I took no pleasure in that," Tomás said. He spread his hands out to the sides. "I only did what I thought was best. You were in pain. I had hoped to relieve you of that."

"Yet here I am," Aidan said. "What kept you from killing me?"

Tomás touched the shreds of his shirt. "Your friend."

Kianna.

"Did you kill her?"

Tomás shook his head.

"It was not the time."

"And is it the time for me to kill you?"

"That depends. Do you feel I've outlived my usefulness?"

Aidan looked around. At the destruction he wrought on his own accord. The purifying fire, the silence in the blaze. None had survived. None, but them.

He didn't need Tomás.

The Kin seemed to gather as much.

"Your power far outmatches mine," Tomás said, "but I can still be of use. You want to kill the rest of my brethren? Let me help you find them."

Aidan considered. Tomás was interested in only one thing: himself.

"You know why I'm doing this," Aidan replied.

"Of course. My brothers and sisters betrayed the Dark Lady. She demands their lives in return. Fair is fair."

"I'm not just here to avenge her."

"I know," Tomás replied. "She gave you these gifts in exchange for something. She gives nothing without a demand in return. And neither do you. If I had my guess…you swore to bring her back."

Aidan nodded. It should have felt like heresy. Instead, it felt like the only way forward. The Dark Lady wanted all of her creations dead? Good. So did he. And he would happily be the one to bring it about.

"That is good," Tomás said. "Very good. I knew you were the one, my prince. The one to make the whole world bend the knee. And that, too, is why I offer myself to you." He knelt. Beside the ashes of his dead brother, as though the corpse was no more than dirt beneath his heels.

"I know where they keep her. Let me help you. We shall kill my traitorous siblings. And then, with their blood staining our hands, we will bring our Great Mother back."

"It is our greatest vanity
to believe we should alter creation.
Demons are born
when men
raise angels."

—Sermon of Brother Jeremiah
1 P.R. (Post Resurrection)

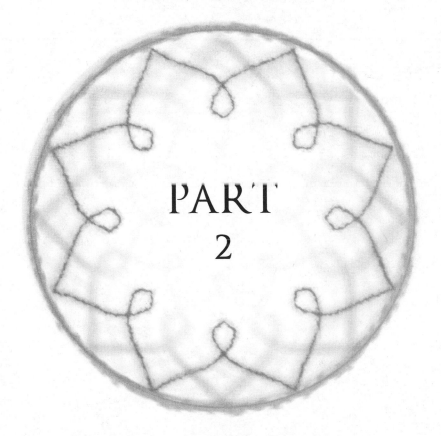

PART
2

GODS AND MORTALS

CHAPTER TWENTY

SILENCE.

Absolute, perfect silence.

Tenn could hear the blood pumping in his veins and the distant drip of water from the ceiling. He could hear his breath rattling in his lungs. He could hear the seconds ticking by with every pulse of blood, every drop of water, every timid breath.

Every second was another Hunter dead on the other side of the world.

Every second was another reminder that he had failed. Miserably. He hadn't saved Aidan. He hadn't saved anyone. As far as he knew, Aidan and everyone else had died in the Kin's attack. And now what? He was just supposed to wait here for the Kin to find him and destroy Outer Chicago? Or did Jarrett truly think that locking him down here would inspire some sort of meditative state, some trance that would let the spirits speak? Tenn doubted that.

He felt like bait.

For the first time in his life, he actually wished he could

reach for Water. Wished the damnable Sphere would drag him down into despair, or dredge up memories to haunt his waking life.

He had been down here for over an hour, with only his thoughts and a guttering candle to keep him company. And right now, neither was good company.

He grunted as he tried to shift positions. The guards had manacled his hands behind his back, and the pendant hung heavy on his chest. He considered trying to go upside down or something to remove it, but that seemed like too much work. Everything seemed like too much work. *Living* seemed like too much work, and without the Spheres to energize him, he couldn't see the point in trying.

It's not like escaping would get him anywhere.

His friends were dead. He had to come to terms with that. Mostly. His friends were dead, and even if he did get out of here, he'd lost. Aidan was gone. He'd failed everyone. The whole world. He deserved to be down here more than anyone else. It was only a matter of time before the Kin came after him and finished what they'd started.

Metal screeched as the door to the cells opened, letting in more torchlight. Tenn flinched. At least he didn't have to worry about it being Tomás—the incubus would never resort to something as pedestrian as a door.

When Tenn saw who it was, he realized he would have rather it be the incubus.

"What are you doing here?"

Jarrett stepped into the room, a torch in one hand and a sad look plastered on his face. Honestly, it was the first time

Tenn had seen Jarrett look remotely remorseful, and he felt a vindictive sort of schadenfreude about it.

"Are you okay?" Jarrett asked. As though *he* wasn't the one who threw Tenn down here in the first place.

"The hell does it look like?" He didn't struggle. He wouldn't give Jarrett that satisfaction.

He felt his world flip as he remembered that a little over a week ago, the roles had been reversed. He'd stumbled into the cell holding Jarrett. Had ripped the ropes from Jarrett's body. Had brought his lover back from the brink of death.

And now, Jarrett had the gall to stand on the other side of the bars, looking down at Tenn as if he was absolutely powerless in this situation.

Jarrett looked at his feet.

"I wish it didn't have to be like this," he muttered.

"Then don't make it be like this," Tenn replied. He made sure to stare at Jarrett's eyes, even if Jarrett refused to return the look. "Why are you treating me like the enemy?"

Jarrett didn't answer, not at first. Then he let out a huge sigh and hung his head even lower.

"You asked why I was sent after you. And I told you the truth. Most of it. The Prophets had seen a power was awakening. One they thought could change the course of history. And they said that like all things, that power could be used for good or evil. I was to ensure you stayed on the path of good."

"Did you know? Did you know who I was before you were sent to find me?"

Jarrett nodded.

"And the rest of it. Did you actually..." The word caught

in Tenn's throat. "Did you actually love me, or was that part of the ruse?"

"I did. I thought I did."

Tenn's heart dropped. It felt like being kicked in the gut.

"You thought you did?" he whispered.

"I don't know. Everything seems so fucked up." Again, it was as if Jarrett were the one in chains, and not the other way around. "When we went over there, when I saw you standing over him. I knew... I knew I didn't fit into your story. Neither of us did."

"What do you mean?"

Jarrett crouched down, still not looking at Tenn.

"I mean, the stories we told each other of the life we would live after this. After all the fighting and the bloodshed and the death. The life with a house and a yard and a herd of dogs. All of that...all of that was a lie."

"You didn't want it?"

"No, Tenn. I want that more than anything. But I don't think you do."

If Tenn could collapse any further into himself, he would.

"What? How could you say that?"

"You aren't destined for a quiet life, Tenn." Jarrett looked up, looked him straight in the eyes. "The moment I saw you next to Aidan, I knew that stronger than anything else. The power you wield, the runes...there is no *after* for you. At least, not the type we'd dreamed of. You and Aidan... I know that story. You're the *chosen ones* and I... I'm just the third in a shitty love triangle."

"You think I'd leave you for him?"

"Haven't you already?"

Silence.

"I don't love him," Tenn said.

"No. And I believe you in that. But Aidan is powerful. He's like a black hole, and you're past the event horizon. Wherever he goes, you will follow. Not because you love him, but because he is the opposite of you, and you will always, *always*, try to help those who need it most. And Aidan needs that help more than any of us."

"Says the man who left Aidan there to die."

"He isn't dead," Jarrett muttered. "I know he isn't. It wouldn't be that easy."

Tenn swallowed. "What about the twins. Are they alive? Did they—"

"They had nothing to do with this. Dreya would have killed me if she knew what I'd had planned. The only reason I got the sigil off Kianna was because I told her I thought you could find a way to reverse it on Aidan."

"So you lied."

Jarrett finally looked at him. His eyes were red, but they weren't soft anymore.

"You're one to talk."

Tenn looked away.

"What do we do now, then? You know Aidan is important. And if he isn't dead, that means he's still out there. It means he still needs our help."

"Aidan isn't the mission. Saving Aidan will never fix the world or end the Howls. Your job is to end this. All of this. And so long as you think Aidan is the one you have to fix, rather than the world...you're a risk. Either he convinces you to join him, or he kills you. Either way, we lose. We all lose."

Tenn didn't know how to take it. If he didn't have this damn sigil against his chest, Water would be clawing at him, trying to drown him in sadness. But as it was, he just felt hollow. Numb.

"Why are there only two options?" Tenn asked flatly. "After everything I've done, why do you believe my only fates are to die or become evil? Why don't you believe that I could save him and all of us?"

Jarrett stood.

"Because one person can't save the world," he said. "What you learned about the runes, the power you wield...that's not enough to end things if you're on your own, if you're out chasing someone who could turn on you at any second. I have to keep you here. Keep you safe. Not just from Aidan, but from yourself. If you go out there...if you go after him..."

Jarrett sighed and shook his head.

"You looked at him with the same worry you once looked at me with. You think you can fix him. He knows you think that. And he will use that against you."

"I saved you," Tenn whispered.

"Some days," Jarrett said, as if to himself. He paused, then headed toward the door. "Some days, I'm not so certain."

CHAPTER TWENTY-ONE

DREYA STARED IN AWE AT THE BATTLEFIELD.

Awe, and fear. Two sensations she was not quite used to feeling.

She looked to her brother. He stared at the carnage with wide eyes, the flames of destruction flickering pink against his pale blue irises. She knew in the deepest part of her soul his Sphere burned inside him with recognition—so much power. So much *anger*. More than the world had ever seen. Pulled from a place the world had never seen.

And she knew her brother felt drawn to it.

Neither of them spoke. Neither of them needed to. He felt her uncertainty just as she felt his struggle.

Aidan had done this. Aidan had done all of this. He had ended the battle before it ever truly began. And then, he had vanished.

Flames licked across the countryside for miles on end, a heat that brought sweat to her brow even here, even with her flickering shield. She pulled through Air and sent her senses soaring, spreading her awareness wide.

Hoping to find someone—anyone—alive.

Even though she knew that hope was futile.

Hope did not change the nature of things.

As far as her powers could go, so too did the destruction, until she reached the very edge of her awareness and sensed even more flames lingering beyond. How had he done it?

That was no ordinary magic, Devon thought.

Dreya nodded. The Witches had taught them everything they knew of magic, and the nature of the world. There were more than the five elements all humans contained, more than Earth and Air and Fire and Water. More even than Maya. There was a balance to it all, and on that fulcrum rested a shadow. A dark to the light.

There were the powers that came from this world, and the powers born only to destroy it.

It should not have been possible, but Aidan had drawn from that darker wellspring. He had drawn the runes that allowed him to do what even the Dark Lady could not.

The Dark Lady had opened the door for evil. Aidan had blown apart the wall.

Once more, she thought of Tenn. Brought his tracking rune to mind. He was far, so far. And when she focused on Jarrett's own rune, she found him to be in a similar locale. Betrayal twisted her heart, but until she knew for certain, she would not entertain the notion. Where had they gone? And why had they done so without telling her?

The questions were troubling. The only consolation she

found was that Tenn was still alive. She had to believe Jarrett had brought him far away to keep him safe.

If that's the case, Devon thought her way, *then why were we not brought with?*

And that was the true question. Why had Jarrett not trusted them with their location? Or was this something else? Had the two of them been captured?

She had no way of knowing, not yet. And she had long ago learned not to fill her mind with worry about things she could not explain. It would not be productive. It would spell her death.

Movement nearby.

She'd been so distracted scanning outside her shield that she'd barely cared to keep an eye on what was occurring within.

She snapped her senses back to the stairwell and felt a small wave of relief wash through her. Devon grunted to himself.

"Kianna," Dreya said the moment the woman stepped out onto the balustrade.

Kianna jogged the last few steps, and slowed as she surveyed the fire-swept field around them. She shook her head absently. Dreya found she could watch Kianna's movements all day and not get tired. There was a strength in each gesture that Kianna seemed absolutely unaware of, and yet made her who she was. Like a lioness. Unknowing of her grace, but confident in her strength.

"Where did he go?" Kianna asked.

There was no point asking who. Kianna didn't care about Tenn or Jarrett. And that, too, was another reason Dreya admired her—Kianna was focused on only one thing. Even if that often led to frustration.

"I do not know," Dreya said. She reached out and put a tentative hand on Kianna's arm. Kianna wore only a T-shirt despite the cold, and her skin was hot to the touch.

Stop flirting, Devon thought gruffly. Dreya glared daggers at him.

Kianna didn't shake off her hand. She just leaned against the railing and stared out at the flames.

"I can sense you now," Dreya whispered. "How?"

"Blondie. Said Tenn needed to study it or something. Hell if I know."

Jarrett took the sigil? But why? Another question she had no answer for, and another she filed away for a future worry. She had to focus on now.

"What did you do, Aidan?" Kianna whispered.

Dreya swallowed down the words she knew Kianna would not want to hear. *Your friend has taken on the words of the Dark Lady. He has harnessed powers no man should wield.*

Kianna looked to her.

"An hour ago, he was close to death. And just now he blasted onto the battlefield like a goddamned comet and destroyed everything. *Everything.* How is that even possible?"

The scene replayed in Dreya's mind. Just as Kianna had said, Aidan had burst from the Guild in a ball of flame and landed in the midst of the battle, sending wave after wave of fire around him. Nothing stood a chance against him. No man or woman, no Howl. Not even the nameless Kin that led the charge. Aidan had burned it all down in a matter of seconds. Dreya had sensed him, out there. She had sensed him kill the Kin with his bare hands. Just as she sensed that he hadn't been alone.

But it was more than sensing. Air was the element of

thought and sound, and she had heard voices amidst the screams and cinders. Aidan's voice. And another's.

Aidan, speaking to someone, saying he would destroy the rest of the Kin. And then, he would bring the Dark Lady back. She had heard them. And Devon had heard them.

It chilled her to the core, those words. The Dark Lady was dead and gone. But so many things that should have been dead and gone had been reviving lately, and though she was not one for flights of fancy, she would never discard a statement like that without absolute proof it was impossible.

Right now, nothing seemed impossible.

Especially because she had heard those very same whispers through her brother's attachment to Fire. The promise that the Dark Lady still lived. The promise that eternity still existed in her ever-burning heart.

Dreya gently tightened her hold on Kianna's arm.

"She has him, now," she whispered. "The Dark Lady. He has discovered her words, has found runes to grant himself new power. I believe…he intends to kill the rest of the Kin as an offering to her. And then, he intends to bring her back."

Silence between them as her words burrowed deep in Kianna's heart. Silence, save for the cinders. Silence—not even screams of the dying. Aidan's wrath had been that absolute.

We have to kill him, Devon thought.

We have to save him, Dreya hissed back. *They are both necessary to end this.*

"Then we have to end this," Kianna said, her grip on the railing tightening. "And if it comes to it, I will be the one to end him."

She didn't brush off Dreya's hand.

Not once.

CHAPTER TWENTY-TWO

"DO YOU WISH TO DO THE HONORS," TOMÁS ASKED, "OR shall I?"

They stood above a man. A Howl. A Kin. Outside, the sun shone on a pale sand beach and clouds skittered across the blue sky. There were seagulls. Swaying palm trees. It was paradise.

But in here, the scene was far from pastoral. Blood splattered against the walls, and the fine silk sheets the Kin lay on were stained with his blood.

It hadn't taken much to surprise and subdue him. The moment Tomás appeared in the palatial house, Aidan at his side, the Kin clearly knew the fight was over.

Desmond was his name. Desmond, a bloodling who ruled the entire continent of Africa from the comfort of his seaside condo. Desmond, who seemed less like a Kin and more like a posh tourist.

Desmond, who was moments away from being ripped out of history.

"Let me," Aidan said. He knelt down and stared the man in the eyes. Hazel eyes. Hazel, and oh so very afraid.

He placed his hand on Desmond's stomach. Felt the Kin's inverted Sphere of Water sizzle and hiss against Aidan's Fire.

"Any last words?" Aidan asked.

Desmond opened his mouth.

Aidan opened to Fire, and one of the most powerful creatures in history was no more.

CHAPTER TWENTY-THREE

"WE SHOULD NEVER HAVE LET HIM GO," DEVON GROWLED.

Dreya stared up at her brother, who paced at the foot of her narrow bed. Morning had come and the remaining troop had assembled back within the Guild's walls.

There weren't many of the remaining troop. Everyone outside the main perimeter had been destroyed.

Kianna had gone to sleep or to pace, Dreya wasn't certain which. Amiina had been killed. And while the rest of small Guild tried to rally and decide on new leadership, she and her brother had retired to the dormitories to figure out what to do next.

"What would you have had me do?" Dreya asked. "We could not keep Tenn here. It was too dangerous. If Aidan had turned on him. If the Kin had gotten through—"

"And now he is back in America. What good is he to us there? Aidan is gone, Dreya. Perhaps he has gone after Tenn? Perhaps even now Tenn burns for our mistake. If we had kept him here, we could have protected him. Now, he is so far away we cannot even warn him of the danger that Aidan has become."

"I have to believe that Aidan has not gone after him," Dreya said. "He has gone after the rest of the Kin."

"Why? Because your *girlfriend* believes so?"

It was like a slap to the face.

Never once had she or her brother had a lover. Never once had they even had an *interest* in romance. There was only death for them. Only duty.

And yet, something about Kianna had kindled a spark deep within her, a knowing as much as a yearning. For her brother to use that against her, when for so many years they'd had only each other, felt like the worst sort of betrayal.

"I believe so because that is what I *heard*." She kept her voice even, pulled through Air to clear the lesser emotions from her head. She had to think logically and rationally. For the both of them. It was the only way they could possibly make it through. "Aidan has gone after the rest of the Kin. And then…"

"And then he plans on doing what no one else could do." He slumped against the wall, arms across his chest, and faced her. "We have failed."

Those three words. They were a spear to her heart.

The three words she had tried desperately to keep from ricocheting through her mind and tearing through the little hope she still had. And now that he had said them, she felt the weight of their truth settling on her shoulders.

"We have," she said quietly.

Sadness fell heavy atop her. A sadness she hadn't felt since watching her entire Clan die at her own hands. A sadness she had tried so desperately to replace with logic and reason and purpose.

She remembered it clear as yesterday. Clearer still. The scent of her people dying and burning, the sound of their screams as they echoed up the canyon walls. She glanced to her brother. To the burgundy scarf draped loose about his neck.

The scarf that had once been their mother's.

The scarf he had pulled from her burnt corpse.

A reminder to them both of their failure. A reminder that every breath he took was because someone else had died. Because many people had died.

Now, it seemed to settle on his shoulders like a noose.

"I'd ask if I'm interrupting," Kianna said from the doorway. "But I can never tell if you two are talking or just brooding."

Dreya jolted at the sound of her voice. She had let herself be taken unawares. Had let her guard down. Even Devon looked shocked. The stress of everything must be getting to her. That must be it. Must be.

"Kianna," Dreya said.

"Yup." She had changed since they last saw her. Out of her ash-covered clothes and into fresh jeans and a long pink sweater. Dreya looked down at her own soot-stained fabric. She must do the same. Death debased her.

Kianna stepped into the room and plopped down on the bed beside Dreya. Inches apart, but still close enough to feel her warmth. Devon's eyes flickered between the two of them.

Should I go? he thought toward Dreya.

Dreya shook her head, almost imperceptibly.

"What are you two discussing?" Kianna asked.

"What there is to do," Dreya replied. "If there is anything we can do."

Kianna nodded to herself.

"Been asking myself the same thing. And it all boils back down to one goal. We have to find Aidan. Before the idiot can do something we'll all regret."

"But how? We have no idea where he might be. And even if we could find him, we have no way of getting there."

"You guys made your way to us just fine," Kianna said.

"Yes. We had runes for travel. But to use them, we would need an Earth mage." She paused. Looked Kianna in the eye before flicking her gaze away. She could feel Devon rolling his eyes. "And in order for us all to travel, you would need to be attuned, as well."

Kianna jutted her jaw. She didn't say anything.

Dreya looked to her brother.

What do you want me to do? he asked.

Dreya had no idea.

"Figured as much," Kianna finally said. "Magic seems to be part of everything anymore."

She readjusted herself on the mattress, leaned back against the headrest and put her long legs on the bed, nudged right against Dreya's side. Her boots, Dreya noted, had been cleaned. But still.

"You know," Kianna said. "I've spent the last four years doing everything I could to prove that you didn't need magic to survive in this new world, and I'd say I've done a damn good job of it. All it does is fuck everything up. I mean, look around. Would any of this have happened if humans hadn't discovered magic?"

Dreya could feel Devon's agitation raise, and his tenuous grasp to keep Fire in check. *Humans would have found a way to ruin things*, she heard him say. It felt like a slight against the two of them. After all, they had spent most of their lives learning magic. Learning to protect and revere it. Not everyone used it as a weapon.

Even though she and her brother had begun to.

"But." Kianna sighed and flopped her head back against the wall. "But."

She went silent for a moment. Then closed her eyes.

"But it's becoming increasingly clear that Aidan is so far up shit's creek that the only way to get him back is to swim. And by swim, I mean use magic." She opened her eyes and tilted her head forward, looked Dreya dead-on. "You say I gotta be attuned to get to the wee bastard? Fine. Attune me. But don't you dare tell him about it."

CHAPTER TWENTY-FOUR

"WHERE ARE WE?" AIDAN ASKED.

Snow swept around them, blanketing everything in pale blue and white. The sun was rising—or was it setting? he couldn't tell—and blanketing the horizon in pink. Aidan knew he should have been freezing. Knew the snow whipping around them should have cut him to the core.

But for once in his life, he was warm. Blessedly warm. Fire burned within him, and in that heat, there was no room for weakness.

Tomás squinted through the snow.

"Russia," he said. "We're here to pay my sister a little visit."

"Your sister lives here? There's nothing around."

Nothing but rolling dunes of snow and a horizon that seemed to stretch into infinity. Not even trees.

"My sister has a flair for the dramatic," Tomás replied. "Come. You'll see."

He strode through the snow, his feet melting deep footprints with every step. Aidan followed. The hiss of steaming snow and ice sounded like screaming. So much screaming.

He smiled at the memory of the battlefield, even if a small part of him whined that it had been too easy. Far too easy. He glanced to his arm and the network of cauterized runes he'd scratched there. A new Hunter's mark. A new promise. If only he'd had them sooner, he could have ended the Kin's reign before it ever began.

"Who was he?" Aidan asked as he strode to keep up with Tomás. "The one I killed on the field."

Tomás looked over his shoulder and quirked an eyebrow. "Does it matter?"

Aidan shrugged.

Truthfully? No. It didn't matter. None of these lesser Kin mattered. He knew now killing any one of them wasn't a victory. Destroying all of them, though…that was something to gloat about.

"His name was Sigmund," Tomás said. "He ruled Western Europe from Germany. Of all my brethren, he was, perhaps, closest to me. He at least knew how to have fun."

Aidan didn't care to ask what he meant. Just as he didn't care to apologize for killing Tomás's brother. Tomás didn't seem to care either way—he spoke as if discussing the weather.

The very shite weather.

"And what's this one's name?" He didn't care. It was just a way to make conversation. What did it matter what her name was? She'd be dead by day's end whether Aidan had a name for her or not, and his name would replace her own in the annals of history.

"Natasja," Tomás said wryly. "Could you ask for a more

Russian name? She was a homeless orphan when my mistress found her. Unwanted. Unloved. I suppose it's no surprise she became *this*."

"Became what?"

Tomás paused. Stared at something in the snow at his toes. Markings in the ice.

Runes.

He looked at Aidan.

"What do they tell you?"

Aidan stared at the runes. They shone heavy and dark against the snow, shadows burning against the brightness, jagged and serpentine and moving under his scrutiny. As if ashamed. Because as he heard their whispers in his mind—*deceive and be deceived, burn and blister*—he knew they were incomplete.

He knew he could have done better.

"She's hiding," Aidan grunted. He looked up, past the runes, to the unending snow. And he knew that farther in, Natasja waited. Just as he knew that one step over these runes would blow him to pieces, no matter how powerful he was. "And she's scared."

"Scared?"

Aidan looked to Tomás. It wasn't what the runes told him. Rather, it was the *presence* of the runes that spoke to him. These were defensive runes. Ones to hide her away and destroy anyone unlucky enough to cross over them.

"She's heard about me." Aidan smiled. "She knew I'd be coming for her."

He knelt down and placed his fingertips to the ice, ready to redraw the runes. He still hadn't decided if he wanted to negate them, or invert them, making everyone *within* the perimeter a target for the runes' destruction. Then he paused.

She knew I'd be coming for her.

Thoughts swirled. Thoughts he'd been too strung out to understand before.

"What is it?" Tomás asked. "Can you not undo them?"

But Aidan wasn't listening.

He'd known Tenn would come after him, yes. But how had Tenn tracked him? Vaguely, he remembered overhearing a conversation Tenn had had with Kianna. He'd thought it just a fever dream. But as he sorted through the mire of his memories, he remembered. Tenn had shown her a tracking rune on his forearm. He'd said it was how the four of them kept track of one another.

So how had Tenn been able to find him from an ocean away? The only thing they had in common was the incubus standing beside him.

Aidan looked up to Tomás.

"How did he find me?"

"Who?" Tomás asked, his voice shifting from gloating to guarded.

"Don't play stupid. It doesn't suit you." He nodded to the landscape before them, to the Kin that waited within. "You guided me here. How the hell do I know you didn't guide him here, as well?"

"I would never—"

"Bullshit. You would in a heartbeat if you thought it would serve you."

Aidan stood. He may not tower over the incubus, but when he pulled in through Fire, the might of it made even Tomás step back. It filled him not only with warmth, but with anger. He knew he'd been toyed with. He'd just been so focused on his victory that he'd ignored it.

Well, here was the final victory. One more Kin to kill only a few hundred feet away.

One more, besides Tomás.

"No more games, Tomás. The Dark Lady chose *me* to do Her work. Do you truly think she would mourn if that work included destroying you?"

Tomás shook his head, his eyes wide. For once, he actually looked scared.

"I have served you," he said. "Just as I have served her. I had nothing to do with Tenn's unwelcome obtrusion into your life." He swallowed. His eyes flicked away when he said it.

Aidan took a step forward.

"The truth." He grabbed Tomás's arm, poured Fire through his veins so even the incubus's skin steamed. "Or I throw you over those runes and see how you look missing half your limbs."

Tomás's eyes narrowed. "I must say, your newfound confidence is both disconcerting and maddeningly arousing." He sighed. "Fine. I had no say in Tenn's appearance. That I promise you. But when he and I last parted ways, he…he branded me. With one of his damnable little tracking runes."

"Where?"

He removed Aidan's hand and pressed it to his chest. Aidan's palm sizzled against the incubus's skin, but Tomás said nothing about the pain.

"In here," he said. He looked Aidan in the eyes. This time, he didn't look away. "I swear to you, my king. I had no idea he would find you through me. Had I known, I would have ripped out my own heart."

Aidan dropped his hand and grunted a laugh.

"I may just have to hold you to that."

CHAPTER TWENTY-FIVE

IF TENN DIDN'T GET OUT OF HERE SOON, HE WAS GOING TO lose his mind. He was trapped. Barely able to move and unable to use magic, unsure if Jarrett would ever come back and release him. Unsure if the twins had known Jarrett would do this, or if he'd been lying about that, as well. Was it just as he'd feared all along? That they'd all been sent not to protect him, but to use him? Was any of their friendship real?

Knowing that Aidan was still alive filled him with both hope and dread. Aidan was alive. So that meant he could still be saved. And yet Jarrett's words kept replaying in his head—saving Aidan would destroy him. Saving Aidan would cost them everything.

Was it true? Was Aidan already so far gone that there was no way to bring him back?

"What do you want me to do?" he whispered. Maybe to himself, maybe to the spirits he was quickly losing faith in. He wasn't a murderer. So why did it seem like every time he tried to find another way, he was rerouted back to needing to kill Aidan?

Finally, after what seemed like weeks, the door opened again.

Probably Jarrett, coming down to apologize but not do anything about it. Or else a guard, bringing him dinner. When the stench of whiskey and BO hit him, however, Tenn realized he would have happily taken Jarrett's disappointment or a crappy meal instead.

"How did you get down here?" Tenn asked.

He stared at the man before him, at the greasy beard and slicked hair, at the worn suit and sharp eyes.

"God is everywhere," Caius said gruffly. "And since I go with God, I'm everywhere, too."

He grinned and placed his hands on the bars, leaning in toward Tenn.

"Truth be told, I think they're worried about you. Think you might have turned to the Dark Lady. And they want me to make sure your soul is pure."

Tenn flinched back, both from the man's breath and the fear that shot through his heart. Immediately, he thought of Aidan and the wounds he had suffered at the hands of the Inquisition. If the Guild had let Caius in here, if Caius was actually part of the Inquisition...

"Or," Caius said with a chuckle, "I've had many of my followers held down here. So many visits to ease their souls. So many, that I may have learned a secret passage or two for sneaking in. And out." He winked.

If anything, it put Tenn even more on edge.

The Church had overthrown London after Calum had been

killed. Who was to say they weren't going to try the same thing back here?

Caius must have noticed the concern in Tenn's eyes. He laughed. Far too loudly for Tenn's liking.

"My, you've grown much more suspicious since I last saw you. Good. Good. You may just live through all this yet."

"What are you talking about?"

"I'm talking about good and evil, Tenn. You've seen it first-hand, the darkness that stirs in men's hearts. I've heard the stories of what you've done. You've read the runes and all that mumbo jumbo."

"If you're here to tell me I've sinned—"

"Quite the contrary." His voice lowered, grew quiet. "God speaks to me, Tenn. You may not believe it, but it doesn't matter. Just as many don't believe that you have heard the words of gods long past. I say, it doesn't matter who or what you call it. The Witches and the Church are all after the same thing— God's love. When you feel it, you're changed. And you have definitely changed."

That made Tenn's heart flip. How did Caius know about that?

"I don't—"

"Understand. Yes, yes, I know. Why do you think I snuck down here when I learned you were back? It's not safe for you to stay. Your story hasn't ended just yet."

"Why would you help me, though? How do I know this isn't some sort of trap?"

"Because when we last spoke, I told you that the time wasn't right for you to learn the truth of the Dark Lady." His eyes narrowed, and his fingers clutched the bars of the cage tight. "Now, it is."

CHAPTER TWENTY-SIX

NATASJA'S RUNES WERE RIDICULOUSLY EASY TO UNDO.

Aidan knelt in the snow and used a tendril of flame to melt a few small channels in the ice, redirecting the runes' power. He had considered using the runes to kill Natasja, yes. But that seemed cowardly.

He deserved to see her die.

After all, she was the last.

He glanced at Tomás. So far.

The moment he finished his work, the new runes snapped into power, and an archway of sparks hissed into life before him. On the exterior of the arch, the world looked the same—a long unbroken stretch of snow and ice. But within...

"As I said," Tomás mused. "A flair for the dramatic."

Aidan stood in awe, suddenly grateful he hadn't brought the whole place down without ever stepping foot inside.

This was everything a proper palace should be.

The structure towered high above them, stretching up into

the clouded sky like inverted icicles. And that's precisely what they were.

Although the ground floor appeared to be dark stone, the upper towers and turrets had been crafted with a sculptor's grace from delicate, glistening ice. Every window, every arch, every shingle. Beautiful and jagged, powerful and imposing. Impossible in its enormity. So much magic had been fused into this place. Magic, and...

"Why is it pink?" Aidan asked. Because the more he looked, the more he realized the reddish tint to the place wasn't from sunlight or fire. It was part of the ice itself.

"My sister's enemies," Tomás said. "She thought it fitting that those who tried to destroy her should become part of her defenses. She is a bloodling, in case you hadn't gathered by now. And have I mentioned yet that she is dramatic?"

He began to walk.

Aidan followed, though he refused to call it following.

In the minutes or hours after he'd scratched the new runes into his arm, he'd expected to feel...different. But truthfully, even though he'd harnessed incredible power—what was it Brother Jeremiah had said? *What you know of power is but a candle to the sun*—he was his normal self. He didn't have the Dark Lady screaming directions in his ear. He didn't have shadows or demons following him about.

He didn't *feel* evil.

He just felt powerful.

And after all, he wasn't exactly *doing* anything evil in the first place. He'd told the Dark Lady he'd bring her back under two conditions—one, that she'd give him his power back, and two, that she'd bring his mother back to life. Two conditions, and his world had hardly changed.

It was almost disappointing.

Here he was, about to destroy the final Kin that barred the way between him and immortality and his mother and everything he'd ever dreamed of. And it didn't feel any different than storming Calum's castle had barely a week ago. In fact, this seemed even less climactic. He was walking up to the front door of a terribly imposing castle, about to face down what was supposed to be one of the most powerful creatures in the world, and he felt nothing. No adrenaline. No fear. No rage.

He paused midstride.

Was this what being powerful truly felt like?

If he was being perfectly honest with himself, he was almost…bored.

He stared up at the castle. Remembered the throne room that Calum had blockaded himself within—the twisted frozen corpses of Hunters and civilians past, the throne of interlocked bodies. At the time, Aidan had thought Calum to be a nutter.

But only an hour at the very top of the food chain, and he was starting to understand.

Without the battle of life, what was even the point of living?

"Coming, my king?" Tomás asked. He was five steps in front of Aidan, looking back with a quizzical expression. "Don't tell me you're getting cold feet."

Aidan drew in deep through Fire, an inhalation that sent sparks and flame swirling around him, turning snow and ice to steam.

"I don't get cold anymore," Aidan said, his lungs filled with cinders. "And it's about damn time."

As he continued following Tomás, he realized something he'd never noticed before. Probably because the Kin had never turned his back to him. Aidan jogged a few steps and grabbed hold of Tomás's bloody, shredded shirt and ripped open the back.

"My king," Tomás said, pausing but not turning around, "now is hardly the time."

But Aidan wasn't interested in sex or coyness. He was staring at the line of black runes tattooed down Tomás's spine.

"What are these?" he heard himself ask, but he hadn't actually meant to voice the words. He didn't need to.

The sinuous black marks that curved and cut down Tomás's back whispered with the voice of the Dark Lady, as audible as if she were standing right behind him. Runes to change. To control. Runes to command. And he knew as he read them that they were what allowed the Kin to be created. Just as he'd seen on Calum, these allowed the monsters to use magic. Allowed them to maintain a semblance of their original sanity. He reached out and drew his finger down Tomás's spine.

Both the runes and the incubus seemed to curl at his touch.

The runes were good. Better than the ones scratched and scrawled over Calum's chest. Better than the ones on the shard. Hadn't Tomás said that he was the youngest of the Kin? It seemed that the Dark Lady had improved her craft.

Shame she had been halted before she could continue.

Well, almost a shame.

Aidan knew he could have done similar work if he so wanted.

The thought struck him.

He could create more Kin. He could do what the Dark Lady could not.

No.

That would be crossing a line. He snickered to himself at the thought. Of all the things he'd done, he found it hilarious that making a Howl would be the worst.

Maybe I could do it to Tenn, though. Turn him into a mopey bloodling. Aidan looked up to the castle, imagined Natasja brooding away inside. *Nah. He would probably enjoy being miserable too much.*

"Do you like what you see?" Tomás asked, breaking him from his thoughts.

"Not really." Aidan stepped past him. He made sure to look Tomás in the eyes when he spoke. "Her work was sloppy."

A dozen emotions warred on Tomás's face, but Aidan was past him before any one could settle.

"Why aren't they attacking?" Aidan asked idly, making his way up the broad, icy avenue leading to the castle. There weren't any guards, as far as he could see. But any Kin with an ounce of intelligence would sense the threat. "Or did you *prepare* this one for me, as well?"

Tomás seemed to settle on annoyance as he resumed his pacing at Aidan's side, his shirt hanging from him like tattered, bloody wings.

"That is not my sister's way. She prefers to toy with her victims. I think she disdains killing, honestly. I think she prefers when they do it themselves."

Aidan didn't bother asking what he meant.

The great doors before them opened, revealing a crystal-line hall devoid of life. Tomás bowed and gestured forward.

Aidan stepped inside. And, as the doors shut behind him, he felt only the briefest flicker of panic when he realized he was alone.

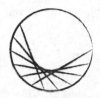

CHAPTER TWENTY-SEVEN

"YOU ARE SURE YOU WANT TO DO THIS?" DREYA ASKED.

Kianna didn't glare, just stared her straight in the eyes.

"Don't make me ask again." And perhaps it was Dreya's imagination, but it sounded if it were less of a demand and more of a plea.

Dreya nodded and looked down to Kianna's arm, to the scarred, unmarked dark skin.

She had already retrieved the tattoo machine from one of the guards—they hadn't asked any questions. Figuring out the ladder of command and what to do in the wake of battle was more important than wondering why strangers needed a tattoo machine. She held the device with a steady hand. It was not the first time she had given someone the mark, but it was the first time she had felt so…unsteady.

Kianna hated magic above all things, for reasons Dreya could not understand. And yet, here she was, trusting a relative stranger to attune her. She sat in the chair with her eyes closed and her breath slow and steady. Intentionally so. Dreya could tell this was not something she wanted to do.

"Normally," Dreya said softly, "I would have you meditate on your chosen Sphere. It is easier that way, I think, especially for an initiate." Kianna raised an eyebrow. "But in this case, I do not believe it is necessary. Just know...this will hurt."

"Pain means nothing," Kianna said.

Dreya felt her brother's disapproving stare on the back of her neck as she opened to Fire and threaded a small spool of energy into the machine. Instantly, it whirred to life. She dipped it into the ink.

Spirits, guide my hand. Grant me the grace to do your work.

Devon grunted.

Dreya brought the needle to Kianna's forearm and began.

When Dreya had been attuned, the moment had been steeped in ritual. Even now, in the basement of some unmarked Guild, she smelled the lingering trace of sage and palo santo, the heavy hum of frankincense. She could almost hear the songs and the chants of her Clan as she worked. They hadn't used a machine to give her the mark. A simple needle on a simple stick, the light tap of a hammer. Hours of focus and distant pain as the concentric circles and runes blossomed on her pale skin.

It had felt like an eternity. Not the pain. But the floating. The emptiness. Every tap a vibration, and she an instrument, strummed.

And then the spark when the final runes took hold, when Air blossomed in her throat, and she felt like she had taken her very first, true breath.

She wondered if it would be the same for Kianna. The same

spiritual intensity. Or if she would see it as donning another weapon.

"I'll never hear the end of this," Kianna muttered. She opened her eyes, peered down at Dreya's work. "That one looks wonky."

Dreya felt herself smile. Because there was nothing wrong with the lines she drew, and there was no accusation in Kianna's voice.

Ugh, Devon thought. He turned and left.

"He doesn't like me, does he," Kianna said. Not a question.

Dreya tried not to let her focus wander. She had just begun working on the runes that would connect Kianna to Earth, and if she messed any of these up, she would render the entire design impotent.

"He does not like many."

Kianna just grunted approvingly.

And then there was silence. Just the buzz of the machine. It made her wonder—how long had it been since she'd truly had silence like this? No war burning on the horizon. No boy to save or protect. At least, not nearby.

"Where did Tenn go?" Kianna asked. Dreya jolted her head up and nearly missed a mark. Did Kianna read her mind?

"Back to Outer Chicago." It was an estimate. But she thought it close enough to call it truthful.

"Why?"

"It is safer for him there." This was a lie, although it bore a note of truth, and was easier than explaining the full situation. Especially when she herself did not understand.

"With lover-boy? Hard to imagine."

Dreya bit her lip and resumed focus.

"Jarrett thought it prudent for Tenn to be away from this battle. It is…difficult to explain."

"Because you're afraid you'll hurt my feelings. Admit it— you were scared that if he stayed here, Aidan would kill him."

Dreya completed another rune. Only a few more to go.

She wondered what it would be like to understand them fully. She had spent years studying the runes, and yet for Tenn, reading them had been as simple as breathing. They had spoken things to him that they never had for her. She would have felt jealous. And yet, the burden on his shoulders was not one she would ever want to bear.

The gods had chosen him to hear their words and remake the world. That was not a burden she wished upon anyone.

"Yes," Dreya finally admitted. "We have no way to fathom what Aidan thinks."

"Used to," Kianna said. She hissed an inhale as Dreya buzzed the machine over her inner elbow. "He used to just like killing and shagging, just like the rest of us. Now…"

Dreya felt heat rise to her face. Perhaps because "shagging" had never been on her radar. It was an act she knew others performed. But beyond that, she had never thought it would be for her.

"What happened to him?" Kianna asked. Dreya paused and looked up. "You said he's reading runes of the Dark Lady. So… what? Is he a necromancer now?"

Dreya shook her head.

"I do not know what he is or is not," she whispered. "We can only hope he has held on to his humanity."

CHAPTER TWENTY-EIGHT

THIS FELT LIKE A TRAP.

It felt like a trap, but with Fire burning in his heart, he wasn't afraid. If anything, he was amused. Tomás thought he could trap him? Natasja thought she could dazzle him with—what?—a glittery hallway? A maze? Please. All it would take was a flick of power and he could turn this entire place into a goddamned puddle. Ice was nothing. Not against the sun.

But he had to admit, he wanted to see whatever snare they had laid for him. This was his final kill, after all. Sigmund had been simple. Desmond ridiculously so. And now that he stood on the precipice of his final victory, he realized he wanted a battle. Even if it was all a farce. He didn't want to just destroy the castle and everyone within. He wanted to savor it.

He walked down the crystalline hall, admiring himself in the many mirrors that lined it. Mirrors and ice and snow in the corners, and if he hadn't had Fire in him, he would have been freezing.

"Come out, come out, wherever you are."

His voice echoed along the hall, reverberating off crystal and glass and stone. He knew this was supposed to be disconcerting. Knew he was supposed to feel like a mouse in a cage. But what could she do that would harm him? He had the primal Fire in his hands. He could unmake her in a heartbeat if he wished.

"This way, young Hunter," came a voice. It echoed, too, but he followed it with a smile. Down the hall. Around the corner. And into a maze of the dead.

Calum's hall had been desolate in its depravity. But this... this was artistic. Whereas the frozen statues in Calum's castle had been dusty and dimly lit, this was clearly meant to be a showpiece. One intended to inspire fear in any who trekked through it. Frankly, Aidan was just bored.

He'd have thought the Kin would at least be a bit more original.

He walked down the rows and rows of giant ice slabs, each lit with bright electric light above. And within each slab was a human. Some with shocked expressions. Some clothed. Some young, some old. But they were each of them posed, each of them floating in eternal ice. And each block of ice had something Calum's hall had not.

Tubes.

Tubes looping from wrists, carved in the ice and into flesh. Tubes sluggishly transporting thick, coagulated blood.

"Do you like what I've done with them?"

Natasja's voice was as cold and crystalline as her subjects. She glided into the hall in a ball gown, a long, glittering, delicate thing of blue satin and diamonds. She was tall and pale, her hair bleached within an inch of its life. Her eyes glittered light gray, and around her throat was a heavy sapphire necklace.

She probably thought it was impressive. A show of power, that in a broken world like this she could walk around wearing finery. No armor, no weapons, no flank of guards.

He just found it terribly outdated.

"I've seen better."

Her eyes flashed, and that serene expression cracked. Just like Tomás, the monster waiting below the surface of her highly polished exterior was craving blood.

"You're here to kill me," she said.

Aidan examined his nails, twining flame around his remaining fingertips.

"Yup," he said. "Is this the point where you beg for mercy?"

She laughed, high and clear.

"Would you expect me to grant you mercy if the roles were reversed? I think not. Creatures like you and me, Hunter, we are not in this game for mercy. We are in it for power. And we fight to the death to maintain it."

"And yet you aren't fighting." He gestured to the emptiness around them. "No guards. No defenses. Save for those ridiculously bad runes you had out there. Who taught you those, anyway?"

"Our Mother," she said, and began walking away. "Come. We have much to discuss before you kill me."

CHAPTER TWENTY-NINE

"ONCE UPON A TIME," CAIUS SAID IN HIS GRUMBLY, SMOKER'S voice, "there was a nun who grew impatient."

Despite the confines of the cage and the stink from Caius's breath, Tenn found himself leaning in closer. The air around them felt heavy, similar to the feeling he'd had when the Witches shared their own secrets.

"This is heresy, you understand," Caius said. "The gravest of sins. But it is the secret the Church held close to its heart with daggers and blood. Knowing is the reason I came here. Surrounded myself with sinners. Because here, at least, the main Church has no hold. They can't find me. If I tell you, though, they will know. I know they will. And they will kill both of us in our sleep."

"I can think of worse ways to go," Tenn said.

"Right you are." He glanced around, but they were alone. "She and I worked together. The Dark Lady. When magic was revealed to the world, the Church sprang into action, creating various arms to gain as much information as they could. It took them by surprise. They thought that all magic had died with pagan times. They thought it had all just been a story to tell kids around a campfire. They were wrong.

"The Dark Lady... Her name was Elizabeth. Such a kind, caring name, for a kind and caring woman. We managed a network of spies and intelligence gatherers, hoarding as much knowledge on magic and runes as possible. We didn't gather much. Not more than the general public knew, but we held hope.

"And one night, Elizabeth and I were in the Church's library, poring over biblical texts and modern magical treatises and reports from the various schools that had sprung up all over the world, and she turned to me and said...she said, *Do you think this means it was a lie?*

"I asked her what she meant, but of course I knew. *Our stories,* she replied. *Our savior. Was it all a lie? If magic is real, if miracles are possible, why are none happening within the Church?*"

He sighed.

"She asked why our savior hadn't returned. I knew this was something she had been grappling with for ages. And I said, *I don't know what stories are real and what are not, but I know the core of the Word rings true. Sometimes,* I said, *we have to be our own saviors.* I never should have said that."

He pulled out a flask from his breast pocket, took a swig and reached it through the bars toward Tenn. Tenn's first impulse was to decline anything that man's mouth had touched, but his head swirled with the weight of what Caius was saying. He brought his head forward, and Caius helped him take a long swig.

It tasted just as disgusting as Tenn had expected, but it bit the back of his throat with warmth and filled his lungs with fire. He coughed, tried to hide the sound. Caius just smiled and took another drink.

"She didn't bring up our conversation again after that. But something in her had changed. Every day she seemed a little more tired. I'd asked her if she was feeling okay, if she'd been sleeping. She never answered me. At least, not honestly. Only once did she hint at the truth. *I've been studying,* she said. And that was it. By the time I learned, well…by the time I learned, she was no longer the Elizabeth I knew. One day, she was just gone. All of her paperwork, too. Not a single damn trace. I was questioned, obviously, but I didn't know anything. Not until I saw her on TV. Knew it was her right away."

He closed his eyes, as if reliving the news scene: the man, strapped in a chair, while the blonde Dark Lady twisted him into a kraven.

"Later, much later, I realized what she'd done. She'd taken my words and run with them. *We need to be our own savior.* Bah! I didn't mean she needed to try playing God and raising the dead. And that's what she wanted to do. Stop death. Reverse it. She thought that if God was just a story like magic had once been, there was no point in dying. There was no eternal glory. Just this bleak, accursed earth. This one life. And she wanted to be the savior of mankind. She wanted to heal the world. She wanted everyone to be their own savior. Their own gods. And look what became of it. Bastardized. Just like everything else we do."

When Caius stopped talking, Tenn realized he hadn't actually breathed since Caius had resumed. His inhale was shaky and harsh.

"She was part of the Church," Tenn whispered.

"Was, at one point in time. They got her, eventually." His eyes leveled on Tenn. "They always get what they want. Eventually."

CHAPTER THIRTY

NATASJA LED AIDAN UP A CRYSTALLINE SPIRAL STAIRCASE, UP to the top of the tallest tower in the castle. The room was sparse, only a small white armchair and a mirror in the corner. It was clear this room wasn't made for lounging, but for viewing. From here, through walls and windows, he saw the great expanse of white stretching out into oblivion.

"Seems rather lonely," Aidan said, pulling a little deeper through Fire to warm his toes. He tried not to draw so much that the ice steamed around him.

"I prefer it this way," she replied. "Being surrounded by those who fear you grows tiresome after a while."

Aidan shrugged. He didn't want to admit that he was starting to understand.

"So what are you going to show me? Or are you just stalling?"

Natasja looked at him, and it struck him just how much the sadness in her eyes reminded him of Tenn.

"Trust me, Hunter, I am not hoping to prolong the inevitable. I am more than ready to die."

"Then why didn't you just do it yourself?"

"Pride," she said.

She stepped over to the mirror.

"There was a time when I delighted in my power. When I thought the entire world mine to control. But as my hunger spread, my discontent grew. There was no joy in my life, no matter the joy I found in killing or feeding. Once, the peasants surrounding me called this the Castle of Blood. The walls ran red with my hunger, and I would freeze and feed dozens at a time. I would make family members watch as I drained their children or parents. I would make them make the cuts themselves. I delighted in it."

She sighed. Aidan was already growing tired of this. As she trailed her finger along the edge of the silver-framed mirror, he considered just ending her once and for all.

"But that was the greatest curse of the runes our Mother bequeathed to me. To us. She allowed us to keep our humanity. And after a time, no matter how strong the monster within, humanity wins out. And when you realize what you have done, you cannot live with yourself any longer."

She looked at him in the reflection. Pointedly. Sadly.

He pulled deeper through Fire. This had gone on long enough.

"I'm not here for a lesson in morality," he growled. "What do you want?"

"The runes here," she mused, brushing the silver frame once more. "They are unlike so many. They can be fueled by any magic. Any magic but mine, that is. I was her disciple, you see. From the very beginning, I worked with her to turn the first of the Kin. We created the Kin first, did you know? Four to help usher in a new age. To help recruit those to Her cause and spread Her word. Four. And then I asked her to turn me. She did so, gladly. I had helped her understand so much. The ancient language, it spoke to me. It whispered in ways she would never understand. And now that I have turned, it has stopped speaking. But I still remembered enough from my studies."

She gestured Aidan forward. He stepped up warily.

"Place your hand to the mirror, Hunter. Channel in your power. These runes will show you my history."

"I don't give a shit about your history."

"And yet here you stand. You haven't killed me. You are curious. Curious to know why a woman so powerful as the Dark Lady was destroyed. Curious to know why she craves the death of her own creations. Curious as to why she chose *you* to do Her work. Your answers rest within, Hunter. Or are you too afraid to seek?"

"I'm not afraid of anything except you boring me to death."

She smiled. And for a moment, he saw a trace of the monster within her, the bloodling struggling to get out.

"Trust me, Hunter. That would not be my way."

He placed his hand to the mirror. Channeled a web of power into the glass.

And as his reflection rotated, as his vision shifted to his mirrored self, he wondered if this had been the trap all along.

It should have felt momentous, this moment. The five of them together for the first time in history. The five most powerful creations in the world. The creatures who should make the world tremble. And they would, in time. But first—

"She has to be stopped." Calum's voice cut through the

heavy silence of the room. Even though he stood tall, even though there was a fresh fire in his eyes, he still reminded Natasja way too much of a corpse.

My greatest triumph, the Dark Lady had called him. *My triumph over life and death. Behold, the rise of a new savior.* Though whether the Dark Lady had meant Calum was the savior, or she herself, Natasja wasn't sure. All she knew was, for all of Calum's vitality, something in him seemed sick with grave dust. They might all be other than human, but Calum's inhumanity made her flesh crawl.

Almost as much as his proclamation. The reason they had all gathered here, in the outskirts of the world, without their Mother's knowing.

It was heresy. Natasja had been turned only a few weeks prior, but it was clear that Calum was right. The Dark Lady had gone public, and the world ripped itself apart. Just as the Dark Lady had predicted it would.

In the ash, they will need a savior, she had told them. *We are those saviors.*

"She means to create more of us," Desmond muttered. "Even now, she works on creating a sixth. She wishes to spread to every country, every continent."

"She doesn't want just to create us to spread Her word," Natasja said. They all turned to her. They knew her well—after all, many had been turned with her watching on. "She seeks to perfect us."

"Perfect us?" Leanna asked.

Natasja nodded.

"The runes she uses…she doesn't fully understand them. With every creation, she gets closer to her true goal."

"And what would that be?" Calum asked. "She has already reversed death."

"No. She stalled it. When you were killed, the runes on your body kept your Spheres alive. You did not truly die—you were kept in stasis until you could be revived. Death only occurs when all five Spheres cease to function." She paused. Should she tell him that even his "resurrection" was incomplete? That with his body so damaged, he would quickly begin to age and fade? No, let him believe himself immortal. It wouldn't change anything.

"She will continue her trials until she has created the perfect creature—one who will never age, can never die, and can use both the Spheres and the runes. And then, she will have the process done to her, so she may outlive us all."

That clearly struck a chord. Although none could use runes, all within this room thought themselves gods. Thought to be above law. But if there were creatures above them...if their *maker* suddenly became more powerful, then what? Then, they would be servants.

"And there is more," Natasja said. "I know her. I know that once she *has* perfected the process, she will not stand to surround herself with imperfections. She will have us eradicated. All of us."

Silence.

They stared amongst each other. Only a handful of weeks after their creation, and they already saw the end.

"So what do we do?" Desmond asked.

"We stop her," Leanna replied. She turned to Natasja. "Do you still have connections within the Church?"

Natasja nodded.

"They have militarized since the Resurrection. They seek to destroy her. And her creations."

Leanna mused, biting her delicate bottom lip.

"But what if we proposed a truce?"

"Truce?" Calum asked. "With the Church? You're mad."

"I am an opportunist." Leanna looked at Natasja. As if there were no one else in the room. As if Natasja's answers were the only ones that mattered.

"What if we offered a trade? We give them the Dark Lady. And in return, we do not step foot in their Septs, we do not attack any under their fold and they offer the same. They will see this as a victory. Their victory over the darkness. Immunity. Think on it—ages ago, the Church ruled all. Now, their influence has weakened. We would give them the world on a silver platter. They would allow us to rule as we will. Humanity can choose once more—serve the light, or serve the dark. They will finally be able to live their own fables."

Natasja's stomach churned. Such an emotion should be beneath her, should be impossible with her broken Sphere of Water swallowing such lesser despairs. But she had known Elizabeth, the Dark Lady, for years. She had been Natasja's dearest friend. And now...

"How do we know a truce would hold?" Desmond asked. "If we kill her, they will just turn around and kill us. And why should we need their support in the first place?"

"We don't, dear brother. We could kill them all without breaking a sweat. But then where would we be? This is much more fun. And as for killing her, well...who said anything about that?"

Leanna looked back to Natasja.

"I assume you have the runes?"

Natasja nodded, uncertainty clenching at her once more. She needed to feed. That was all. She needed to feed.

"Very well then," Leanna said. "We will keep her...safe. Under our care. In stasis. And should they break their treaty, we will set her free."

She finally looked to the rest of the room. "Are we all in agreement? We render the Dark Lady obsolete, and in return, we secure our places in history. We rule as gods, unimpeded."

There was a moment of hesitation. And then, finally, the Kin nodded as one.

CHAPTER THIRTY-ONE

KIANNA'S EYES WIDENED THE MOMENT THE FINAL RUNE CON-
nected.

She inhaled.

"Oh," she said. "*Oh.*"

Dreya set the machinery to the side and hid her slight smile.

"There is much you must learn," Dreya said. "How to channel it properly. The extent of your power. You must remember,
it is like training a new muscle—you will only be able to do a
little before tiring. And if you pull too much, you could drain
yourself. Earth causes very physical drawbacks."

Kianna sat there, mouth slightly open, the Sphere of Earth
timidly glowing in her belly.

"You better teach her quick," Devon said as he stepped into
the room. He looked between the two of them. Even if Dreya
couldn't feel her brother's emotions, she would have known
his agitation from the sparks flying around his clenched fists.
"We've gotten word from the Prophets."

"And?" Dreya said.

Devon shook his head.

He's about to destroy everything, he thought.

Deep in her heart, Dreya knew that meant they were already too late.

CHAPTER THIRTY-TWO

THE VISION BROKE.

Aidan turned, expecting the Kin to be holding a knife to his heart. But she merely sat in her high-backed chair in the corner, watching him with cold gray eyes. She didn't even have a glass of fresh blood in her hand for the ambience factor.

"Where is she?" he asked.

He couldn't even feel anger at the Kin's betrayal. Hadn't he done the same when promised immortality and power?

Now he understood why the Dark Lady wanted her own creations dead. They had handed her over to the Church. Or rather, they had done the Church's dirty work for them.

Natasja stood slowly.

"She is here. I thought it best to keep her within my own walls. Until you, none had been able to find me, let alone get past the runes. I suppose I should thank Tomás for that?"

Aidan nodded.

"Am I the last, then?" she asked.

Another nod.

"I thought as much." She began walking down the steps. "You know you cannot trust him, correct?"

"I don't trust anyone," Aidan replied. He gestured to the stairs. "That's why I'm letting you go first."

"And here, I thought it was because you were a gentleman."

"Clearly you don't know me very well."

Aidan didn't ask why the castle was empty. He figured she'd just grown bored or hungry and had started murdering her subjects—especially if she thought her own death was coming. Fire burned impatiently within him. He wanted to kill her and get this history lesson over with.

He wanted to find the Dark Lady so she would bring his mother back.

He was so close to getting everything he wanted, everything he'd fought and sacrificed for. So close. He just had to endure this a few more minutes, and he would have his mother back. A few more minutes, and he would have everything.

She led him in silence, first down the crystalline steps of the tower, back through the maze of frozen corpses and then into a dark tunnel leading far beneath the soil. Aidan *did* shiver, then. Being underground made him think too much of being snuffed out. It was almost as bad as being surrounded by water.

"In here," Natasja said. She stopped outside the door. Silver runes covered every surface, from the wood to the walls and the floor. They whispered in Aidan's mind, runes of concealment and containment, stasis and eternity.

"Open it." He curled flame around his hands, casting the walls in flickering shadows and highlights. The runes seemed to writhe at his presence.

She nodded and placed her hand on the door. There was no magic. When the door opened, Aidan was almost disappointed.

It was a basement room just like any other. Concrete walls, concrete floor. A bare fluorescent bulb on the ceiling. Completely empty, save for the pedestal of stone in the center of the room. And on it…

Her arms crossed over her chest like a mummy, her long dress a deep violet. Her hair, the palest blond, spread in a halo around her head.

The Dark Lady.

He took a step forward. As the light from his flames shifted, he saw the runes that traced their way over every surface in the room, runes dug into the walls and stone. Runes to preserve, to protect, to hide away. Runes to keep her young and contained forever. *Forever.* Runes to protect her from magic, barriers that no mage could pass. These, he noted, were much stronger than the ones he'd crossed to get here.

"You've made her a prison," Aidan whispered.

Natasja said nothing for a moment. Then, "I kept her safe."

Aidan looked over his shoulder at her. She stared at the Dark Lady's body, sadness once more filling her eyes. And once more, that made him think of Tenn. Trying to keep everyone safe. And failing.

"You betrayed her. That isn't saving."

"I did what we had to do. To protect myself. To secure my rule. That, I'm sure, is a motive you can understand."

Aidan grinned.

"Yes," he said. "I can."

He pulled through Fire, drank deep of the eternal flame and sent it coursing through Natasja's chest.

A flick of power. It felt like so very little.

And yet, when he turned his attention back to the Dark Lady, he heard the satisfying thud as Natasja's corpse toppled to the floor.

"Your final sacrifice, *Mother*," Aidan said, stepping toward the Dark Lady's dais. "Now, it's time you give me what you owe."

CHAPTER THIRTY-THREE

"NOW YOU UNDERSTAND," CAIUS GROWLED. "NOW YOU understand why I had to hide away here, amidst you heathens."

"But what happened to her?" Tenn asked. "She was human. She was part of the Church. So what happened after?"

Caius shrugged.

"Beats me. I ran as soon as the Church realized who she was. Knew they'd start drawing parallels, knew they'd come after me. All I know is, she pissed off the wrong people."

"It doesn't matter. Even if she was part of the Church, she's dead now. She's just a story."

"You know that in your heart to be false." Caius stared at Tenn, and in that moment he didn't look like a mad drunk. He looked as wise as Dreya. "Evil never dies, Tenn. Think about it. The Church got in the Dark Lady the answer they'd always needed, a dark to their light. Why do you think there has always been an uneasy balance? Why do you think Septs are never targeted by the minions of the Dark Lady, when they refuse to use magic?"

Tenn looked to the amulet against his chest.

"I just assumed it was from this," he muttered.

Caius grumbled, reached between the bars of the cage. And snapped the amulet from around Tenn's neck. It felt like waking from a bad dream—the flood of familiarity and power as Earth and Water rematerialized under his senses. He gasped with pleasure.

Maybe he was as addicted as Aidan.

"This," Caius said. "This is just a party trick. It doesn't keep you from being murdered in your sleep by a dagger. No, the Church and the Dark Lady have an alliance. Somehow. And you don't kill the person you hold an alliance with, no matter how tenuous."

"You think she's alive," Tenn whispered.

"I know it. And so do you."

Tenn swallowed.

"Do you know where she is?"

"No," Caius said. "But I know she is gaining strength. Darkness stirs in the world, Tenn. And if you do not act fast, it will swallow all of us."

His words speared Tenn's heart.

Why me? Why does it always have to be me?

Before he could ask, Caius jerked upright.

"Company."

Without another word, he turned and scurried off into the darkness. Tenn never heard a door open or close, but he didn't hear Caius again.

He sank against the wall and closed off to the Spheres. He didn't want to give away his ace. When whoever this was went away, he would make his escape.

Though where to, he had no idea.

Footsteps down the hall.

Many footsteps.

The door burst open, blinding him with light as the strangers crowded in.

No, not strangers.

"Dreya?" he gasped.

She barely acknowledged him. Just strode in with Devon and Kianna close behind.

"Where's Aidan?" he asked.

"That's what we are hoping to find out," she said.

Jarrett, he realized, was nowhere to be found.

"Come." Her words were rushed, and it was then he realized she was still open to Air, still scanning. She hadn't come here under Jarrett's orders. "We must get you out of here."

Tenn opened to Earth and undid the manacles at his back, then crumbled the lock on the bars between them.

"What's going on?"

"Didn't you hear?" Kianna said. "The whole world's turned upside down." She opened to Earth and opened the cell door. Tenn gasped. She'd attuned? "And Aidan's the one behind it. He's been on a rampage, killing Kin left and right. We have to go. Now. Before he does something we'll all regret."

"But I don't know where to find him," Tenn said. It's not like he had a rune on Aidan or anything.

Dreya looked at him with an eyebrow cocked.

"You found him before," she said.

Tenn's gut clenched. He'd told her he could find Aidan when he brought them to London. He hadn't admitted he was chasing Tomás.

Tomás.

If Aidan was out killing Kin, he had to believe that the incubus would be at his side, guiding his hand. He had to believe. It was their only shot.

"Okay then." He didn't ask if they should bring Jarrett. It was clear Jarrett had already decided what side he stood on. And it most definitely wasn't Tenn's. Tenn pulled through Earth and scratched grooves into the stone at their feet, the runes of travel unfurling between them like a jagged rose. He brought the rune he had seared in Tomás's heart to mind.

"Let's end this."

CHAPTER THIRTY-FOUR

AIDAN STARED AT THE DARK LADY'S CORPSE.

He'd expected a sort of gravity between them. Or, at least, a gravity to her presence. After all, this was the woman who had guided him all this way. The woman who promised to turn back the hand of fate and bring his mother back to life. The woman who had set the entire world on a collision course with extinction.

And here, in this room, she looked like just another body on a cold stone slab.

"You're still in there, aren't you," he muttered.

There was no response, but there didn't need to be. He knew it was true. He knew it in the pit of Fire, in the strange resonance in his chest. Her face was pale and smooth, her hands delicate—painter's hands, his mother would call them. Her dress was layered in deep violet silk, her hair so fine it reminded him of Dreya's. Bloodred lips. Sharp, angular cheeks.

He stared at her, and he wondered how this woman, who looked to be the same age as his own mom had been, this frail, delicate woman, had sown so much destruction. She had become the face of evil incarnate, and yet she was stunningly beautiful. There was nothing truly malicious in her features. Nothing that made her to be a monster.

And yet.

Hadn't he learned that evil could be hidden behind any beautiful mask? He reached up and touched his face, his scarred palms scratching against his stubble. If anything, he looked more the part of monster. The cuts and bruises from the Inquisition, the missing fingers, the lacerated Hunter's mark, still pink and tender on his arm. He was the monster, and he would play his part.

He looked at the mark, at the runes he'd inscribed. Those had been her words. And also, not. They had been his, as well. He reached down and pulled at the sleeve of her dress, revealing her own mark. The runes scrawled across her forearm were similar to those most Hunters wore. Nothing special.

She had never given herself the runes Aidan had. She had never felt power like he.

Realization struck him—he wasn't following the Dark Lady. She wasn't his superior. They both channeled the same energies, read the same runes.

They were equals.

His lips quirked in a smile.

Maybe he didn't need her to rule, after all.

And wasn't that always the intention? Not to serve her like her mindless necromancers and minions, but to use her—get her to bring back his mother and show him the doorways between life and death. Teach him the runes that would grant him immortality. And then, when she had served her purpose, destroy her. He could only hope she couldn't read his thoughts as well as she could his heart. She knew he wanted to burn the world down.

She didn't know she was included in the funeral pyre.

He took a deep breath.

"So, then," he said to her motionless body. "How do I bring you back?"

He knelt at the base of the pedestal and examined the runes, let his mind settle and the words sink.

There were runes for longevity, for preservation, but there were others, too. Darker runes. Runes for imprisonment, for destruction. They hissed through his mind, serpentine shadows, and as he let them swirl through his consciousness, he knew that Natasja had done more than just preserve the Dark Lady here for eternity, had done more than hidden her away.

This room—this pedestal—was a prison.

Natasja had ensured that no one would take the Dark Lady from here. At least, not alive.

The runes preserving her body also snared her to the pedestal. If someone so much as tried to move her an inch, the snare would snap, and the threads keeping her alive would unravel.

The only way to bring her back would be to undo the runes of this damned prison, to reignite the stilled spark of life within her. She wasn't dead, not really. Just in stasis. The web of runes wove tight over her, and he knew that one small mistake would cost more than the Dark Lady's life. It would cost him his only chance at bringing his mother back. He glanced over his shoulder at Natasja's corpse; perhaps he should have kept her alive a bit longer. Perhaps she could have been useful.

Perhaps. But then, where would the fun be in that?
He smiled in spite of himself.

"Finally," he muttered. "A challenge."

CHAPTER THIRTY-FIVE

SNOW SWIRLED AROUND THEM, SNOW AND A COLD SO BIT-
ing Tenn immediately regretted their decision. Everywhere he
looked he saw only snow. No houses, no settlements, not even
trees. Just snow and windswept hills and a frozen gray sky.

"Where the hell are we?" Kianna asked. She burrowed
deeper into her trench coat, which seemed hard to do with
all the weapons strapped to her body. Even after attuning to
Earth, it was clear she didn't trust magic enough to be un-
armed.

"I don't... I don't know," Tenn admitted.

He'd tracked Tomás to here. And yet there was no one to
be seen. He pressed his senses deep through Earth, tried to
find some trace of where the Howl could be. Because he *felt*
Tomás in front of them, not far at all, even though before them
lay only snow. What if the runes had failed him? What if this
was all some sort of trap?

"Tenn," gasped Dreya.

She pointed. And there, through the swirling snow, he saw

it. An archway of sparks. He couldn't see anything beyond besides more snow and those sparks, at least not from this vantage point, and when he tried to push his awareness there with Earth, he found nothing but emptiness.

"That must be it," he said. Tomás had to be in there. And Aidan.

A castle loomed through the opening, all stone and crystalline pink glass. Or no…was that ice?

"Look," Devon grunted. He kicked the ground.

Runes were scratched into the frozen soil, glowing faintly. They sifted through Tenn's mind in a haze, a language he barely understood—these were not the runes he was used to, but their meaning was clear. Runes for distraction and destruction, stronger than the ones he had used before, more diabolical than the Witches'. These would maim any who crossed over. Except someone had managed to divert the runes and create this arch.

Tenn knew precisely who that *someone* might be.

"He's through there," Tenn said. "Just make sure you only go through the arch. Those runes will kill you."

But something else pulled him forward. A tug in his chest. A hook in his gut. Something about this place was off. A force that made Water churn uncomfortably. He wanted to run the other way—and that, more than anything, was how he knew this was precisely where they needed to be.

They walked.

CHAPTER THIRTY-SIX

SWEAT DRIPPED FROM AIDAN'S FOREHEAD AS HE WORKED. Fire twined around his fingertips, charring against stone, reworking the runes delicately, one at a time. Changing not only the words, but the phrases, the sentences. It felt like rewriting an epic poem in a language he only half understood.

So far, at least, he hadn't cocked it up.

"What the hell are you doing?" Tomás asked.

Aidan was so focused he hadn't heard the incubus come in, so entranced he didn't even start at the voice. He kept working. He couldn't lose focus. Not now.

"We have to go."

A hand on his shoulder. Aidan glanced over. Tomás had changed out of his bloodied shirt, but he still wore very little—black silk button-down, clean slacks. Aidan was so consumed in his work, he barely registered the Kin's attractiveness.

"I'm nearly done," he said.

Tomás stared at the Dark Lady, at the flames flickering over her pedestal, caressing her pale skin.

"Our Mother…" he whispered. "What are you doing to her?"

"Saving her."

Tomás said nothing. Then his eyes jerked up. His hand clenched tighter on Aidan's shoulder.

"You must work faster, then," he said. "Or leave her for another time. We are no longer safe here."

"I'm safe anywhere," Aidan replied. Fire sang in his veins. Whatever was going on, he could handle it. He had nothing to fear. Nothing.

"That is what the dead think." He continued staring at the ceiling. Aidan continued his work.

"What is it?"

"Your friends have arrived."

The words shouldn't have struck a chord, but they did. *Friends.* Aidan didn't have friends. Not really. Not anymore. He had enemies, and those who would become enemies— those he must snuff out before they could try to rise against him.

"They don't scare me," Aidan said, focusing on the next rune. He was close. So close.

"They should. Come, this can wait. We must get you somewhere safe."

Tomás pulled at his shoulder. Aidan broke his concentration and turned on the Kin, sending a wash of flames between them.

Although it didn't hurt Tomás in the slightest, it still made him step back.

"Why the hell would I go with you?" Aidan said. "Why should I even trust you, after everything you've done?"

Tomás shook his head.

"I would never abandon you, my king. We both seek to bring our Mother back. I vowed to her, and I have vowed to you, and I have kept my vows. It is clear that *you* are the only way to bring her back. I would give my life to ensure that happens."

"Then why do you want me to run? Why not just kill Tenn and the others now and get it done with?" Fire sang in his veins, telling him he could do anything he wanted. Fire didn't run. Fire consumed.

Tomás's words were careful, considered.

"Because you may hold the power, my king, but you cannot take these four on your own. Not now. Not yet. We still may need them."

Aidan imagined them, the twins and blondie and Tenn, parading into the main room as if they were the saviors. As if they were the ones who would go down in history. But they were wrong. Wrong.

He didn't need them. He didn't need anyone.

"You're protecting them," Aidan growled. His eyes flickered up as a rumble shook the earth, making the light in the room sway. "You don't want them dead."

Tomás's jaw corded.

"He has a knowledge that is useful to her." He looked to the Dark Lady. "I do not question. And if you were wise, neither would you."

"How dare you? I'm—"

"A god, yes. And one of great power. But do not forget that the very forces that give you your might once gave *her* the very same. And now look at her. She was rash. She ignored those she should obey. And she nearly lost everything for it." Tomás swallowed. "I know you think you are omnipotent, my king.

And you will be. Soon. But there is still much that neither of us knows, and we must play our cards right to ensure we live to learn it. We must trust her. In her stasis, she has dwelled amongst the dead gods, the ones whose power flood through your veins. She knows more than we ever could. If she believes we need Tenn alive, we must follow."

Tomás gingerly touched the crown of Aidan's head, where the fifth Sphere, the elusive Sphere of Maya, rested.

"We wish to remake the world. And for that, we need a power the world has never seen. The Dark Lady believes she has found the way. We must listen."

Anger burned heavy and hot in the back of Aidan's chest. He wanted to refuse. Wanted to prove Tomás wrong.

But the Kin was right—this was just the beginning. Especially if Tomás thought the Dark Lady could access Maya.

Fire sang at the thought.

Maya could remake the world. Could burn apart the very fabric of creation.

If he could tap into that Sphere, he would truly be a god.

Tomás jerked away, looking toward the door, barely glancing at his sister. "We must go."

"No," Aidan said. He was a king. He was a god. He wouldn't begin his reign by fleeing. "I have another idea."

He smiled. Pressed a burning hand to Tomás's face.

"Don't worry. I won't get hurt. And I won't kill them. I promise."

"But—"

He moved his hand to cover Tomás's lips.

"That wasn't a request, Tomás," Aidan said. "That was a command. From your new master. From your king. And you don't want to disobey me. You've already seen what happens to those who betray their masters."

Tomás swallowed, but he didn't move Aidan's hand away. He stared deep in Aidan's eyes. Aidan knew that look. Tomás was finally realizing the shift in power. Finally realizing the monster he had created. The king he must now serve.

Tomás nodded. Stepped back.

"As you command," he said, bowing low. His eyes flickered once more to the Dark Lady. To Natasja's corpse on the floor. "But I will not leave your side, my king."

"Then follow my lead."

I have a surprise for you, Tenn, Aidan thought, and went back to work.

CHAPTER THIRTY-SEVEN

THIS HAD TO BE A TRAP. *HAD* TO BE.

Tenn's skin practically crawled off his bones as they made their way through the castle, first through the grand entryway, then through the crystalline maze of frozen bodies, following the tracking rune seared on Tomás's heart.

Tomás didn't move.

Nothing in this accursed castle of ice and frozen blood moved.

No guards. No necromancers. Not even a kraven.

Tenn knew Tomás could sense them. Anyone with a lick of power could sense them. All four were open to their Spheres, scanning and ready to defend or attack at the drop of a hat. He sensed Tomás's rune down in the cellars, but try as he might, he couldn't feel him with Earth. He strained his senses further. He felt the tunnels and stairways, a veritable beehive of chambers. But there was a void surrounding Tomás. Tenn couldn't sense anything—not a room, and definitely not the people inside. It reminded him way too much of the Witches, of the runes that had made them invisible to the outside world. Invisible to anyone who didn't know the right runes.

Something was hiding within that void. Something much, much worse than Tomás.

Nothing good could be hidden in a place like this.

"Do you feel anything?" he asked the others.

No one answered. No one felt a thing.

Kianna stood at his side, a sword in one hand and pistol in the other, Earth a twining green in her gut. Only a few hours in, she had gotten a handle on her power far better than Tenn had when he first attuned. He would have been jealous if not for the necessity of their circumstance, if not for the knowledge that to her, magic was just a weapon, and if there was one thing she had a handle on in this world, it was weaponry.

The twins stalked behind him, flames from Devon's agitation flickering around them. They cast shards of light over the ice, which almost looked beautiful, if not for the nightmares illuminated inside. Dreya pulled through Air, a constant whirlwind that billowed all of their clothes and sent goose bumps over his skin.

They all knew the weight of this situation. All knew they needed to be on the highest alert.

Even if they didn't know *what* exactly they were walking into, it didn't take insight to know they were nearing the end of their story. Caius's words still rang in Tenn's ear. The Dark Lady had been part of the Church. The Dark Lady was still alive. She was at the center of this. All of this. And as Water churned in his gut, sucking him forward like a whirlpool, he knew in the darkest shadows of his bones she was here, too.

He hated to guess what that might mean Aidan was doing here.

He wanted so badly to sit Aidan down and talk to him, reason with him. He was destroying the Kin, and Tenn had to believe that was a good thing. But something wasn't right. Whatever Aidan was doing here wasn't good. Couldn't be good.

He had to help him.

You can't be trusted around broken things. Jarrett's words rippled through his mind. But no. He wasn't here to be a martyr. He was here to stop Aidan from doing something he would regret. There had to be reason in Aidan's mind. Had to.

Tenn glanced over to Kianna. If nothing else, she should be able to change Aidan's heart. Right?

Something about the set of her jaw told him she was just as uncertain as he was

Then, halfway down the darkened steps leading into nothingness, Dreya gasped.

"Tenn, there is a body," she whispered. Her eyebrows furrowed. "Part of one, at least."

Tenn stalled. Memories of stumbling upon half a Witch's torso replayed in his mind.

"Part?"

"I sense legs. But the rest...the rest I cannot sense."

Tenn pushed harder through Earth. Dimly, he could make out what she was saying. Legs on the ground. And the rest fell within the void he could not sense.

"Maybe it's someone sleeping?" Kianna suggested.

They all knew that wasn't the case.

Dreya took a deep breath. The air around them flickered, the faintest shield.

"Let us go," Dreya said. "Carefully. We do not know what we will face."

Tenn nodded. He didn't need a reminder.

They walked toward the unknown, and he wondered if he should have prepared them better. Scrawled runes of hiding into their flesh or something. But, just like with Leanna, he didn't think it would do much in the face of the Kin. Or Aidan.

He hated that the thought of facing Aidan filled him with more dread than facing the Kin ever had. Or could.

At the bottom of the stairs, his fears were realized.

A woman's body lay half in the doorframe. Her dress was beautifully intricate, her skin pale as snow. He knew in that one glance she was of the Kin—no one in this world was so beautiful, so untouchable. She was also undoubtedly dead.

"Don't be rude," came Aidan's voice from within. "It isn't polite to stare."

From their vantage, the door half-closed, they couldn't see who or what was inside. All Tenn could see was stone. Kianna growled and made to step forward, but Tenn yanked her back. Her pistol was at his forehead in a heartbeat.

"Don't," he whispered. "Let me."

"Like hell." She shook off his hand and lowered the pistol. With a quick kick, the door slammed open, and she strode inside with weapons raised.

Tenn was close behind.

It took a moment to realize what was happening. Aidan on the other side of a stone dais. Tomás at Aidan's side. And a woman on the stone before them. A woman in purple, with pale blonde hair. As beautiful as the Kin at his feet, but more so.

It clicked.

He remembered her from TV. He remembered her face.

The Dark Lady.

They had found the Dark Lady.

CHAPTER THIRTY-EIGHT

AIDAN DIDN'T THINK MUCH COULD SURPRISE HIM ANYMORE. Not with all the power running through his veins, not with the body of the Dark Lady splayed out before him. He was wrong.

When Kianna burst into the room, shock pulsed through him.

"What the hell are you doing here?" he asked. "*How* are you here?"

They were in Russia. A thousand miles from where he'd left her. Even if she'd somehow taken a plane, there was no way she could be here. Unless...

He looked. Really looked.

And there, curled in the pit of her gut, glowing green behind the black of her trench, was the Sphere of Earth.

"You let them *attune* you?" he spat as the others—the Hunters he expected—crowded in behind her. Well, he'd expected all of them, except blondie wasn't with them. Maybe they'd had a lovers' quarrel?

"Aye," Kianna said. He didn't fail to note that her gun was

pointed straight at his chest, the sword at Tomás. "And I blame you for all of it."

"Well, well, well," Tomás said. "Here we are at last. All of us. How pleasant." He glared at her, but the scowl broke into a grin. He pulled aside his shirt to reveal his smooth flesh. "No hard feelings, of course. It takes a bit more than a few gunshots to kill me."

"I look forward to it," Kianna said. She took a step forward, but Tenn put a hand on her arm.

Surprisingly, she didn't lop it off.

"Wait." He looked at Aidan with those damn watery eyes, and Aidan had to fight down the memory of Trevor looking at him the same way. The sadness. The fear. The absolute ache of betrayal, right before Aidan had burned him to ash on Calum's throne. "Aidan," he continued. His voice smooth. Calming. The way you'd talk to a feral dog. Fire sparked at the indignation. *No one* should talk to him like this. And yet, something in the way Tenn said his name… "Aidan, I don't know what you're doing. But it doesn't have to be like this."

Aidan laughed. "Please. You don't even know what *this* is." He gestured wide, sparks racing across his arms. "What, you believe that just because you're the *chosen one*, you have a part in all this? You don't. This has nothing to do with you." He looked to Kianna. "With any of you."

"Then what does it have to do with?" she asked. "Because it sure as hell looks like you're standing over the woman you vowed to kill, beside a monster you swore to kill, as well."

Tomás chuckled and bowed at the word *monster*. Aidan was impressed. Normally, that was enough to set Tomás off.

Then he realized why everyone was static. It wasn't just because they were uncertain. It was because he held this entire situation in the palm of his hand. He could kill them in a heartbeat if he wanted. He could bring the very castle down around their heads. Or, he could be a merciful god and let them live.

He looked to Kianna. His only friend. Then he looked at the pistol pointed at his chest. Perhaps she was no longer his friend, Fire purred. Perhaps she has joined with *them*.

"Things aren't so black-and-white," Aidan said. "Not anymore." He clenched his fingers, brought his destroyed hand in front of him. Lowered his voice, tried to level the burn. "Don't you understand? After everything we've been through, there isn't a pure good or pure evil. Just power. *She* knew this." He pointed to the Dark Lady. "And I'm quickly learning. This world doesn't give a shit about good or bad. It never has. It only bows to one thing—power. And we either use that power, or we are chained by it. I know precisely which side I want to be on."

He placed his hand on the Dark Lady's chest, right over her heart. Felt the shiver of life within. Just as he felt the words of the runes snaking over his skin. He had undone them. Most of them. But there was only so much he could do.

There had been another curse hidden within the runes.

A requirement.

He looked to Tomás.

"I suppose I should thank you," Aidan said. "You taught me that good and evil are just what we make of them."

Tomás nodded, but his grin was slipping. Probably because Aidan's was slashing into place.

"The true heart of everything is power. You showed me that.

That life was only about the burn, the acquisition. No matter who we have to consume along the way. You've taken me far, Tomás. Here to the very end."

He paused, let them linger on the word *end* while he looked at the others.

"And you are also to thank for bringing us all back together again. You and that treacherous heart of yours."

He traced lines of flame over the Dark Lady's chest.

"You have risked everything to bring me here. To help me achieve everything I desire. You've given your life to bringing your mistress back, when all your brethren were content to lock her away. All because they were too weak. Too frightened to see what she might create."

He looked to Tomás as he burned the final runes into the Dark Lady's skin, as the runes of the pedestal fell away, and a new language took their place. He reached to the blade at his hip, his fingers wrapping around the hilt.

"You were imperfect. All of you. And you had hoped that by bringing me here, by aiding me, I would overlook that imperfection."

Tomás growled in the back of his throat. But he didn't take a step forward. Didn't try to rip out Aidan's tongue. Everyone stood silent. The whole world waiting to see what he would do.

"But if there is one thing I have learned from you, Tomás, it is that weakness has no place in the world. Your mistress knew that better than most. You say you would do anything to bring her back? Good. Because she requires something of you. One more little thing."

Aidan struck.

He lashed the final runes into the Dark Lady's chest, deep into her static heart, and twined tendrils of flame around his arms as he thrust his dagger into Tomás's chest. Tomás screamed.

It shouldn't have been enough to kill him. On their own, the dagger or the flame would have been nothing to the incubus. But the runes…

The power of the runes Aidan seared on the Dark Lady's heart twined with those he burned into Tomás's chest, linking one to the other. As Tomás's heart failed, as his spark winked out, the runes on the Dark Lady dragged that power in.

Tomás's eyes widened.

"What's the matter?" Aidan asked, making sure to stare deep into the Howl's copper eyes. "You told me you would die for me. Did you truly think I wouldn't call your bluff?"

Distantly, he heard commotion. As if in another room, another world, he heard the other Hunters leap into action, felt the flares of their power. But the power he wielded billowed around him, the fire a cocoon of searing warmth. The power of his own inner flame. The power of Tomás's dying light.

The spark of her awakening.

Maybe the Hunters attacked. Maybe they didn't. It didn't matter.

He watched Tomás sink to his knees, the dagger still in his chest.

He felt the Kin's heart stutter against the blade.

Felt the Kin's power flood through him. Past him. And into the woman who warmed beneath his fingertips.

"The Dark Lady does not forgive treachery," Aidan said. "And neither, my prince, do I."

Tomás's heart stalled.

He crumpled to his side.

And as his eyes closed and his head thudded to the floor, the woman the world had thought dead was reborn.

"There is no death.
There is no darkness.
There is only truth
and that truth
is me."

—Teachings of the Dark Lady

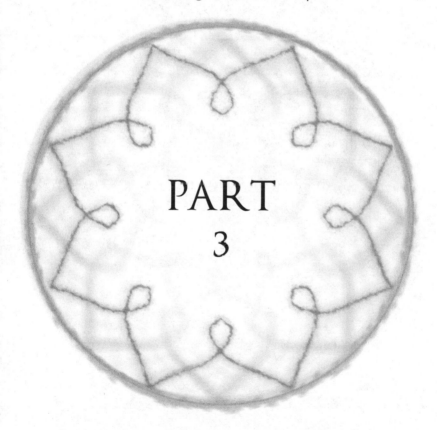

PART
3

BLOOD LIKE POISON

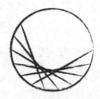

CHAPTER THIRTY-NINE

"GO!" DREYA YELLED. SHE SHOVED THE REST OF HER COMRADES back, pouring as much Air into the shield between them and Aidan as she could. "Go, now!"

But they did not move. Of course they did not move.

Tenn screamed out even as Devon pulled him back. Kianna fired her gun into the hellstorm, but her bullets melted the moment they hit the flames. Everything was heat and hatred, and in her heart she heard the screaming.

The screaming of the spirits. The Ancestors. The very souls that had sent them here, the very gods who thought that they could make the world anew.

Screaming at their failure.

Screaming that the end had come again.

She watched in awe and terror as the incubus dropped to his knees, his fingers fluttering like birds' wings over the hilt of the dagger in his chest.

Watched as the runes connected, as the swirl of the incubus's final life force was ripped from his body and channeled into the woman at Aidan's side.

She watched as the power snapped through the woman's veins. As her eyes opened and her lips parted in a gasp.

She watched as the woman looked over. As the eyes that had haunted her nightmares since the Resurrection's beginning locked on her own.

Then she grabbed onto Tenn's arm, to Kianna's wrist. *Do it!* she yelled in her thoughts to Devon.

He nodded.

Seared the runes of travel into the dust at their feet.

She poured her own power into the runes, prayed that Kianna and Tenn were doing the same.

But as the world vanished around them, she knew hope was already lost.

CHAPTER FORTY

"FUCK!" TENN YELLED.

He kicked the low stone wall, but he was so numb, so shocked, he didn't even feel the pain.

Where they were, he had no idea. Somewhere dark and wet and desolately urban. It was fitting.

With Tomás dead, he had no way of using the tracking runes, no way of telling how far they were from the boy he had failed to save.

He thought it was just raining. Then he realized the pools in his eyes were tears.

Someone placed a hand on his arm. He tried to shake it off.

"Tenn," Dreya whispered. Her voice barely cut through the screaming in his head. His own voice, calling himself a failure. A failure. "You must get a hold of yourself. We must be rational. We must *think*."

Think.

Think of what? The way Aidan's eyes burned with purpose as he stabbed Tomás in the heart? The bodies of the Kin that had fallen at Aidan's feet? Or did she want him to think about the power? The power Aidan had wielded like it was nothing, the runes that had burned holes in Tenn's mind with their might, words and whispers this world had never—and should have never—seen. Aidan had done the unthinkable.

He had brought the Dark Lady back to life. He had unleashed the worst darkness the world had ever known.

And now…now…

"We're right fucked," Kianna said.

She paced at Tenn's side, and Devon sported a nasty bruise on his eye from where she'd punched him in the chaos. She had wanted to leave Aidan even less than Tenn.

"I can't believe the wee bastard," she said, her accent thickening in her anger, becoming more Scottish than British. "I knew he was getting dark. I didn't realize he'd gone *that* dark. That was the Dark Lady, wasn't it? He brought the bitch back."

Tenn nodded and forced down the sadness, the defeat. Water roared within him, the betrayal fresh as a wound. He was still alive. That meant he still had a responsibility.

He'd thought his purpose was to save Aidan. Perhaps not. Perhaps Jarrett had been right all along—perhaps he was meant to end him. The Violet Sage had warned that Tenn could sway Aidan to the side of the living or the dead. Clearly, Tenn had fucked it up and sent Aidan spiraling into the Dark Lady's clutches.

"She's back." He stared up in the dreary night. Even saying the words didn't make the truth feel real. Nothing actually *seemed* different. Surely her return should have been more apocalyptic—heralded with blood raining from the clouds and the dead rising from the soil. Instead, there was just the gloom and the haze and the already-destroyed buildings around them. He almost wanted to laugh. "The Dark Lady is back."

Was there really much worse she could do?

Even thinking that made his stomach clench. Of course there was. Of course.

In that moment, all the futures he'd ever dreamed of having—a house and Labs with Jarrett, a happy-ever-after, a *future* at all—were crushed under the weight of the new reality. Aidan had damned them all.

Tenn had damned them all. The Violet Sage told Tenn to make Aidan trust him. He had failed. This was all his own doing.

Water delighted in the misery of it.

"So what do we do?" Kianna asked. "I should have put a bullet between his eyes when I had the chance."

"There is no use dwelling on what was," Dreya said.

"No," Devon interrupted. "She's right. We should have killed him."

"Hey." Kianna brandished her gun at him. "That's my mate you're talking about. The only one who gets to threaten the wanker is me."

Devon glowered at her, flames flickering around him like fireflies. But he didn't say or do anything. Tenn couldn't tell if Kianna was joking or not.

"We don't need to fight amongst ourselves," Tenn said. He swallowed. Remembered all too well how touchy everyone had been around Aidan when his Sphere had been damaged. Maybe this was the aftershock of what they'd seen, what Aidan had done. "That's what he would have wanted us to do."

"And what do *you* want us to do, oh fearless leader?"

Kianna asked. "Teleport back there and kiss his boots and beg for mercy? Because we sure as hell can't kill him now. He's gotten a taste for power and he won't stop until he has it all."

"But he has it," Tenn said. "He *had* it. He killed the Kin like they were nothing. He was the most powerful mage in the world. Why would he bring her back? It just means there's someone else more powerful than him in existence. Someone else to kill."

"Not if he thinks he can use her."

Kianna's words made Tenn's heart flip.

"What? That's...that's..."

She grunted.

"I never said he was smart. Fire's gone to his head. Always told him magic would get the better of him. Always said he was addicted. And look what he's done now."

"It's not him," Devon said. "Not really."

"Oh?"

"It's Fire. He's consumed by it." Devon's eyes glittered with the flames around him, his entire body haloed by firelight. To think, there was a time when Devon's might intimidated Tenn. Now, even this display of agitation barely bothered him. Still, it was a good reminder that Aidan wasn't the only one playing with, well, fire. "He is no longer the man you once knew. That has been burned away. He will crave only one thing— to spread. To consume. He will do everything he can to burn the world down. And if he thinks he can use the Dark Lady to do so, he will."

Tenn shook his head. How could Aidan be so naive as to think he could *use* the Dark Lady? He must be really desperate.

Of course he is, Water seethed. *You felt his pain. The boy hurts more than all of us combined. You should have saved him. You could have saved him. Now you are too late. Too late...*

He forced the thoughts down, drowned them under Water.

"But what can she possibly offer him?"

Kianna shrugged.

"Power changes people. Before and after the Resurrection, people have always been the same. Taste power, and you won't settle for anything less than more."

Tenn knew she was telling the truth. He'd seen it in Aidan's eyes. Aidan had tasted power none of them could dream of.

"I have to believe there's still good in him."

Kianna cawed with laughter, so loud Tenn jumped.

"Jesus, Mary and Joseph, Tenn," she said through tears. "You really don't know anything about him, do you? If you think we're going to find some good left in that one, you're in for a serious disappointment."

"I'd say all of this has been a serious disappointment."

Kianna nodded. "That it has been. That it has."

They stood in silence, the rain drizzling around them.

"Where are we?" Tenn asked. The place looked like any other ruined town in America.

"Near Outer Chicago," Dreya whispered. It was one of the few times she'd ever sounded timid.

Tenn bit down his anger. *Back to where Jarrett locked me up.*

"I thought it safest," she continued. "And the most prudent. We must let the Guild know what we have seen. They must prepare. They must tell *others* to prepare."

"No one can prepare for this," came a girl's voice.

For a split second, Tenn recognized the voice. So much that he just assumed it was one of his party. Then the moment passed, and he realized it wasn't Kianna or Dreya. It wasn't anyone he knew.

He turned on the spot—all of them did—weapons raised and Spheres blazing.

But it wasn't a Hunter or necromancer standing in the street before them.

No, it wasn't human at all.

The silver fox stood in the haze, glimmering like moonlight on water.

"The true end has come," the fox said, bowing its head. *"And only together can we face it."*

CHAPTER FORTY-ONE

AIDAN ONLY BRIEFLY LOOKED AT THE PLACE HIS EX-COMPANIONS had stood. He had watched Kianna and Tenn try to fight their way forward. To fight *him*. To kill him. He had known it from the look in Kianna's eyes even before she pulled the trigger of her gun.

Their friendship was over. She would see him dead.

It pained him. In a distant corner of his burning heart, it hurt. To know that he had incinerated years of friendship in a moment. To know that his hope of ruling with her at his side was gone.

Then the fire burned it away.

Had he ever wanted her to rule at his side? No, *no*. Fire seethed that there was only room for one throne. Only one ruler. And that would be him.

All his thoughts burned away in a heartbeat.

Because there, on the pedestal before him, the Dark Lady awoke.

He knew he should tremble. Knew he should bend his knee.

After all, this was the woman who brought all of humanity to the dirt. The woman who had unleashed hell on earth.

The woman who could bring back the dead.

And yet, with Fire humming in his veins, he didn't kneel or grovel. He stood only a foot away from Tomás's bleeding corpse, dagger still in hand, with Tomás's blood burning on the blade.

He watched her blink. Watched her slowly move her fingers and toes. Watched her carefully push herself up to sitting, facing away from him. Facing Natasja's body. In all of those movements, she looked terribly frail, terribly human. It made him wonder if he had made a mistake, if perhaps this wasn't the Goddess of Death, after all.

"They are dead," she said. Just hearing her voice made shivers race down his sweating skin. Her words were oceanic in their pull, laced with power. He knew, then, she was indeed the one who had spoken to him through Fire's urgings. She looked over to Tomás's corpse. In death, the Kin didn't seem all that seductive. He was nothing more than a bloody sack of meat. "All of them."

To think, there had been a time when Aidan thought he and Tomás might be equals. That Tomás might be able to grant him everything he desired.

"As you asked," Aidan replied.

"I did not ask you to kill Tomás." She still didn't turn to face him. Didn't look him in the eye. And for some reason, that dismissal, that tone of her voice, sent a chill of doubt through him. Fire quivered.

"I needed a life to bring you back. Tomás had pledged his life to your return. I thought it fitting the he be the one to bring it about."

"The poetry is not lost on me. But you, Hunter, are no poet. You killed Tomás because you feared him."

"I fear nothing."

"Not even me?" she asked, glancing at him over her shoulder.

That look, that flash of her eyes, made Fire stutter out in his chest. On the slab, she had been beautiful. Delicately human. With a model's cheekbones and pouting lips. But now, those features were feral. Hungry. She was beautiful, yes, but it was a terrible sort of beauty, the kind that destroyed you the moment you crossed its path.

"Yes," he admitted.

The word fell from his mouth before he could stop it. Something about her demanded the truth.

She stood slowly and elegantly, stretching as if from a long nap, and not four years of imprisonment. Then she stepped over to Tomás and knelt at his side, placed a hand on his brow.

"He was a good subject," she mused. "My finest creation."

And there it was, the tiniest spark of fear within him. That he had pushed too far. That he had overstepped.

Instead, she sighed and stood, her dress swirling as she turned to face him.

"But we will make more, will we not?" she asked. "Better. Far better. We will be gods."

I already am a god, he wanted to say. He bit the words down. "Yes. But first, you owe me."

Her eyebrow quirked as she smiled. He could tell she wasn't used to having people stand up to her. Demanding things.

"I brought you back from the brink of death," he said. "I saved you from obscurity. From an eternity of *this*." He gestured around the room, to the pedestal and stone walls and the two corpses littering the floor.

Her smile widened. She stepped forward, her long dress dragging over Tomás's face. She reached out and touched Aidan's cheek, and he realized her fingers still dripped with Tomás's blood.

"Brazen," she said. Her fingers were cold on his jaw. "To demand a life from the Goddess of Death."

"The Goddess of Death that nearly died," Aidan said. He had to play his cards right. He had to prove he wouldn't be beaten down. He had to get her to pay her half of the bargain.

She laughed.

"You cannot kill one such as me. Even if my body fades, my name will live forever." She leaned in. "I have watched you even in stasis, and I know you are not as cold as you would like to believe. You desire one thing more than anything else. Even more than ruling. And I can give her to you."

"As you said you would. As you *promised*."

The last word came out as a squeak. He couldn't sound like he was begging. He had to remain in power. But how could he hold on to that power when it all seemed to stream from her?

Her eyes searched his face, and her other hand reached down and took his broken fingers in hers. "I will bring your mother back, Aidan. I am a woman of my word. I am no monster, not like the Church who tortured you so. I will bring her back, but not yet."

He took a step back.

"Not yet?"

"Not yet. There is much that must be done first. The Church will find out I have been set free, and they will come for me. As will those you thought to be your friends. We must be ready when they arrive. We must prepare."

He shook his head.

"No. No, I already killed all of the Kin for you. I brought you back from the dead. You promised me you'd bring her back. Now."

"And I will," she said. "But what use is her life if she is killed immediately after? We must wipe out all threats."

"And how do you propose we do that?"

She smiled.

"With a little help from your friends."

CHAPTER FORTY-TWO

"THE HELL IS THAT?" KIANNA ASKED, HER GUN POINTED AT THE fox. "Did you hear that? Is that thing talking?"

Dreya put a gentle hand on Kianna's arm, but she couldn't get her to budge. She couldn't take her own eyes off the fox. The boys stood, dumbstruck.

She had heard the voice, clear as day. Just as they all had. She knew it deep in her core.

"That is not the enemy," Dreya said. She kept her voice low, soothing. "It is an emissary."

"Emissary? Emissary of what?"

"The Violet Sage."

The fox bowed its head again when she spoke the name.

"The hell is a Violet Sage?" Kianna asked.

"The only human to ever wield all four Spheres at once," Dreya said.

"That looks like a fox to me."

"It is her voice."

Tenn took a hesitant step forward.

"Why are you here?" he asked. "What do you want?"

"*You have let the boy unleash terrible evil,*" the fox said. "*We must prepare to fight it.*"

"But how?"

"*You already know,*" the fox said. "*Come.*"

It turned and walked away, down the alley. Tenn glanced to the others. Dreya nodded.

"We will need her help," she said. "We should follow."

Tenn nodded. Began walking forward. Then Dreya heard the voice again.

"*Not you,*" it said. She knew the voice was meant only for her. "*It must be him. Only him.*"

But there is so much I wish to ask you, Dreya thought back. So much I wish to learn.

"*And you will,*" the Violet Sage replied. "*Soon. But for now, he must go alone. There is much that must be done back here. She will come for you. And you must be ready when she does.*"

A vision filled her mind. The sky in flames, clouds roiling as lightning struck and earthquakes toppled buildings. Figures scattered on the ground. Men and women and children, running and screaming as thousands of Howls poured through the streets like blood, like so much blood, and it was then she realized it was Outer Chicago she saw. And there, at its beating, burning heart, was Aidan.

She gasped.

Tenn looked back at the three of them. They had all stopped moving. She wondered if the others had received a similar message, or were simply too stunned to go.

"You must go alone," Dreya said. She swallowed. "We will be here when you return. We must let the others know."

She could see the struggle within him. The desire to tell them he wasn't going alone. But he saw the logic in it. This was no time to let emotion override logic. The war was no longer coming—it was *here*. And they needed to prepare.

She worried the vision she had been granted proved there was no point in preparing. They had already lost.

Is that what will be, or what might be? she asked within.

"It is what the Prophets have seen," the Violet Sage replied.

It wasn't the answer she'd hoped for.

There was not much more in this world to hope for.

"Okay," Tenn said. As if to ready himself for whatever was to come. "Okay. I'll… I'll see you soon."

She nodded. They all did.

Then the last hope the world had walked away from them, and Dreya felt the weight of knowledge settle on her shoulders.

This was the end.

No matter what Tenn tried, this was the end.

CHAPTER FORTY-THREE

THE LAST THING TENN WANTED WAS TO BE SEPARATED FROM his friends.

He felt like a raw nerve, felt like everything that could have gone wrong had. Everything felt wrong. Absolutely, horribly wrong.

And it was all his fault.

But he knew he had to follow the fox. Knew it was his destiny just as he'd known in the depths of that internal cave that finding Aidan had been his destiny.

This destiny, at least, he wouldn't let himself screw up.

It felt like something out of a fairy tale, trailing a fox through the abandoned streets. It leaped over potholes, its feet barely making tracks in the mud, its fur somehow dry despite the rain.

What have I gotten myself into? he thought.

If the fox heard him, it didn't respond.

He followed the beast down an alley that led to what appeared to be a dead end. With every step, the dread in him grew deeper. This has to be some sort of trick or trap; there was no way the most powerful mage in existence lived here. This close to Outer Chicago.

No way she lived in a place like *this*.

"*Here*," the fox said in the Violet Sage's voice.

He looked around.

There was nothing. Battered garages and crumbling brick walls and fences choked with dead weeds. Abandoned suburbia at its finest.

"Here?" he asked. "But there's nothing—"

Images flooded him before he could finish his sentence. A rush of color and sound and sensation that washed from the crown of his head down to his feet. He fell to his knees as the vision overtook him, as the sounds and whispers grew louder, drowning out the rain and the city, until all he could see were the symbols, all he could hear were the whispers.

Runes.

Dozens of them.

They poured through him, racing across his vision, pumping through his blood. He pressed his hands into the cold puddle before him, trying to stay upright as the runes continued. No, not continued. They were repeating. A dozen or so, flickering through his mind, their meanings sinking deep into his bones.

It felt like it went on for eternity.

And then, like the snap of a finger, the sensation stopped.

He shuddered as reality closed around him. The rain. The gray. The mud.

As if it had all been a dream.

Except, he remembered.

With shaking limbs he pushed himself back up to standing.

The fox just stared at him with its head cocked to the side. That pose made him think of Tomás.

Tomás.

Tomás was dead.

The final member of the Kin was dead. The one who had haunted and tormented and threatened Tenn all this time. Tenn should have been relieved. There was no longer an incubus stalking his bedside. No longer the looming threat that this creature would come in and kill all those he loved if he said the wrong thing.

So why did that movement fill him with sadness?

Tomás was *dead.*

Tenn swallowed and looked to the garage door in front of him, trying to push the loss down. He shouldn't despair over the death of the monster. Even if it did make him feel more alone. A little more cold. Without Tomás, the world would always be a little colder. A little less, well, *fun.*

He opened to Earth and held up his hand, scrawling a dark, long line of runes vertically along the door. They hummed with meaning in his mind. Some, he already knew—runes for travel, for speed. Others were more precise, more ethereal. Runes for bending, for stalking, for binding to a course. On their own, they wouldn't do much. But together, they spelled one of the most powerful equations for travel he'd ever seen.

Unlike the other runes of travel, these didn't require him to have a destination in mind, nor did they require him to use Air. He only needed to feed them power, any power, and they would take him to a preset destination. This, he knew in the corner of his mind. They would take him to the Violet Sage.

He stared at his creation for a moment, marveling at the language that simmered in his heart.

"Are you coming with?" he asked the fox.

When he looked over, however, the fox was gone.

"All right, then," Tenn said to himself. He glanced once more to the entrance of the alley, toward where his friends had parted ways with him. A pang of sadness strummed through his heart.

He had a terrible feeling he would never see them again.

Before the fear or the prophecy could get to him, he stepped forward and placed his hands to the runes. Then he opened to Earth, and let the language take him where it willed.

CHAPTER FORTY-FOUR

AN UNEASY SILENCE STRETCHED OVER THE THREE OF THEM the moment Tenn left. Dreya could tell Kianna didn't want to be here, that she wanted nothing more than to travel back to Aidan and beat sense into him. Though they all knew such an act would be fruitless.

Otherwise, Dreya might very well be inclined to comply.

Devon snorted.

I thought I was the one who was supposed to prefer violence, he thought at her.

Desperate times, she thought back.

"I must be losing my mind," Kianna mumbled. "A fox. A bloody *fox.*"

Dreya watched her pace. She wanted to reach out and calm her. But she knew there was no calming her, not now. Kianna had just seen her best friend revive the very force he was sworn to destroy. There would be little comfort for any of them from here on out. Even though Dreya would very much like to be that presence…

Get your head in the game, Devon growled.

Dreya glared at her brother, but he had a point. They must be rational. As she had told Tenn they must be. She drew through Air, a cleansing inhalation, and let clarity breeze away her doubts.

"No one has lost their mind," Dreya said. It wasn't much of a comfort, but it was a start. "Outer Chicago is only a few blocks from here. We need to go and warn them of what has happened."

"Don't you lot have the Prophets and all to warn you when things go to shite?"

"Yes. But we cannot rely on them. We can only rely on ourselves."

"That, at least, is a motto I can stand behind," Kianna said. "All right then. Lead on."

Dreya was not used to leading. She glanced to her brother, expecting him to step in front and guide them to Outer Chicago. When he just stared at her, she realized that would not be the case.

Sometimes you are insufferable.

Beneath the folds of his scarf, she knew Devon grinned.

She reached through Air and spread her senses throughout the suburb, her mind's eye racing over ruined streets and abandoned houses. Nearly a mile away, she caught sight of the wall separating Outer Chicago from the rest of the world.

She began to walk.

Why didn't you just take us to the interior? Devon asked.

Because I could not risk Tenn being taken prisoner again, Dreya replied.

They both knew Jarrett wouldn't risk Tenn's freedom. Now,

more than ever, Tenn needed to be kept safe. Not only from Aidan, but from himself. Water was a tempestuous Sphere, and when it felt pain, it dragged the user toward it like a moth to flame. Hopefully, resisting that temptation was amongst the skills the Violet Sage could teach him.

Hopefully, he could learn quickly.

No one spoke as they walked toward Outer Chicago's perimeter. The sky above broke into a heavy rain, and even though Dreya put up a shield to prevent the worst of it from staining their clothes, they were still soaked through and sullen. Not necessarily with water, but with the message they carried with them.

The end has come.

The end has come.

Dreya tried to formulate what she would say, and how she would say it, to make Tenn's involvement seem even less than it was. She tried to think of how she would explain rescuing him from the prison.

She tried to think of how she could rally the troops, when in the deepest pit of her heart she knew it was a dying cause.

She looked to Kianna, who even now walked with her head held high and a dozen weapons strapped to her body. Who, after attuning to Earth, seemed even taller, stronger, more stable in her body. It made Dreya feel tiny and frail in comparison.

Everything about this situation made her feel tiny and frail.

There is no point giving up just yet, Devon thought. *We have never given up. Will never.*

And even though he didn't play the images she knew were running through his mind, she felt the ash in his words, smelled the char of her family's flesh.

She still had all of them to avenge. Somehow.

She felt the presence before they reached the gate. For a moment, she thought it an enemy. Then she felt the stirrings of the tracking rune she always held loosely in her mind.

Perhaps she would have rather it be an enemy.

Perhaps it still was.

"You helped him escape," Jarrett called through the deluge when they came into view.

Even those words were enough to rise the ire in Dreya's chest. He may as well have called them traitors. For what? For doing what the spirits had told them to do, rather than what the ego-driven Guild had decided?

They may have been sent after Tenn for the same reason as Jarrett, but after meeting with the Witches, they knew what their true duty was.

"We had to," Dreya said. She amplified her voice with Air, filled it with power. She would not back down. "He was never meant to be taken prisoner."

"No." They had neared enough that he didn't have to yell. Dreya stepped up to him, though the others lingered behind. "He was meant to be kept safe. And now where is he?"

"Safe. Which is more than you could say."

Jarrett lowered his voice. And for the first time since they'd traveled off to find Aidan, he actually looked as she had once known him. Human. Hurting.

"Do you think I wanted to do it?" he asked. "It killed me, Dreya. To see him struggling. To see myself losing him. I thought if I took him here, if I kept him safe—"

"If you locked him up and severed him from magic. That is not saving. That is inhumane."

"You don't understand—"

"I do understand. You were angry. Aidan and his broken magic was only partly to blame. You were angry because you feared you would no longer be important to Tenn, that duty and another would take him from you. You forgot that he is a grown man. That he is able to make his own choices. And from the day he met you, he chose you."

Jarrett swallowed.

"I didn't mean—"

"What you did or did not mean to do is no longer relevant," Dreya said. "The past is done. We have larger things to worry about."

"I thought you said Tenn was safe."

"He is. For now. But we must hurry."

Jarrett took a step back and looked over the three of them. Air burned brighter in his throat, casting away all doubt, all emotion.

"What have you done?"

"We didn't do anything," Kianna said, stepping up and patting Jarrett on the shoulder as she walked to the main gate. "But my mate brought back the devil incarnate. Things are about to get really fun around here."

CHAPTER FORTY-FIVE

THE MOMENT THE DUST OF THE RUNES CLEARED, TENN WAS smacked with the overwhelming weight of heat. Heat, and a dampness so profound, his clothes stuck to him like a second skin.

He blinked against the brightness. Everything green and vibrant and lush, so bright he thought perhaps he had died. Minus the heat, this place had to be heaven.

Dense jungle foliage draped all around him, giant fronds and lush grass, as close and cloying as the heat and the air that filled his lungs. A shudder coursed through him—in the last few years, even the summers had been cold and damp and unpredictable. To have this heat, this lush beauty, was more a sign than anything else that he was somewhere altogether new. Somewhere, well, *magical*. He stood awestruck in the copse and stared at the green and the flowers and the sunlight filtering in from above.

Maybe he *had* died. Though he doubted he would go to heaven after everything he'd done.

It was then he realized what truly felt strange.

He heard birds.

Dozens, if not hundreds of them, singing in the trees, calling out in a myriad of voices. Birds, and other animal noises, too. It felt like being in a zoo, an aviary. How long had it been since he'd been in a place that had really seemed alive? Most everywhere in America had been stripped bare of life—anything with a pulse had become food for the Howls. How had this place escaped that fate?

"Welcome, Tenn," came a woman's voice.

He turned slowly, like he was moving through honey. And there, on the path before him, was the girl who could be none other than the Violet Sage.

She couldn't have been older than fourteen or fifteen. Her long white dress draped around her in folds and layers like the petals of an orchid, her black hair hung loose down her back. At first, he thought her skin was mottled by the sunlight, but when she moved he saw that in fact her skin was a blend of light and dark, brown and pale pink. And her eyes… He knew her eyes were what gave her her name. They were stunning amethyst, and he swore they saw straight to his core.

She smiled at the look on his face.

"You will get used to the heat," she said. She turned and beckoned him to follow. "We do not get many visitors here, and I'm afraid that time is of the essence, so I cannot give you the full tour…"

"Where are we?" Tenn asked. He jogged to catch up with her, giant leaves smacking wetly against his shoulders as they moved.

"An island." She looked over at him. "Forgive me for being

discreet. We cannot risk this haven becoming known. We have already lost so much. To lose those who live here would be catastrophic."

"Who lives here?"

"My disciples. Those who seek to understand Maya. You call them the Prophets."

Despite everything, Tenn felt a hitch of excitement in his heart.

The Prophets lived *here*. The mysterious mages who could tell the future, that had dictated the movements of so many battles, had held the lives of so many Hunters in their hands. Including his.

They were also the ones who sent Jarrett and the twins after him. They had set all of this in motion. Fitting that here, at the end, he would finally meet the ones who caused the beginning.

"Is that what I'm here to learn?" Tenn asked. "How to access Maya?"

She nodded.

"That is our hope."

They walked in silence after that, even though Tenn was overflowing with questions. He had felt the weight of destiny heavy on his shoulders before, but this…this was more than he could comprehend.

No one really knew what Maya was, beyond that it existed, beyond that it had more power than the other Spheres combined. The ability to change creation. A Sphere that was almost sentient.

To have Water act up was one thing. To be told he needed to access the Sphere that—to his knowledge—no one ever *had* wielded was quite another. What chance did he have? He

could barely control Water. How the hell was he supposed to
control a Sphere that was truly omnipotent?

Thankfully, he wasn't with his thoughts for long. The path
veered and opened, and the sound Tenn had thought was wind
through the trees turned out to be waves crashing on a beach.
Despite the urgency, he stared in wonder.

The beach before them was crystal white, stretching far
into the distance and out into the sea in an undulating curve.
Farther out, the beach gave way to thick grass tumbled with
stone paths and small platforms. And behind those, nestled
amidst the jungle, were huts of raw wood, windows open to the
sea breeze. Dozens of huts in all shapes and sizes, all of them
with large porches that jutted toward the sea. From here, he
could see a handful of white-robed people milling about the
paths and buildings.

"This is…"

"Paradise. A reminder of what we are fighting for. And what
the world could become again."

He felt the words she didn't say ringing between them—*if
you don't fail, that is.*

But that wasn't what he'd wanted to say, not precisely. Because beneath the awe, another emotion bubbled to the surface. Anger. *This is unreal*, he'd wanted to say. *This is unfair.*

"How?" he asked. She'd begun walking again, and he hurried to her side.

"How can we re-create this?" she asked.

"No. How can you live like this?"

The anger intensified as he looked out at the pristine waves,
the idyllic blue skies. The scent of flowers and baking bread

filled his nostrils. It should have made him feel peaceful, but instead it stoked the flames.

These people were living in bliss, while the rest of the world crumbled away. People were starving, literally living in their own shit, wondering if they would even have the luxury of waking up in the morning or if they'd be eaten or turned or destroyed in the night. This may as well have been another planet. How could they live with themselves when they knew humanity was suffering—no, not suffering, *going extinct*—on the other side of the ocean?

"I do not understand," she said, her smile dropping.

Maybe it was from being around Aidan too much, but the hypocrisy of this burned in his chest, a rage at all the injustices in the world coming to a fine point.

"You live in paradise," Tenn said. "And we're out there starving. *Dying.* Every day, dying and fighting and failing just so we can survive another day, and you get to live here. No Howls or necromancers or danger. How the hell can you live with yourselves? If we had known…"

She studied him, her purple eyes pensive if not a little hurt, while around them the seagulls and waves mocked him with their ease.

"Years ago, humans were given the most powerful gift the world could give. And they used it to destroy themselves and the very planet that bore them life. We live here, in paradise, cut off from the entirety of the world, not because we believe we are better, not because we believe we deserve a special life apart, but because we carry the burden of knowledge, of a power even greater than that which humanity has already bastardized. We must be kept apart. If the rest of the world

found us, if a single necromancer made his way here, civilization as we know it would be doomed."

"It's already doomed," Tenn said. "What knowledge could
you possibly have that would make things worse?"

"Maya. The ability to erase or reform creation itself."

It felt like too simple an answer, a brush-off.

"If it's so powerful," he growled, "why haven't you used it
to save us?"

"We have tried," she said. "And we have failed. And every
time, we lose another great mind, another guardian of a power
nearly lost. Maya does not give readily, Tenn. The Creator
owes us nothing. No, the Creator owes us only spite. For what
we have done with the gifts, the world, the very life beating
in our hearts. Maya will not restore what we have destroyed.
That is not nature's way."

It didn't make sense, not really.

"Then why am I here?"

"Because we must try. Time and again, we must try, and we
must hope, and we must pray. Pray that Maya will answer our
cries, and heal our wounds."

"And you think Maya will answer me?"

"I think there is a chance," she said.

"Why not before? Why wait? For Aidan to do what he did.
For the Dark Lady to rise again. If I'm here so you can teach
me something that will change the world, why wait until now?
You could have prevented all of this."

Her eyes cut straight to his soul.

"Because attuning to Maya may very well kill you. We knew
you were important, in ways we still do not understand. We
could not risk losing you. If we had, there would have been

no chance at turning Aidan, and our future would have been moot. We had to let you try to convince him on your own. And when that did not work, we have only one option left."

"And you think that will work? You think I can attune?"

"No," she said. "But I think you will try. I have watched you, Jeremy. I know you will throw your life on that altar, that you will sacrifice everything, if there is even the slightest chance it will help those who suffer. And that is why I have summoned you here. Not just because you are special or powerful, but because you are willing to give up your life to save the world. Because, in so many ways, you already have."

Tenn swallowed hard. Thought of Jarrett and the future that had disintegrated before his eyes way before his lover had tossed him in the prison cell. Once, he thought he was willing to be a martyr. Now, he wasn't so certain the world deserved it.

Now, he thought Aidan and Kianna might have been right all along.

There wasn't anything worth living for. Only things worth killing.

"You don't know me as well as you think," Tenn said.

Again, that long, soul-searching stare. Tenn tried not to shuffle his feet in agitation. Tried not to let his anger drown in the pity and doubt that curled in the waves of his mind.

"Pray that you are incorrect," she said. Then she turned and walked away.

CHAPTER FORTY-SIX

"WE DON'T NEED HIM," AIDAN GROWLED.

He paced back and forth in front of a fireplace twice his height in the dusty library. They hadn't left Natasja's castle, and even with the blaze in the hearth and the burn in his chest, he was cold. Or maybe it wasn't ice scratching at his limbs, but boredom. Agitation.

They had been here for hours.

Hours.

Him and the Dark Lady and a castle of corpses, and the corpses had been more engaging than the Dark Lady.

She sat in a large wingback chair before the fire, nursing a veritable goblet of red wine—at least, he assumed it was red wine—and watched him pace. She hadn't divulged the secrets of the netherworld or announced some diabolical plan. She just sat. Silently. As if she hadn't just spent the last four years in a similarly catatonic state. As if she had all the damn time in the damn world.

As though she weren't the most powerful mage on the planet, who could take over it all with a cock of her finger.

Well, second-most powerful. He had to keep reminding himself of that.

He wasn't her lackey.

She wasn't his superior.

Which didn't make waiting around for her to open her bloody mouth any easier.

"Where is he now?" she asked.

Aidan brought Tenn's tracking rune to mind. He could feel the boy out there, distant. Not the same place as before. But he couldn't place where. Could only point like a needle to due north.

"There," he said, gesturing out the window. "Somewhere."

The Dark Lady shifted forward in her seat. Swirled the wine in her glass.

"That is not good enough."

Finally, something new.

"If you're so all-powerful, why can't you find him yourself?"

She stopped swirling her wine. He stopped pacing.

He stared her down, Fire roaring assurances in his chest. A tiny voice inside him questioned if he'd pushed her too far.

Then she smiled.

He smirked, let out a chuckle.

Her eyes narrowed.

Pain shot through his chest.

He staggered back, clutching his heart as it screamed and froze and *he* screamed and froze and fell to his knees before the fireplace, digging at his chest as if to scrape it open.

She rose and stood before him, her dark dress a billowing

shadow at her feet, the air around her wavering with power, or perhaps it was the tears staining his eyes.

"You forget your place." There was no vitriol in her voice. No passion. She spoke to him as if he were nothing but a pedestrian passing on the street. She stepped forward and placed her foot on his chest. He howled as more pain flooded him, as she pressed him to the rug. "Pray that it does not happen again," she said. "For your own sake."

The pain stopped.

He lay there, gasping, sweat drenching his skin as shivers raced through him.

"Sorry," he choked.

She sat back down and picked up her goblet. "Sorrow is for the weak." She took a sip. "I do not tolerate weakness. Now, I ask you again, *where is he?*"

Aidan tried to force himself up, but his body refused to cooperate. He settled for crouching, hunched over before the fire, trying not to fall back into the flames.

"I don't know."

"Then you are weak. Do you require another reminder?"

"The runes," he said. "They don't show me where he is exactly. Just a direction."

"Then create new runes."

It struck him silent.

Create new runes?

Shivering, he looked to his arm, pulled back the sleeve to reveal the cauterized marks he'd scratched into his skin. He'd done it before. He'd thought they had been her words, but he realized he had been wrong.

The runes weren't the words of the Dark Lady.

They were older. A source outside of both of them.

But she couldn't hear everything he could. She needed him. She needed *him*.

He swallowed hard and let his sleeve drop. He didn't ask what to do. Didn't say he couldn't. Because he could. He already had.

He shuffled and turned to face the flames. Fire had always spoken to him. Through him. But it wasn't Fire he needed now. It was the voice behind it, the power that fueled it. He let his eyes unfocus and stared into the flames as Fire ignited within him.

Show me how to find him, he thought. *Show me.*

He pulled through Fire, but he didn't use it to manipulate, didn't use it to burn. Instead, he fed himself to the flames, let them burn through his consciousness, until he was no longer Aidan. No longer a Hunter. No longer human.

Until he was nothing but a flame, *the* flame, and he burned with the spark that turned the wheel of time.

Show me, he thought, the words echoing in the fire, the bliss, the *heat*. Knowledge coursed through him, but it wasn't words. Fire didn't speak in words. Only emotions. Only in action.

Distantly, he felt his body move, felt his arm reach into the flames, his fingers digging into the coals and ashes. It should have burned his skin, should have melted fat and flesh from his bones, but it was a distant tingle, the barest brush of sensation.

Flame couldn't hurt flame. It could only embolden. Burn brighter.

Fire took over, and he pressed his other hand to the fibers of the rug. Tendrils of flame laced from his fingers, webbing over the rug, searing a circle of symbols around him. The stench of burning dust and fiber filled the room, distant to his senses. All he knew was the flame, the vibrating pulse in his chest that flooded from the heart of the flame before him, through him, into the rug and around him. A circle of sigils, burning through his consciousness even as they burned through the rug, seared themselves into the stonework below.

Runes completed.

Flame connected. Burned a brilliant orange around him, a tapestry of glimmering power as his eyes fluttered to the back of his head, as the room flooded orange, orange, brilliant and bright. Power swirled. Vision blanked white.

And then he saw.

Granules. White granules. Sand.

Heat reflecting off white sand, sunlight touching everything, *everything*, a land of brilliance, a land of flame.

Save for the water washing around them. An island. He flinched back from the waves, focused instead on the sparkle in their curl. His sun. His light. His power. Light reflecting off waves. Off sand. Off leaves.

Off *them*.

Tenn, walking through the sand, light flickering off the wetness coating his skin. A different sort of light. A different sort of power.

Power.

Beside him walked a girl. So young. Yet the power around her blinded even him, made his eyes avert on their own.

Aidan was the sun. She burned like a galaxy.

He couldn't hear their words. Could only see the brilliance, the light. But he knew them. He could find their light anywhere, beacons burning in even the deepest darkness.

He could find them.

Then she looked at him. The girl.

Their eyes met. Hers, a violent violet.

Purple flooded him.

This need not be your way, she said, her voice reverberating through him.

The vision broke and he was back. Back in the dusty library, one hand still in the cinders of the fireplace, the other pressed to a dark burn stain in the carpet. Sigils smoked around him, their power spent.

But it had been enough.

Slowly, he withdrew his hand from the flames. Sat back.

Felt, even with Fire burning in his chest, exhausted.

"I found him," he whispered. Smoke curled from his lips.

Perhaps he had hoped for praise. An exclamation of shock. He had created new runes. He had found what the Dark Lady could not.

Instead, when he looked to her, he found she wasn't even watching him. She stared out the window at the gathering darkness.

"Good," she replied, and sipped her wine.

CHAPTER FORTY-SEVEN

"WHERE THE HELL IS HE?" JARRETT ROARED.

They'd gathered in Cassandra's study, a large, lavish room of thick wooden furniture and oak bookshelves, plush curtains covering any spare bit of wall and light filtering in from crystalline chandeliers. Dreya had always found Earth users lavish in their tastes, but Cassandra had both the thirst for comfort and the wealth and power to see it through in spades. Frankly, Dreya found it mildly grotesque.

Cassandra herself sat behind a table littered with maps and paperwork, gems and crystals acting as paperweights. Kianna toyed with one, a chunk of emerald the size of a fist. Cassandra watched her suspiciously.

"Yes," Cassandra mused. "That question exactly. Where is Tenn, and where is this friend of yours? I had left the former in your care, when it seems I should have sent you after the latter instead."

"No clue," Kianna said. She picked up the emerald and tossed it, catching it lightly. Unlike the others in the room, she wasn't open to magic. Devon stood in the corner with flames flickering around him, Jarrett and Dreya both held Air in their throats, and Cassandra and her two commanding officers were open to their own powers. It didn't seem to bother Kianna in the slightest. Neither did their glares at her nonchalance. "Left him over in—where was it?—Russia I think. Somewhere cold. Snowy. Doubt he's still there. Prick hates the cold almost as much as he hates Tenn. So maybe if you find Tenn, you'll find Aidan with a knife to his throat."

She inspected the emerald, then looked to her silent spectators.

"What? Too far?"

She tossed the emerald up once more. Cassandra snatched it from the air before Kianna could reach for it.

"Nice one," Kianna said.

"Do that again, and you'll lose your hand," Cassandra said, not breaking eye contact.

Kianna just snorted, picked up another paperweight—a cloudy crystal ball—and walked over to an unoccupied corner.

Cassandra set the stone on the table, then turned her attention to Dreya. Dreya filled herself with Air's clarity. She would not be cowed by a mere Earth mage, even if she did control Outer Chicago. Dreya bent to no one.

"You say you brought him back here," Cassandra said. "And then conveniently lost him to a fox."

Dreya nodded.

"The Violet Sage summoned him. It was not my place to intervene."

"Or a necromancer parading as the Violet Sage," Jarrett growled. "How could you be so stupid?"

Dreya bristled. As he knew she would. She wanted to lash out, but she kept her emotions in check, smoothed them down with Air.

"Do you know many who can control foxes?" she asked simply. She turned her attention back to Cassandra. "All we can assume is that he is safe. The Violet Sage has been kept hidden since before the Resurrection."

"That is an assumption none of us can afford to make." She sighed and sank back into her chair. "All right, then. Two of the most powerful mages are missing. One on our side, one against, both a threat to our existence just *from* their existence. And the dangerous one has managed to not only find but bring back the Dark Lady. Do I have that correct?"

Dreya nodded.

Cassandra closed her eyes, rubbed her temples. Dreya wondered idly if it was all an act. Cassandra was nothing if not ever in control.

"What do you think they will do? Aidan and the Dark Lady."

"They'll raise an army," Jarrett said. "All she has to do is proclaim her presence, and the necromancers will rally like never before. They'll topple us."

"So you would have us rally our own army?"

He nodded.

"Send envoys to every Guild and Outpost in the country. We don't stand a chance if we spread out. But if we gather together, we might have a chance."

"Yeah," Kianna snorted from the shadows. "A chance to be slaughtered."

Cassandra looked to her.

"Do you have an opinion you'd like to share?"

"Always. Though I guarantee you'll never like it." She took a step forward, rhythmically tossing the globe up like a baseball. "I'm saying that if my mate comes here—and that's a big *if*, because I don't think he's that stupid—you're just going to make it easier for him and the Dark Lady to wipe everyone out. I mean, think about it, you don't just toss all the leaders of the free world into one room during a nuclear war, do you? That's mass suicide."

"So you say we scatter?"

"I say you fortify where you can. Spread your defenses. Lay traps. Let him slip up and then take him when his defense is down. But again, he ain't going to do that."

"Why?" Jarrett asked sarcastically. "Is he going to have a sudden change of heart?"

"No. Aidan doesn't ever do what you expect him to. Trust me on that one. He wants to rule. He'd happily burn the whole world to the ground. But he could have done that himself. He didn't bring the Dark Lady back to take over. He brought her back because he wanted something."

"What he wants doesn't matter," Cassandra said. "What matters is that he brought *her* back. And we know what she wants. She wants what she's wanted all along—to divide and devour us." She looked to Jarrett. "Send the envoys. Bring in the forces within a hundred-mile radius, and fortify all major hubs. I want America to be empty save for the major Guilds by the end of the week."

"You're making a mistake," Kianna said.

"Then I'm sure you'll be around to laugh over our graves when it's all over."

Kianna smiled at her, tossed her the paperweight. Cassandra caught it.

"That's probably the only thing you're right about," Kianna said. Then she turned and left.

Dreya hesitated. Jarrett and Cassandra had already begun discussing their plans, and a part of her wanted to stick around and learn the details, absorb as much as she could.

The rest of her knew it wouldn't do any good, and she could sense Kianna getting farther down the hall. If she waited much longer, she would look desperate.

Wait here, she thought to her brother.

Without waiting to see if he agreed, she slipped from the room.

She caught up with Kianna halfway down the hall, walking swiftly.

Kianna didn't even look over her shoulder.

"You know it's a mistake."

"I do," Dreya said. "And I also know they will not listen. We have done what we intended to do. We have warned them."

Kianna paused. Looked at her.

Dreya felt her heart skip. Slightly.

"Then what do you propose we do now?" Kianna asked.

"They will not listen or help us. So we seek out those who will."

"And who are these miraculous beings?"

Dreya dropped her gaze.

"Those we have betrayed," she said. Even after saving Rhiannon's Clan, it was not enough to undo what she and her brother had done. "And those we will spend our lives trying to avenge."

Kianna placed a hand on her shoulder. It was surprisingly gentle, even if her words were not.

"Betrayal and vengeance? This plan sounds better already."

CHAPTER FORTY-EIGHT

THEY WANDERED UP THE BEACH, PAST THE BEAUTIFUL HOUSES
that were more cabanas than anything, their sheer white curtains billowing in the sea breeze. Everywhere he looked were
young men and women dressed in white robes. Some carried
bowls or books between buildings, others meditated in the
sand. Most were silent, though a few sat together and talked
in languages he couldn't place. None seemed to be past their
early twenties.

Every one of them paused to watch him pass by.

One young boy dropped the book he was reading to the
sand.

Tenn wanted to pretend it was because he was an outsider,
the only one here covered in black and rainwater from another
continent. But he knew it was because they recognized him.

"Are they the Prophets?" he asked.

"No," the Violet Sage replied without looking.

She led him to a large building, the biggest on the beach,
with long open windows and a high-peaked roof.

"Do you have a name?" Tenn asked. "Or am I just supposed to keep referring to you by your title?"

A small part of him marveled at his boldness, or maybe it was rudeness. The rest was just so, so tired of being led around blindly.

She paused then, and looked up at him. Considered.

"Kara," she said, and continued on.

He didn't know what he expected when he stepped into the house. All of this was entirely out of left field; after the last four years of rain and cold and bloodshed, being here felt like stepping out of his life and into some sort of fairy tale. One where good things actually happened and evil could be vanquished. It wasn't his reality. And the space they entered wasn't some grand room of learning or power.

There wasn't a chamber of wizened monks balancing on precarious stones or anything even remotely magical. It was just a large room overlooking the sea, with two brocade pillows in the center and a small porcelain tea set on a tray beside them.

"Sit," she said, gesturing to a pillow.

Tenn did so, fidgeting with his clothes. He opened to Water and pulled the rain from them, but the moment he did, the humidity snuck back in and stuck to his skin.

Kara sat on the opposite pillow, a small smile on her lips. Then she opened to her Spheres. All four of them.

Instantly, the windows closed and the air in the room dropped to a comfortable temperature. The humidity vanished. Small lanterns burst into flame around them, casting a warm, soothing glow over the scene. Sticks of incense in ceramic holders began to smolder, trailing tails of smoke up into the rafters.

Even though they were small acts of magic, and even though he had known she could channel all four Spheres, it still filled Tenn with a sense of awe.

"Tea?" She raised the pot and filled both cups before he could answer. The scent of peppermint and something more pungent drifted around them.

"So how does this work?" he asked as she handed him the tea. "Is there some sort of secret ritual or something?"

He couldn't help the sarcasm laced through his words. He knew he was being childish and insolent, but Water churned and bruised within him, an ache and injustice that just wouldn't go away—why did these people get to live in peace, while everyone else suffered? Why was he even trying to help them?

You aren't helping them, he told himself. *You're helping everyone else.*

If she noticed the tone of his voice, she didn't let it bother her.

"How else? Through the runes."

She took a sip of tea, and he did the same. It tasted...gross. Like someone had mixed mint in with a lump of dirt and roots and called it good. But it seemed to clear his head a bit, and even though a part of him resented all of this, he didn't want to seem rude.

He took another sip.

"There are runes to attune to Maya?" he asked. "I thought it was the one Sphere no one could attune to?"

She nodded.

"That is correct, in a fashion. One cannot attune to it. It is not simply like an electrical socket one can plug into. No, the runes are to bring you to Maya's doorstep. To open you to its mystery. Then, it is up to the Sphere to decide."

"Okay, then." He set the tea down. "What are they?"

She hesitated. And had he not been watching her carefully, he would have missed the uncertainty that flashed over her features.

"There is one thing you must know," she said.

Of course there is.

"You mean beyond the fact that this most likely won't work and might kill me?" he asked.

She nodded. "Yes. There is a cost to failure. In order to open to Maya, one must give oneself to the Sphere. Fully. And should the Sphere refuse you…"

"You die."

"No," she said. "Not fully. Not quite."

"How many have successfully attuned?"

"None."

"Then how do you know the runes work? How do you know you can actually attune?"

"The same reason you believe you can fight the Dark Lady. Your heart tells you it is so. We have faith. We have simply not been worthy enough for Maya's grace."

Tenn swallowed. It wasn't exactly heartening, but what choice did he have? If he left here without attuning to Maya, he'd either be killed by Aidan or the Dark Lady or one of her spawn, or else Jarrett would throw him back into prison until everything was over—which it would never be, because they didn't stand a chance. He was as good as dead either way. The only real chance he had was attuning to Maya. And after everything he'd been through, a small part of him believed that this would work.

That he was special.

He was the one the Spheres bent toward. The one the spirits spoke through. And even though it was somewhat egotistical, he felt like that should be more than enough to prove his worth to a Sphere.

The moment he thought that, however, doubt flooded through him.

If he had been so special, so powerful, why had he failed so many? Why hadn't he been special enough to save his parents? Why had he failed when he'd needed to succeed the most?

"Why me?" he asked. "What makes me so special? And don't tell me it's because I'm willing to die to save people. A lot of people are." He swallowed. Thought of the dozens of Hunters he'd watched fall in battle. "I should know. I've fought beside many of them."

She considered for a while, her cup poised beneath her lips, untouched. That stare made him want to take his question back.

"Why should it *not* be you, Jeremy?" It still unnerved him that she called him by his old name. "It has nothing to do with being 'chosen,' and everything to do with being willing to answer the call. You answered. You followed the trail. And you believed. Which has brought you here, and once more you have the choice—believe not in yourself, but in the call, or turn away from both?"

In a way, the answer was disappointing.

He wasn't special.

He wasn't some chosen one.

But then he thought about it. Did it not make him stronger, to think he had been equal? That he hadn't been chosen, but had chosen to take this on? It made him feel less battered by the Fates and more in control. He had a duty. There were people to save. And in the end, that would always be his highest calling, *chosen* or no.

He took a deep breath and nodded.

"Okay, then," he said. "Show me."

She set down the cup.

"I cannot write them down. Not for fear they will be discovered by the wrong sorts. Just as you must promise never to share these."

"I promise."

Kara gestured at her side, Air glowing brighter in her throat. A stick of burning incense floated over, smoke trailing behind it.

"Let your mind relax and the symbols flow through you," she said. "These runes require only thought to activate, much like the tracking rune you know. As they settle in your mind, they will begin to work their magic. And then...well, then it is up to Maya. The process can take seconds or minutes, or even days. For some, the process never truly ends."

She looked at him. "Are you ready?"

Despite himself, his heart thudded in his chest.

He knew there was no turning back from this. He succeeded, or he failed. Whatever that failure looked like, he knew it spelled death. For him, and for many, many others. He wanted to say of course he was ready, he didn't have a choice. But he did have a choice. And he chose this.

He had to hope that was enough.

"I'm ready," he said.

With a curt nod, she closed her eyes and twined her fingers through the incense smoke. It curled over her skin, serpentine, but rather than dispersing or dissipating, it moved. It twisted before her, a thread of gray, and began to form shapes. Runes.

They unfurled before him, a long, sinuous line of smoke and power. With every breath, he inhaled the heavy, heady scent. With every breath, he felt them settle into his bones.

His vision swam. The room faded, became a darkness that felt familiar. Comforting. Like the heavy black he'd felt in the Witches' vision. He was safe here. Safe.

And then, he heard the Violet Sage scream.

CHAPTER FORTY-NINE

DREYA HAD HER HAND TO THE GUILD DOOR WHEN SHE heard it. *Felt* it. In the very depths of her bones, she heard the scream.

She gasped, her breath catching in her throat.

It wasn't a scream of pain. No.

Despair.

The worst type of despair.

The knowledge that all was lost.

She turned to her brother, whose eyes were wide.

"Did you feel—?" she asked aloud, so shocked she couldn't even think it his way.

He nodded.

So did Kianna.

"The hell was that?" she asked.

They looked behind them. Other Hunters had similarly paused, faces slack with shock.

"Dreya," Kianna said. And there was no mistaking it—there

was fear in her voice. Just as there was no mistaking that it was not a sensation Kianna was used to. "What was that?"

Dreya couldn't answer. She couldn't even swallow. She stared at the frozen Hunters behind them, at her brother, at Kianna. All she could feel was the shock of that scream. All she knew was that the worst that could happen, had happened.

"The Violet Sage," Devon said for her. "She has been discovered."

Dreya shook her head. *Tenn. What has happened to Tenn?*

"We are too late," Dreya whispered. "The Dark Lady has found her. She has been taken."

CHAPTER FIFTY

"AND HOW EXACTLY IS SHE GOING TO HELP BRING MY MOTHER back?" Aidan growled, staring at the creepy girl bound to the chair before them.

The Dark Lady prowled around the chair like a panther, staring at the Violet Sage with a smug look on her face. Runes formed a ring around the girl on the floor, runes in a language Aidan found he knew as well as his own, even though the Dark Lady had carved them. They were similar to the ones on the Dark Lady's tomb—runes for imprisonment, for silence. And others he knew far too well, runes that weren't runes at all, but the mark the Church had used against him, to cut the girl off from magic.

Which was good, since she could apparently use all of it.

The Dark Lady didn't answer. He was used to that by now.

The girl didn't struggle against the ropes. He'd tied them himself, his one contribution to this entire bit of fuckery. He'd had plenty of practice tying knots, and plenty of guys to practice them on. Before. Now, he couldn't even imagine finding a partner worth his time.

Now that Tomás was gone...

He pulled through Fire and tried to ignore the fact that the incubus was still nearby, lying in a pool of blood in the dungeons. Tried to ignore that he had killed the Kin, even though...even though, yes, he had fallen for the creature.

That was why he'd had to kill Tomás. Not just because he couldn't trust the Kin—after all, Tomás had already tried to kill him once—but because he couldn't trust *himself* around him. Aidan had to keep a clear head. And that meant things like romance were a liability.

Something he understood much, much better than their other prisoner in the room next door.

Tenn had put up even less of a struggle than the Violet Sage. It probably helped that he looked drugged out when Aidan and the Dark Lady had swept in and dragged them both back here.

"Do you remember them?" the Dark Lady asked Aidan. "The runes she showed him? The ones he used to access Maya?"

Aidan nodded. He also remembered the Violet Sage's warning. He wanted power, but he didn't want to risk dying—or whatever she meant—if Maya refused him. He couldn't imagine the Sphere would take too kindly to his history.

"Show them to me," the Dark Lady demanded, finally bringing her attention back to Aidan.

"You don't have to do this," whispered a voice in his head. He knew it was the Violet Sage. Just as he knew she was wrong.

He pulled deeper through Fire and twined the flame around his fingers, arcing a line of fire before him, manipulating and twisting it into runes. Even just looking at them made him feel funny, heavy, like he was stoned. The room wanted to give way, wanted to swallow him. So he looked at the stones at his feet and tried to stay grounded.

"Good," the Dark Lady said. She stepped forward, the hem of her violet dress the only thing he could see. It pooled at her feet like oil. "Very good."

He couldn't help it. Even that little bit of praise helped win him over. A smile flitted over his lips.

He let go of the runes; they flurried around his fingers like fireworks. When he looked up, she was standing once more before the Violet Sage.

"You worked your whole life to hide this knowledge from me," the Dark Lady said. "You were nearly successful. Nearly."

She prowled around the girl, her glee palpable. But there was a darkness there, a hurt that ran deep.

"I have watched you. All of you. From the doorstep of death I have watched as you fling yourselves at Maya. And I know what you think. I know you believe you must be worthy to attain that power, that the Sphere would never bend to one such as me. You believe it is a god. You couldn't be further from the truth. You must merely be willing to die, to give your soul over. Maya is no god, holds no judgment. Maya is the Sphere *of* gods. And I, little one, have been close to death for four long years. I am already a goddess in the hearts of mankind. Now, I may take the powers of one."

She turned to Aidan.

"Watch her. Ensure that she does not escape." She smiled. Maybe it was his imagination, but she actually looked happy. "It is time for me to ascend."

He didn't need to ask her what she meant. She was already considered the Goddess of Death. Now, she wanted to truly take on that role.

"And then you help me get my mother back," he said.

Something shifted in her expression. The smile stayed, but it no longer looked sincere. Or maybe it was his imagination.

"Of course," she said. "Once I have Maya, we will do everything we desire."

She turned and left the room, leaving him alone with the Violet Sage and a terrible feeling in his gut not even Fire could burn away.

"You can still make this right."

The girl's voice echoed in his head. He sat in front of her, hands to his temples, staring at the runes glowing on the floor, trying to pick them apart, to understand them, to find ways to manipulate or restructure them. Not because he was inquisitive, but because he was bored, and it helped him ignore the voice in his head that would. Not. Stop.

He growled in the back of his throat and considered just opening to Fire and shutting her up for good. Though he had a feeling the Dark Lady wouldn't appreciate that very much. He was beginning to not care. What had she done for him so far? He'd given her everything she'd asked for, and she hadn't delivered on a single promise. He didn't rule the world. He didn't have a throne. He didn't have omnipotent power. And he didn't have his mother back.

All he had were more promises, more demands.

More pleas from the bound girl before him.

The runes around her stopped magic. Maybe he could figure out a way to make them stop her telepathy, or whatever it was.

"Please, Aidan," she continued. "*I know what is in your heart. You don't want to do this. You have no idea what she is planning. She is using you. Only using you.*"

"Shut up!" Fire flared around him, sparks burning bright, missiles ready to launch. He jumped to his feet and glared at her, hands clenched into fists. "You don't know anything. I'm not being used. I'm using *her.*"

"*We both know that is not true,*" she thought. Her eyes were pleading, but they weren't afraid. At least, not for herself. She seemed terrified for him. That, more than anything, pissed him off. "*Release me from here. I can help you. I can—*"

"Right," he growled. "You can help me. Just like you've helped me all these years. Just like you helped save my mother and the rest of humanity, oh great and powerful one. Oh, wait, you haven't. You haven't done jack shit with all of your power. You know what I think?" He took a step closer, the flames around him burning brighter. "I think you're just scared that someone else has come along that is more powerful than you. You don't want to be usurped."

"*She will never be more powerful than I. Even with Maya, she—*"

"Not her, you idiot. Me. You know I could break this world if I wanted. That scares you. You want me to let you out so you can try to kill me. So you can keep me from becoming the king I'm meant to be."

She shook her head. "*That is not true. I can help you, Aidan.*"

"You say you've seen into my heart. If that's so, can you bring my mother back?"

She didn't answer.

"I thought not," he said.

"Neither can she."

"But she'll try. And if she fails, I'll kill her."

"You cannot kill the Goddess of Death. Not with what she is about to become."

"Watch me," he replied. "Now shut the hell up. You're giving me a headache."

He went to sit back down, but her words stopped him.

"She would never have wanted this of you. You know that, deep in your heart. Your mother would never have wanted you to hurt like this. Or to cause this much hurt."

"Don't you dare!" he yelled. "Don't you dare talk about her. You never knew her."

He pulled through Fire until he was nearly blinded by the brilliance around and within him.

"I know more than you think," she said.

And there, through the light, he saw her.

She stood behind the Violet Sage wearing the same cardigan she'd worn the last day he'd seen her. Only this one wasn't ripped to shreds. She smiled at him sadly, her hands on the Violet Sage's shoulders. He nearly dropped to his knees.

"It's okay, honey," his mother said. "Everything is going to be okay. I know you never wanted this. I know you've just been hurting. We can make it right, I promise. You just need to untie this girl. Get her and the boy out of here. And then we can end this. We can make it right."

"Mom," he gasped.

She nodded.

"No." He squeezed his hands to his forehead, blocked out

his vision. "No, you aren't here. You're dead. I saw you die. This is just an illusion."

"No illusion, Aidan. I am here. I have waited so long to reach out to you. There's still time to fix this. To fix everything. You just have to trust me, baby. You just have to let her go."

"No!" Fire swirled around him, a billow that swept across the room and would have incinerated the girl if not for the wards imprisoning her. And protecting her from him. It was enough, however, to make the vision of his mother disappear.

He didn't want it to disappear.

"Get out of my head," he growled. He tapped his temple. "Stay. Out. Or next time I'll make sure the flames hit you."

"Aidan—"

He stumbled. The room tilted. Wavered. As if a heat mirage on the brink of dispersing, before solidifying again.

The Violet Sage's eyes widened.

"The hell was that?" he asked.

She didn't answer, not right away. When she did, even her thoughts were hushed.

"She succeeded. Maya has embraced her."

CHAPTER FIFTY-ONE

"WE MUST HURRY," DREYA SAID.

Hunters scurried around them, shouting out in confusion as, deep within the Guild, a bell tolled—a signal for an emergency meeting, for order. Everyone had felt the Violet Sage's cries. But did they know the true weight of that fear? The true penalty to Aidan's crime? Perhaps only she and her companions understood the threat. But they could not risk hesitating or turning back. They couldn't aid the Guild. Not like this.

"Where are we going?" Kianna asked.

Dreya looked to her brother. He nodded.

"To the Witches." She looked to Kianna. "That was the Violet Sage. Aidan has brought the Dark Lady to her. We must rally all who can use magic. All who can read the runes. The final battle comes."

Despite everything, there was no excitement on Kianna's features. Dreya knew her well enough to know she lived for bloodshed and battle, just as she knew Kianna understood the true weight of this proclamation.

"And Aidan?" she asked. "Tenn?"

Dreya shook her head. "We have to hope they are both still alive. They have created this. They must end it."

"But what have they created?"

A pause.

"There is only one reason the Dark Lady would seek the Violet Sage. She wishes to attune to Maya. And then..."

"And then? Isn't that enough?"

Dreya shook her head.

"The Dark Lady will continue her work. She wanted to create a true immortal, a creature not even God could bend. A force the world has never seen." She swallowed. "Once she has Maya, she will learn how to drain it from others."

Kianna's eyes widened. "She's going to create a Wight."

"Yes. The question is simply whom she will pick as a host."

But deep down, Dreya already knew. The Dark Lady wouldn't seek to create a simple Howl. She would want to create a Kin. One who could wield magic. And she wouldn't settle for Tenn or Aidan, mages who could wield two Spheres at most. She now had the one mage who could wield all four.

"We have to stop her," Kianna growled. "We can track down Tenn. Finish them before it begins."

"That would be suicide. The Dark Lady cannot be taken unawares. If she is already attuned to Maya, we would be killed before we even had a chance. We must gather our defenses."

"But we could still—"

"No. It is already too late. The boys will be fine. I know it in my heart. But they will need us. They will need to return to something safe. They will need an army to lead. And only we can create that."

Kianna swallowed. She didn't like this. Truth be told, neither did Dreya. She would much rather teleport in and steal the boys from the Dark Lady. But she knew Aidan was lost to them, and they would have Tenn under lock and key.

She also knew her words were a lie.

The boys couldn't finish this. The boys would never make it out alive.

They were on their own.

"Come," Dreya said, brushing the fear away with a gust of Air. "We have work to do."

She traced the runes of travel in the dust at their feet, and as they opened to their powers, she prayed to every spirit listening that they still had a chance to make things right.

CHAPTER FIFTY-TWO

AIDAN TOOK AN INVOLUNTARY STEP BACK WHEN THE DOOR opened and the Dark Lady stepped through. The very air around her wavered, as though she were the center of a rippling pond. Her dress billowed in an unfelt breeze, her blond hair a halo. She practically floated above the concrete floor.

"My Hunter," she said, her voice once more its oceanic hum, a thrum that vibrated deep in his chest. "We have succeeded."

Her words filled him with a new sensation: dread.

Because in those words was another proclamation: she had everything she needed, which meant she no longer had use for him. His single ace of reading the runes was spent. He just had to hope she still wanted him around. That his insight into the runes might still prove useful.

As he watched her fucking billow toward the Violet Sage, he doubted that insight accounted for much anymore.

"And now," the Dark Lady said, "I believe we have some unfinished business."

"My mother—" Aidan said, his voice quiet.

The Dark Lady turned to him, her eyes flashing, the air moving about her like a living, breathing thing. He stepped back.

"Your mother can wait. We still have many who would oppose us. Many who will rise up to defend this wretch the moment they realize she has gone. The moment they realize what I have become."

Immediately, Tenn's face flashed through Aidan's mind. But the boy wasn't a threat. He was bound and gagged and magically sealed off next door. What threat could he be? What threat could anyone else pose against...this?

"Go back to the island," she said. "Kill all who dwell there. We cannot risk the powers of Maya falling into anyone else's hands. We cannot risk a true rebellion."

He almost wanted to tell her to do it her damn self. Almost. He might have been angry, but he wasn't an idiot.

This would prove him useful to her.

Would endear him to her.

And maybe, when he was done, he could have his mother back.

Maybe, when he was done, he could turn against her.

Though...he doubted he had a chance in hell of killing her now. He'd need to attune to Maya. He'd need Tenn's help. The thought made anger roil inside him—he'd come so far, and he was still relying on the help of others.

Weak. Tomás's voice floated through his brain. A phantom, but no less potent. Or true.

Aidan pulled through Fire, burned the voice and the weakness away.

"Your will be done," he said. "Killing them will be a pleasure."

What surprised him was that he wasn't certain he meant it.

* * *

Aidan expected some sort of commotion on the island. Torches and pitchforks, battle cries and armor. But nothing had changed. Birds still sang in the trees, the ocean churned endlessly against the white-sand beach. And the acolytes he'd seen earlier still wandered or meditated, their white robes making them look like seagulls in the breeze.

It was peaceful. Idyllic.

You don't have to do this.

He wasn't certain if it was the Violet Sage still speaking to him, or the echo of memory. He stood in the doorway of the room from which he'd stolen the Violet Sage and Tenn away, staring out at the beach, and doubt churned through him. He reached through Fire, but even though the heat filled him, the rage wouldn't come.

These were humans.

Peaceful, innocent humans. They weren't Howls or necromancers, they weren't serving the Dark Lady...

He jolted.

They weren't serving the Dark Lady, but *he* was. Doing her bidding like a dog. All so—what?—she might fulfill her promise and return his mother to him? Was it worth it?

For a moment, he wondered what Kianna would say. Only for a moment, though, because he knew without doubt she would have a sword in his back or a bullet in his brain before he'd even had the chance to ask. He'd betrayed her. He'd betrayed everyone.

He was no better than the Howls. No better than the necromancers.

You don't have to do this.

His mother's face floated through his mind.

But he did. He did.

He'd already gone too far. If he crossed the Dark Lady now, she'd kill him, and the world would go on and her reign would be unchallenged, and everything, everything would have been for nothing.

He wasn't going to let his life be for nothing.

He *had* gone too far. And he had to go further if he wanted to make any of this worth it. Once he had his mother, he could stop. Then, and only then, could he start to question himself. Until that time, there was no turning back.

Closing his eyes, he reached deep into his treacherous Sphere, wrapped himself in heat and energy, fed himself to the flame. The doubt. The pity. The innocence.

He fed it all to the flames, and when he opened his eyes again, he fed his flame to the world.

In a blink, the acolytes on the beach crumpled, fire filling their lungs and veins and winking out without a trace. He turned, cast his Fire farther, seeking out the sparks he felt within the huts, the lives completely unaware they were about to be snuffed out. Another snap of Fire, and they flared and extinguished in a heartbeat.

It unnerved him, the ease with which he killed everyone. A half dozen dead. A dozen. All humans. All innocent. All seeking what he had thought he had wanted—an end to the darkness. Now, he was the darkness.

He snapped his fingers, and the huts went up in a blaze. Infernos, each of them, bright as the sun. It wasn't right, that sun. He'd committed murder before, but it had been cold then.

Dismal. The right weather for a massacre. This…this wasn't right. None of it.

Still, he killed.

He stepped out from the building, onto the boardwalk, and behind him the bamboo and timber erupted in flame, wood snapping and crackling like skeletons beneath a boot.

There was no one around to scream or race to the buildings. There already were no survivors.

Except…

He felt them, farther in. A few dozen sparks, a few dozen lives, all huddled together like offering candles in a church. They must have felt the magic, the inferno. They must have known something was wrong. None of them moved, however. None of them seemed to know he was here, or what he had done.

You could leave them. The thought was most assuredly his own, and the voice of reason felt so alien that for a moment it froze him in place. *You could let them live. She would never know.*

It was true. He could turn back whenever, and the Dark Lady would believe he had done the job. He was a murderer, but he didn't have to commit genocide, not like this.

At first, he thought the waver in the flames was from his eyes watering, from the heat and the smoke. Then he realized he was crying.

"I have to," he said to her ghost. "I have to get you back. I have to make this right."

Only there was no making this right. There was only going deeper. He could only make it worse.

That, it seemed, was all he was good at.

He squeezed his eyes shut. Blocked out the voice of reason in his head, his conscience coming to light all too late.

Then he turned and headed toward the sparks still wavering in the jungle, the lives he would end so he alone could carry on.

CHAPTER FIFTY-THREE

HE IS NOT FORSAKEN, SHE WHISPERED IN THE DARKNESS, HER voice strained and tinged with tears. *For all he has done, for all he has become, he is not lost. Only together will you defeat her. You must remember this, Tenn. You must remember. You must—*

CHAPTER FIFTY-FOUR

BLACK STONE STEPS BURROWED DEEP INTO THE EARTH. LAMPS
glimmered along the walls—not magical, but fuel-burning, and
the sight felt like an anachronism. Despite the lanterns, shadows lay deep and heavy farther in. He didn't want to go down
there. And yet, that was where the sparks flickered.

He could have ended them. He knew this. He could snap
his fingers and extinguish all those sparks without ever seeing
them. But something drew him forward. Curiosity, or something stronger.

He was a monster, yes. But he was still, in some ways,
human. He descended.

The air grew colder and wetter with every step, and with
every step he pulled deeper through Fire to try to fend it off.
He wasn't successful.

There was no door at the end. Only a stone archway and a
mist lying heavy on the ground, illuminated faintly by lights
farther in. He stepped through.

Fog coiled against black rock columns, sconces carved

within them and flickering candles dripping forth. Stone formations littered the floor, small heaps he could barely make out through the roiling mist. The light was too dim, the fog too heavy. And everywhere, echoing through the fog, was a sound. Murmuring. Mumbling. He'd thought it was water at first, but as he stood there, he realized it was a voice. Voices. Human. So where—

"What are you doing here?"

Aidan jumped back, nearly lashing out with flame at the voice.

It was a young man, wearing not the white robes he'd seen on the beach, but dark gray.

"I'm—"

Murdering an entire island? How had you not noticed?

Then the fog parted, just barely, and he realized it wasn't stones resting between the columns, but people. Huddled, mumbling people, wearing the same gray robes as the man by the door. The fog curled back in, obscuring them from view.

"Who are these people?" he asked.

The young man considered Aidan. He wasn't open to any magic; Aidan couldn't understand why the guy didn't attack, or raise an alarm, or seem to even be aware that anything bad was happening in the world outside. Maybe he wasn't attuned to a Sphere? If so, what was he doing here?

"These are the Prophets," the man said, his voice curled as if to ask, *How did you not know?*

"What?"

Aidan took a step toward the figures, as if in a daze. Fog curled around his ankles as he walked toward the nearest Prophet. It was a girl, maybe the same age as he, robed in gray and curled in on herself, mumbling constantly. *These* were the all-knowing figures that guided the motions of men?

They weren't prophets. They were madmen.

"These are the souls that Maya cast aside," the young man said behind him. "Although they are not deemed worthy enough to wield the Sphere, they remain…attached to it. As though a part of them is always open to Maya, in tune with a frequency the rest of us cannot hear. A sort of cosmic radio. Most of the time they mutter only nonsense. Gibberish. But occasionally, they speak in riddles we can understand. That is my job. To watch, to translate and to relay."

Aidan barely heard him. To think, he'd almost offered himself up to Maya. What would have happened? Would he have become like this?

"It is strange," the boy said. "I have watched over them for years. This sounds different. They almost sound afraid."

Yeah, Aidan wanted to say. *They're afraid of me.*

He couldn't believe that this was how armies moved and humanity was influenced. A group of madmen in a cave in the middle of nowhere. Despite his doubts regarding their wisdom, a part of him wanted to shake one of them, to demand some sort of answer: How do I get out of this? How do I get my mother back?

"Who are you, anyway?" the boy asked. "A guest of the Violet Sage?"

"You could say that."

Aidan walked back toward the entrance.

He expected one of them to reach out and grab him, to utter some dark prophecy. To tell him he'd damned the world, that only he could undo it.

He'd read enough books in his lifetime to know how it was supposed to go.

But he walked straight to the archway without any nonsense. There was no need for prophecy, not anymore.

He knew he'd damned the world. Just as he knew there wasn't a way to undo it, not really. There wasn't any secret, there. The Dark Lady was free. The Dark Lady had Maya and the Violet Sage. All he could do was follow her orders and hope she kept her promise.

The tide had turned on him.

Even with all the might of Fire, there was no way he could kill her.

He could only obey, and obey he would.

Behind him, flames lashed through the lungs of the Prophets, instantaneous and relatively painless. No pyrotechnics. No intimidating blaze.

There was no victory in this kill. No glory.

He didn't even feel like a murderer. He just felt like a butcher, harvesting his meat.

The only sign that the work was done was the silence that cut through the hall. Suddenly, the cavern echoed with emptiness.

The boy at the archway gasped.

Aidan looked to him, his expression grim.

"What have you done?" He ran forward, knelt by the woman Aidan had just passed. Checking for a pulse he knew he wouldn't find. He looked back at Aidan, eyes tight and angry. "Murderer."

Aidan shrugged.

"I've been called worse."

"Are you going to kill me then, too?"

Aidan considered it. The Dark Lady had ordered him to kill everyone on the island. But this boy? He wasn't a threat. He wasn't even attuned to magic—if he was, he would have felt the power Aidan had used to wipe out the acolytes. He would have attacked Aidan by now. Instead, he just knelt at the dead Prophet's side, tears welling in his eyes.

"No," Aidan said. He began walking up the stairs. "This way, you can tell your friends that Aidan Belmont is merciful."

There was no conviction in his voice, no emotion. Aidan felt hollowed out. Not even fire could burn the sensation away.

Without the doubt or the drive or the pleasure, there was nothing. Not even a spark. Just a shell guided by a fading light, walking through the cold dark.

The boy called out something. Maybe a curse or threat. Maybe some lingering prophecy.

Aidan didn't hear it. Whatever he said meant nothing, just as the Prophets had meant nothing.

Everything meant nothing.

He drew the runes of travel in the air before him, flames flickering off the cave walls.

When he wrapped the power around him and felt the world melt away, he realized he *had* in fact killed the boy.

He had no magic, no way to escape, and the island was deserted, filled only with the dead. It was only a matter of time before the unnamed boy joined them.

CHAPTER FIFTY-FIVE

THE AIR IN NATASJA'S CASTLE FELT *WRONG*.

He couldn't put his finger on it. Not really. But there was a sensation, like an oil slick, that stuck to his skin and coated his lungs. He wanted to leave the moment he arrived.

And not just from the feeling of wrongness, but from the power. The castle reeked of magic. Of Maya. More power than he had ever felt. More than he could ever hope to harness. And it emanated from the closed door in front of him.

It wavered, undulating slightly, as if his vision were off, as if he were high or drunk or sleepwalking. He felt like he was all of those things. He didn't want to walk through that door. He didn't want to see what was happening on the other side.

For a moment, he considered turning around.

He could still leave. He could teleport back to…where? To Kianna? She was with the other Hunters, and she—and they—would kill him the moment he showed his face. No, he couldn't go back. She was lost to him.

Honestly, the thought kind of hurt.

He looked over his shoulder, to the door opposite the one holding the Violet Sage. Tenn was in there. What did the Dark Lady have planned for him? She'd gotten the runes to attune to Maya. She'd gotten the Violet Sage. She had everything she needed. What use could she have for two mortals like them?

You are no mortal, Fire seethed within him. And yet, when he looked to the wavering door, he had never felt more so.

But no. He couldn't leave. Not yet. The Dark Lady knew him. Had marked him. She would soon take over the world, he knew without a doubt. Fuck being on the right side of history. He would be on the victorious side.

He burned up the little worry he had left and opened the Violet Sage's door.

Aidan had never been one to believe in good and evil, right or wrong. Everything had a consequence, every action a reaction. Sometimes they worked out in your favor, sometimes they didn't. What helped one harmed another. Saving someone damned someone else. To him, morality was just a construct to keep weaker people in line.

But when he stepped into the room, he felt all that resolve fade away. He had never believed in good and evil.

He did now.

The Violet Sage sagged against her chair, the runes on the floor around her glowing like lime beams up to the ceiling. She looked dead, or nearly so, her skin sallow and her eyes bruised, her flesh gaunt, as if the Dark Lady were drawing out more than magic from her. As if she drew out her very life force.

The Dark Lady hovered at the edge of the rune ring. Her dress billowed around her in deep purple waves, her hair a halo but far from angelic. Cracks formed in the concrete around her, small pillars of stone jutting up around her feet, a dais her toes barely touched. Above her, around her, both from the crown of her head and somehow not, the Sphere of Maya bloomed.

A purple lotus of a million petals, unfurling and uncurling infinitely around her. The sight of that Sphere alone dropped Aidan to his knees.

What she did with it nearly made him retch.

He had never seen someone drained of their Sphere before, but he knew that was what he witnessed.

The Dark Lady held a crystal in front of her, an obsidian shard the size of his forearm that glowed an unearthly purple. Runes seared and simmered across its surface, ones he understood at once: runes for containment, for locks and seals, runes of unquenchable thirst and unending hunger. She held a veritable black hole in her hands, and as she funneled the purple power of Maya into it, the stone drew that very same essence from the Violet Sage.

She was turning the Violet Sage into a Howl.

She was turning the greatest mage who ever lived into a Wight.

He didn't know how long he knelt. Time seemed to pause here, as if the gods themselves refused to turn creation in the sight of this unholy act. He knew, then, there was no hope. The Dark Lady had no intention of bringing his mother back. She had used him. As he had hoped to use her.

He couldn't even be angry. It's exactly what he would have done, and if anything, he felt stupid for not catching on sooner.

The Dark Lady would never help him. She wanted a Wight. She wanted to rule the world. She would. Aidan had ensured it—he'd killed everyone with the slightest knowledge of Maya and brought her the greatest weapon the world would ever know.

She had no need for him any longer.

As soon as the Violet Sage was turned, the Dark Lady would use her against him. He knew it in the pit of his heart.

He would never get his mother back.

But soon, he would join her.

They all would.

Because of him.

If he was smart, he would just end it right then and there.

Not the Dark Lady—he had no hope of killing her like this. But himself.

He couldn't even do that. He just knelt and watched and waited for his time at the guillotine.

The Violet Sage didn't squirm or cry out. The Dark Lady didn't cackle or gloat. They stared at each other in silence, the Dark Lady with scorn, the Violet Sage with pleading pity.

Then the Violet Sage flicked her eyes toward him. Just briefly. The barest twitch.

When her purple eyes connected with his, he felt it in his chest.

A spark. A light.

A hope.

You must save him, he heard her whisper. *Before it is too late. Before you both are gone.*

She paused. Silence echoed. He thought that would be the end.

And when the time comes, she said, even quieter, *you must help him kill me.*

CHAPTER FIFTY-SIX

DARKNESS SURGED AND SWAM AROUND TENN. NOT A PEACE-ful, oceanic swell, but a thrashing, raging chaos that shook him to the core. He drowned in it. Screamed out in it. But it wouldn't give. The surface never came.

In the dark, he heard the screams.

Her screams. The Violet Sage.

And their screams. Thousands upon thousands. Voices the world had all but forgotten. The spirits, shaking the cosmos imperceptibly. Demanding he wake. Demanding he make this right.

Demanding he rise, when all he could do was sink.

Sinking.

Sinking.

And then, another jolt in the darkness. Heavier. Physical.

"Come on, you twat," he heard someone grumble. "Wake up. Wake the fuck up."

Another jolt. A slap. And with a sting, Tenn stumbled his way back to consciousness.

"What…?" he managed. The room swam back into view, but it kept on swimming, the walls moving on their own accord like oil, like rippling water. It didn't stop.

"We need to get out of here," Aidan said.

Aidan. What the hell was Aidan doing here?

And where was—

Memories snapped.

Him in the pavilion with the Violet Sage. The scent of smoke, the runes of Maya burning in his mind. He remembered the feeling, the ascension, the glowing door. And he remembered the screams that dragged him back, that kept him inches away from opening to its power. Screaming, a thud, and then the sinking, ever-present darkness.

"What did you do?" Tenn asked.

Aidan paused from undoing the ropes binding Tenn to a chair. Since when had he been bound to a chair?

"I managed to outdo myself." He looked back, continued untying. "I've damned us all twice over. And you're going to help me fix it."

CHAPTER FIFTY-SEVEN

AS DISORIENTING AS THE POWER OF MAYA WAS, MORE SO WAS the shock when the power cut off.

Aidan's heart froze as the world solidified once more. Tenn jerked to attention, his arm over Aidan's shoulders as Aidan awkwardly tried to help him to stand.

"No," Aidan whispered. They were too late.

"What was—"

The door exploded from its hinges, sucked back into the hall with unearthly force. Violet light and smoke poured through, and Aidan knew they were screwed. The Dark Lady stepped through. She clutched the shard in one hand, purple light dripping from it like molasses, shadows curled between her pale fingertips. She wasn't open to Maya, not that Aidan could see, but she wore victory on her smile like a crown.

She raised her hand and cocked a finger toward the hallway. Fog parted, and the Violet Sage floated in.

Even knowing what to expect, even knowing he had been

okay helping bring it about, the sight of her made Aidan blanch.

The girl floated, but she looked held up by strings, her arms and head bent at odd angles—suspended, rather than flying. Her eyes were pale, vacant, staring off into shadows unknown, and her skin had bleached itself almost silver, the barest shimmer of her old color traced on her arms and face.

"Behold, perfection," the Dark Lady said. Her smile widened. She lowered her hand.

And, as if on cue, the Violet Sage opened to all four Spheres, the lights burning like St. Elmo's Fire in the gloom.

"And before you get any ideas," the Dark Lady continued. She opened to Fire, a ball of flame curling to life in her hand. It burned white and hot, enough to make sweat break out on Aidan's skin.

With a flick of her wrist, she launched the fireball toward the Violet Sage. It sputtered apart only inches from her skin, breaking into sparks that flurried and faded to dust.

Aidan swallowed. He knew it wasn't just Fire the girl was immune to, but all magic. She was a Wight. The one monster that should not be.

And she was under the Dark Lady's command.

"Kill them." Her eyes narrowed on Aidan. "*Both* of them."

Aidan didn't think.

He wrapped the runes around himself and Tenn, and fled.

"This is how the world ends.
Not with a whimper or bang,
not in fire or ice.
Our world ends in greed.
Our world will always
end in greed."

—Diary of the Violet Sage
5 Oct, 3 P.R. (Post Resurrection)

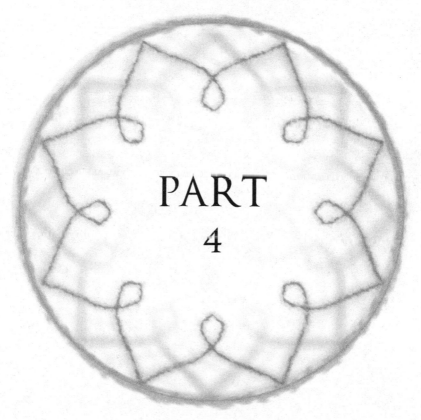

PART
4

CHOSEN

CHAPTER FIFTY-EIGHT

"WHERE ARE WE?" TENN YELLED. "AND WHAT THE *HELL* WAS that?"

Aidan paced back and forth in the rain before him. Not with the anger Tenn had started associating him with, but with, well, despair.

It wasn't a look Tenn enjoyed seeing on him.

Tenn reached out and grabbed Aidan's arm. Aidan immediately shook him off, Fire blossoming open in his chest and searing Tenn's palm.

Tenn took a step back and stared at the boy, at the way his chest heaved, at the way rain sizzled on his skin. Tenn felt like he'd seen the full circle transformation—from a broken, muttering wreck to a Fire-wielding god and now this. Broken in a different way. And somehow, a worse way.

Tenn tried to find pity within him. Surprisingly, in that moment, he found none.

"What did you do, Aidan?"

Aidan looked away.

"What the hell did you *do*?"

Water unfurled in his gut at the question, a wave of anger that overtook him. The rain around them shuddered. Hardened. Pushed back against Aidan, shoving him over and nearly knocking him off his feet.

Aidan growled. He answered the only way he knew how.

Fire bloomed in his chest, white-hot and fierce, and he lashed out, sending a torrent of fire straight at Tenn's face.

Tenn whipped up his arms, crossing them over his body, and the puddles below him rose in a heartbeat, formed a barrier of water five inches thick. Aidan's flame billowed against the shield, steam curling up in a haze. But Aidan didn't give in. He pushed harder, threw more fire at Tenn, a practical beam of heat that pulsed against the shield, battered at it.

Tenn knew he didn't have Aidan's anger. Not even his own pain was enough to mirror the broken boy's. Tenn wasn't a killer. Not like Aidan.

Tenn growled. He wasn't going to die at the hands of this asshole. He wasn't going to let the world fall to a man-child.

But he wasn't going to be able to hold this shield for much longer.

His eyes caught on the steam floating above them. He reached his senses toward it, wrapped it around his fingers, and sent the burning steam toward Aidan, engulfing him, choking him out.

Aidan cried out as Tenn thickened the steam, made it impossible for Aidan to breathe, burned at Aidan's skin with boiling water.

Instantly, the fire died.

Tenn dropped his shield, water splashing back down to his

feet. He didn't let go of the cloud. He wrapped it tighter around the boy, a boa constrictor of burning mist.

Aidan howled, his voice muffled through the steam.

For a moment, Tenn considered continuing. He could feel Aidan's pulse deep within the cocoon, frantic and frail. A few moments more and the boy would die.

He deserved it.

He more than deserved it. He'd killed dozens if not hundreds of innocents, and damned a hundred thousand more.

Who are you to say who lives and dies? Who are you, if you killed the boy you were burdened to save?

Tenn groaned.

Then, with more force than it should have taken, he dropped the mist.

Aidan gasped, breaking through the fog and stumbling almost to his knees. He righted himself at the last minute, glaring daggers at Tenn. But he didn't attack.

Tenn wrapped a tendril of water around his wrist, sharpening it into a point before freezing it solid, a dagger aimed straight at Aidan's chest.

"Talk," he growled. "What the hell have you done?"

Aidan panted, his skin pockmarked with blisters from the steam.

"She lied to me. She bloody lied to me."

He had no idea what Aidan was talking about, but it didn't take a genius to figure out *whom* he was talking about. Tenn had always known Aidan sided with the Dark Lady to further his own end. He wasn't the type to serve. He'd wanted something out of it. And he hadn't gotten it.

"Of course she lied," Tenn said. "Who the hell did you think you were dealing with?"

Aidan opened his mouth, then slowly closed it.

"She told me to bring her the Violet Sage. To help her attune to Maya. She said she would help me. So I did. And she created...she created *that*."

"But why? Why would you help her? She's the *Dark Lady*, Aidan, not some fairy fucking godmother."

Aidan lowered his head and stared at his feet, at the puddle of rippling rain and his spark-lined reflection.

"She said she'd bring my mother back."

Tenn had expected to hate Aidan until his dying day. After all, Aidan had been nothing but a terror since the moment they'd crossed paths. But those words broke something in Tenn's heart. Water churned and seethed, and between one second and the next the power took over, dragging him down to memory.

He watches her go. Watches her and his dad drive by, the dorm mother standing at his side as they both wave goodbye. She tells him it will be okay. Tells him that it will be break before he knows it, and he'll be home again.

She lies.

Even when she says it, weeks before the Resurrection, Tenn knows she lies.

He watches his mother as the car turns and drives off. Watches the tears stream down her cheeks as he tries to stay strong, tries not to cry, because he is here to study magic and it was his idea all along. There's no use feeling bad for himself. No use making a bad first impression on his new classmates. His new family.

"Come," the dorm mother says. "Let's go meet your roommate."

She turns and guides him into the dorm. He pauses. Looks back. His family is gone.

Gone.

He stares at his phone as, around him, the rest of the dorm runs about in terror. Stares at his phone and wonders how he can have a signal, but still can't connect to his family.

"They have to be okay," he whispers. He tries the numbers again. Mom's cell. Dad's cell. Neither work. He even tries his grandparents, and gets the same unending ring, followed by a mechanical voice mail. He hangs up. Stares around.

Everyone is running. Running to the buses that will bring them to...where? To home? Family? Tenn has no idea where they will take them, save for "out of here," and no one else seems to know either. No one else seems to care. Right now, movement feels like life. Like being proactive. Movement feels like the only way to get the dead back.

They aren't dead, he tells himself.

He looks down at the phone again. Soon, he will hop one of those buses and head back to his hometown. He doesn't know what he will find along the way. Monsters? Creatures that shouldn't exist?

It doesn't matter. He has to save them. He has magic now. He can save them. He has to try.

He dials his mother's number again, holds his phone to his ear.

"Come on come on come on," he whispers, a mantra falling on deaf gods' ears.

The phone rings for what feels like an eternity. Clicks.

"Hello," his mother's recorded voice says. "I can't come to the phone right now, but if you leave your name and message, I'll get back to you as soon as I can. Thank you. Goodbye."

"*Mom,*" *Tenn whispers, his voice shaky, tears coating his eyes.* "*Mom, I'm coming back for you. I love you. I'm coming back. I'm coming back.*"

"What's wrong with you?" Aidan asked, his voice cutting through the memory.

Water sloshed away in a tide, the puddles around him rippling. Tears spilled down Tenn's cheeks, though they were thankfully hidden by the rain. He took a deep breath. Looked at Aidan for the first time.

The boy was hurting. Aidan didn't want to destroy. Not really. He just wanted his family back. He'd played the hand he'd been given and hoped for the best.

Unsurprisingly, it hadn't worked at all.

Could Tenn say he wouldn't have done the same if he'd been dealt the same cards?

"Water," Tenn managed. He pushed himself up to standing. He wasn't at all surprised that Aidan didn't help him up. Aidan just watched him warily, as if at any point Tenn might attack again.

And maybe he should. After all, Aidan had brought the Dark Lady back. But as he stared at the boy, he realized he didn't have it in him. Aidan was trying to do what he thought was right.

He was trying, and he was failing, but that wasn't reason enough for him to be killed.

You can't be trusted around broken things.

Jarrett's voice was a curse. Tenn shook it from his thoughts.

They stared at each other for a long time, in the pouring rain, one sodden, one steaming and dry.

"What do we do now?" Aidan asked.

Tenn's gut turned over. He had no idea. And now, the guy he'd been charged to find, the one who'd seemed the absolute farthest from wanting his help, was asking him for guidance.

"We regroup." He looked to the horizon. He had no idea where the Dark Lady was. He also had no doubt she knew *precisely* how to find them. "You helped her create a monster. Together, we're going to have to destroy it."

CHAPTER FIFTY-NINE

THEY SAT AT THE TABLE IN MARA'S TRAILER, A POT OF TEA FOR-gotten between them as they discussed what they could possibly do to turn the tides of the coming battle.

"It's not our fight," Benjamin growled. He was an elder of the Clan, one of the few men Dreya had seen live past forty in this new world. His beard was grizzled and his flannel torn—he looked more like a lumberjack than a wizened Witch, but she had learned long ago that appearances were deceiving. "They brought this curse upon the land. Let them rot in it."

"You want me to curse an entire country—no, an entire species—to die?" Mara asked. The girl took after her mother. Soft-spoken and gentle in the best of times, but fierce as a lion under pressure. Dreya admired her. She had been Clan Mother for only a few weeks at most, but she took to the role as if it were in her blood. And, Dreya supposed, with the loss of her mother, Rhiannon, it was. "That would be genocide."

Benjamin shook his head, but it was clear those words cracked his conviction.

"I say we do what we have done from the beginning. We seek a way to end this. War begets war, violence begets violence. We have the runes to hide away. When we learn how to utilize them to undo the Howls—"

"That is your wise plan?" Dreya asked. "Simply sit around and wait in the hopes that one day, the Ancients will finally answer your prayers and tell you how to reverse the Howls?"

Benjamin shrugged.

"Cowards," Kianna muttered. She leaned all the way back in her chair, cleaning her nails with a dagger. Dreya had to concentrate on not staring at her.

"It is not cowardice to harbor knowledge. It is our charge to keep the language of the gods safe. Look what happened! Not even an hour passes after someone learns of Maya and the damned Dark Lady is back and has a Wight under her control."

"Theoretically," Dreya said. "We have no proof that is what she has done."

"You expect her to have done anything less?"

Quiet twisted between the five of them. Devon leaned against the wall, kept to the shadows, his scarf wrapped tight and his silence speaking volumes.

Dreya thought she would die before she saw the day, but her brother actually sided with Kianna.

"At the very least," Mara said, "we must gather the Clans. We may have the runes of protection, but they will not last forever, and if the Dark Lady was able to thwart the runes of the Violet Sage, ours don't stand a chance. Gather the Clans, and let the elders decide as a whole. We will call a council—"

"We'll all be dead before you lot agree on anything." Kianna peered up over her dagger. "The Dark Lady is coming for you. All of you. And if you think she's going to be content to let you watch the slaughter from the sidelines, you're dead wrong."

Benjamin opened his mouth, but Mara interrupted him with a raised hand. Amazingly, he said nothing.

"What would you suggest, then?" she asked.

"Call the Clans, yes. Have them teleport or ride their Pegasi here or whatever the hell they want. But rally them for war, not negotiations. The Dark Lady isn't going to rest now that she has Maya. She's already waited four bloody years for this. If I was her, I'd attack immediately, before anyone could rally. Humans have grown weak since she vanished. She knows it, too. She'll crush us before we even realize she's here."

Mara looked to Benjamin, then to Dreya and Kianna.

"You would have me declare war."

"We're already at war, sister," Kianna replied. "We're just declaring sides."

Mara inhaled. The subtext was clear—*fight for the living, or fight for the undead.*

"The Witches have a charge to restore balance, do they not?" Dreya asked.

Mara nodded.

"Then we must fight with Tenn. He is the one the spirits spoke of. He's the one who can end this for good."

"How?" she asked.

Dreya swallowed.

"I have no idea. But I have hope."

"Hope is what got us into this mess," Kianna growled.

Before Dreya could ask her what she meant, she felt a snap of power in the distance. A snap of power, and a rune she dared not hope still existed. She gasped.

"He is here."

CHAPTER SIXTY

WINTER FOREST ROSE UP BEFORE THEM, TREES DRAPED IN snow and the sky a haze of gray. Beautiful, pristine, the snow untouched. The last time he'd seen this place, there had been blood in the snow. The last time he had seen this vista, he'd gone to war.

Not much had changed.

The snow had fallen and covered up old sin, but the stench of it was still there. Or maybe that was just the land itself, every inch of America, blood-soaked and sodden, but ever willing to endure more.

Tenn swallowed. It felt like he was describing himself.

"What are we doing here?" Aidan asked.

He hunched beside Tenn, snow melting around him by the second, like he was a one-man furnace.

"Finding reinforcements."

He considered waiting. Considered sending up the runes and symbols he'd seen Devon work before. It seemed like the polite thing to do. *The Witches must be entreated.* But there was no time. He brought the tracking rune on Dreya's wrist to mind, felt it drawing him forward like a thread in the night, and followed it into the trees.

Ahead, he felt the tingle of runes. The first line of defense.

"You'll want to take my hand," Tenn said.

"Like hell."

"That wasn't a suggestion," he said, surprised to hear the steel in his own words.

Aidan glowered. Then reached out and took Tenn's hand in his own.

It wasn't his imagination—the moment their palms touched, sparks raced over Tenn's skin, along with a crashing, falling, soaring sensation that nearly dropped him to his knees. It wasn't love or lust, but something cosmic, the snap of gravity connecting two planets. He looked to Aidan, the briefest glance, to see if he had registered the feeling, too. But Aidan's poker face was absolute; he stared forward resolutely, unreadable. Tenn turned his attention back to the forest and the first line of runes.

He felt the runes quiver around him, felt the caress of their warnings—*turn away, this is wrong, this is a trap*—but he was used to them by now. He knew their language, and they washed over him without much hassle.

Aidan, on the other hand, freaked.

"Where are you taking me?" His eyes were wide, his palms slick with sweat. "The hell is this?"

"It's okay." Tenn tried to keep his voice calm and comforting, even though a part of him wanted to laugh. Aidan thought he was a badass, and yet here he was, cowering from some simple magic tricks. "It's just the runes. They're meant to dissuade visitors. Turn you around. Just hold my hand and keep walking. And breathing."

Aidan took a deep, gulping gasp of air. Tenn gripped his hand tighter—Aidan's fingers shook.

"The next line is coming up," Tenn said. "Nearly there. I should warn you, they're a bit worse than the first."

He couldn't help but notice Aidan's breath was faster, and even though he nodded, there was no conviction in his features.

The runes were designed to scare off intruders. What could they be showing Aidan that would freak him out this much?

The next line washed over him.

Aidan's grip tightened painfully.

"No," Aidan gasped as he crossed the line. His eyes were wide. "No no no, where are you taking me? You're working for her, aren't you? You're working for *her*!"

"Calm down, man," Tenn said. "I'm not working for anyone. It's okay. Just one more. Just one more."

Aidan didn't respond. His eyes darted everywhere and his palm was so slick that even though he held Tenn's hand in a death grip, it was sliding away.

"Almost there," Tenn said.

He crossed the final line of runes; the Witches' caravans came into focus, along with the twins and Kianna, who jogged toward him with Mara in tow.

He smiled. Felt his heart lighten.

Then Aidan screamed and let go of his hand, and before Tenn could stop him, the boy vanished into the woods.

CHAPTER SIXTY-ONE

MONSTERS HOWLED DEEP WITHIN THE WOODS. TENN WAS A distant memory. Tenn had betrayed him, had wanted him dead. This had been a trap. A trap. And he had to get out.

He ran, and when Tenn vanished from sight, another figure appeared. A figure in a purple raincoat, blood dripping from the seams.

"Mom?"

She nodded. Her raincoat was slashed in a dozen places, and her skin a dozen more. But she was whole. He took a step toward her. Her eyes widened, focused on something behind him. Then she turned and ran.

She darted through the trees as the howls increased behind him, and he ran after her, uncaring about the creatures chasing him, his vision twitching every other footstep. The forest shifting this way and that, the snow beneath his feet now fresh, now churned, now covered in her blood.

"Mom!" he yelled. He crashed through the undergrowth, but she was too fast. She was always ten steps ahead, just out of sight, nothing more than a flash of purple between the trees while behind him the monsters were gaining and screaming, and he was lost, lost, but he had to find her, had to find her, had to—

"Hello, Aidan," she said.

She stood in a clearing. And around her, fallen like dominoes, were bodies.

Tenn and the strange twins, Jarrett and Kianna. Those, and more bodies he didn't recognize. Dozens of them. Hundreds. They spiraled out around her, a dull array of color. Beneath them, the snow ran crimson.

"Even now, you aid me," his mother said. Only she was no longer his mother. Her features shifted. Sharpened. Until it was the Dark Lady surrounded by the dead. "Even now, you bring me closer to them."

Aidan swallowed. Backed up and ran straight into a tree.

"I'm not helping you," he said. "You tried to kill me."

She smiled.

"I didn't *try* to kill you." She stepped forward, her feet squishing atop a body. A new body.

His mother.

His true mother.

"I don't *try* to do anything, stupid child," she said. She continued walking, uncaring of whom she stepped on to get there. Just as he had been. "I have set the trap. And now, I get to watch as you stumble into it. I can follow you anywhere, Aidan. I know your heart. And soon, I will hold it in my hand." She pressed her hand to his chest.

Into his chest.

Fire shot through his veins.

He screamed.

"You scream like a bloody girl."

Aidan collapsed against the tree, panting, his breath hot in his lungs. He clutched his chest with both hands, expecting to feel blood.

Nothing.

He looked up to see Kianna a few feet away. Farther, beside a tree, was Dreya. She stood like a ghost, white on white, and when he focused back on Kianna, Dreya practically vanished. It was only then he realized Kianna had a pistol pointed straight at his head.

"I promised you," she said. "Ages ago, I promised you, you ever let Fire take over, and I would be the first to put a bullet between your eyes. You remember that?"

He swallowed. He couldn't find the words. What even were the right words?

"You remember!" She took a step forward, shook the gun. "Say something, you bloody twat. Speak!"

"Do it." His voice was gravelly. Behind her, he could still see the shade of the Dark Lady, the bodies of everyone he had condemned to die. Kianna's included.

"What?"

"I said *do it!*" he yelled. He looked her in the eyes. "Shoot me, Kianna. Put me out of my fucking misery. You're right, you promised. Keep your bloody promise."

She shook her head, biting her lip.

He knew she would do it. He wasn't trying to call her bluff.

He realized, in that moment, he truly wanted to die.

Every time he closed his eyes, he saw the people he'd murdered. The Prophets, the acolytes, and farther back—Brother

Jeremiah and Trevor and Vincent and a hundred others. All of them stained his palms and heart with blood, but now, Fire couldn't burn the guilt away. Fire only inflamed it. He squeezed his eyes shut as if he could block out himself.

He had murdered. He had betrayed.

He'd told himself it was so he could get ahead, so he could rule, so he could end the Howls for good, because only under his reign would the world finally fall back into order.

All he'd done was give the world over to the one creature he should have been sworn to kill. Because she had promised to do the one thing he could not. And she had lied.

Which meant it—all of it—had been for nothing.

Kianna should have killed him the moment she met him, back at the abandoned hostel ages ago.

"Damn it," he heard her growl. "I hate him like this."

"You must be patient with him," Dreya whispered. "He has been through a great deal of pain."

"He's *caused* a great deal of pain. And it's only going to get worse from here."

"He was manipulated."

"He manipulated himself."

A crunch of boots on snow, and then there was a hand on his shoulder, gruff and firm. He opened his eyes to look straight into Kianna's.

"If I'm going to kill you," she said, "it's going to be on your feet. And you're going to take it like a man. This is just pathetic."

"That may be the most chauvinistic thing you've ever said," he whispered. He coughed, closed his eyes. "I killed them."

"You've killed a lot of people."

"No," he said. "The Prophets. Everyone on that island. I killed them. She told me it would get my mother back."

"That sounds like a *you* problem. Come on, up."

She hoisted him to standing.

"We cannot kill him," Dreya said. "He's too important."

Kianna looked him over once. "Doesn't seem that important to me. Except for in his mind."

Dreya shook her head. "No. He cannot die here. Not by your hand. Not yet. He has seen the Dark Lady's language. He has spoken her tongue."

"Yeah, and he brought the bitch back with it."

Dreya stepped toward them. Her pale blue eyes speared Aidan to the spot, unraveling him, reading the shadows on his soul.

He almost wished Kianna had put a bullet in his head.

"He did," Dreya said. "And that which is brought back cannot simply be put away. But we have been seeking the end to the Dark Lady's scourge for years. We have used all the runes the Ancients allowed us, and still it was not enough."

"Aye. We know it's hopeless."

"Not hopeless. Misguided. Perhaps we were simply speaking the wrong tongue. Perhaps, with his knowledge and her words, she and her work can be undone."

CHAPTER SIXTY-TWO

IT WAS A FOOLISH NOTION. BUT AS SHE WATCHED AIDAN AND Kianna talk, as she watched the boy struggle with himself, the idea struck her like a bolt of lightning.

She had known Tenn was key to destroying the Dark Lady and all of her progeny. But Aidan…he had been another key, one to the same door. And Dreya knew, somehow, the two were required to open it.

Besides, she had had her fill of murder. She would not stand around and watch Aidan be massacred. No matter if he deserved it. She must believe he still had good in him, that he could still help their cause. Too much had happened to have him snuffed out in the forest like a common animal. He was important. She just had to figure out how, before he turned on them, or Kianna decided to follow through on her vow.

She knew, if Devon had been here, he would have helped Kianna pull the trigger.

Once more, she was grateful she did not have her brother's rage.

Kianna adjusted her hold on Aidan, and together, the three of them began making their way back to camp.

"Remember," Dreya said. "The runes will try to dissuade you. You must stay strong. They are naught but illusion."

"You don't understand," Aidan said, his voice scratchy from tears. "*She* isn't an illusion. She's watching me. She knows where I'm going. I'm just guiding her to you."

Dreya forced down the chills that traced her spine.

"Be that as it may, we are stronger together than apart."

Kianna looked at her. The unspoken question hung on the air between them—did Dreya actually believe that, or was she just trying to make Aidan feel better? She had to hope it was the former.

She led Kianna and Aidan through the forest, back to the safety of the Witches. In the back of her mind, she wondered how long that safety would last. Aidan and the Dark Lady had broken through the Violet Sage's defenses. What hope did they have?

Kianna kept her grip on Aidan while Dreya held her hand. It was easier this way than to risk Kianna wandering off accidentally. She told herself she felt nothing when Kianna's fingers closed around hers. It wasn't the time.

Aidan muttered the entirety of their walk, but he didn't let go. Or rather, Kianna didn't let go of him. The final two lines of runes washed over them, and when they arrived at the camp, she found they weren't alone.

Tenn and the others were gathered outside Mara's trailer, arguing. They parted when Dreya and Kianna appeared, revealing the last man she expected to see, and a woman who seemed more out of place here than ought to be possible.

"Detain him," Jarrett commanded, pointing at Aidan.

Kianna jumped in front of Aidan, shielding him. Not that there was anything to shield him from; no one moved. Not even Cassandra.

"What is this?" Dreya asked. She poured herself through Air, tried to blow away the unease, the shock. She had sworn to the Witches she would never reveal their location to the Guilds. She had broken that vow bringing Tenn here. And now, somehow, the vow had been broken again.

Cassandra stepped forward. Even here, she emanated power, the aura that she was used to being in command, and having that command taken without question.

"Have you not heard? The end has come with the help of that boy. And we are here to make the final stand."

CHAPTER SIXTY-THREE

"YOU CAN'T DO THIS," TENN GROWLED. HE AND JARRETT stood farther off from the rest of the camp. Cassandra and Mara conferred with the twins, and Kianna and Aidan kept to themselves, apart from the rest but under close watch.

"Do what?" Jarrett said. "Try to save the world?"

"No. Barge in here and take over like this. This isn't your—"

"Not my fight? The world is ending, Tenn. And not in that hypothetical, far-off street prophet sort of way. People know. I don't know how, but they know that the Dark Lady is back. There's rioting in the streets, Tenn. Half of Outer Chicago is on fire and the other half is abandoned. We have reports from every single Guild and Outpost in our network that the Dark Lady's forces are rallying. She's back, Tenn. She's back because you couldn't do your duty."

"My duty was never to kill him."

"Then what was it? Because it sure as hell looks like you've done nothing but help him kill us all."

Tenn went silent. He looked to Aidan, the perpetual ques-

tion, the wild card. Aidan had apologized. But even thinking that seemed ridiculous. How could you just apologize for
murdering hundreds and damning thousands more? What was
repentance when you ended civilization?

"Why are you here?" Tenn asked.

He stared at his commander, at his lover, felt the distance
between them like a punch to the gut. Even now, even after
everything Jarrett had done, after all the lies, all the betrayal,
he wanted to touch him. Wanted Jarrett to hold him like the
first night in Outer Chicago, to make him feel safe and cared
for. Was that a lie, too? Was that a past he could ever resurrect?

"The Dark Lady has rallied, and we need to rally, too. We
know the Clans of the Witches are connected, just as we
knew that you would be able to find them." Jarrett *did* reach
out then, and his voice softened as he touched Tenn's forearm.
"And you, I could find anywhere."

"So you were using me," Tenn said, wrenching his hand
back.

"If you want to look at it that way." His voice was still soft,
still hurting. "I prefer to think of it as caring enough to keep
track of you."

"Is that why you locked me in the dungeon?"

Jarrett swallowed.

"You already know why I did that. And it sounds like if you
had stayed, we wouldn't be in the mess we're in now."

Tenn wished he could argue, but Jarrett was right.

Aidan might have been the one helping the Dark Lady,
but he was the one who opened the door for Aidan to step
through. Water sloshed in his gut, heavy with regret. If not for

Tenn, Aidan never would have gotten the Violet Sage, never would have gotten access to Maya.

Maya…

"I know how to attune to it," Tenn whispered. "Maya. She showed me the runes."

"And you remember them?"

He nodded. Jarrett looked to Cassandra.

"Then maybe we still have a chance."

High above, the sky darkened with storms.

It was decided within the hour they couldn't stay there. The Witches harbored not only fighters, but children and elderly. If Aidan was being hunted—and there was no doubt he was—they needed to take the battle somewhere else. Somewhere they could fight on their own terms.

And that meant going back to Outer Chicago.

Not many Witches could fight. At least, not as many as Tenn had hoped, and a few had opted to remain and protect those who stayed behind. Still, a dozen or so had joined in, and that was more than they had before. He taught the runes of travel to a few of them, those who knew the locations of the other Clans, and watched as they vanished into thin air.

Hopefully, it would be enough. Hopefully, they would be able to bring more Witches to the cause.

Tenn drew the runes of travel into the frozen dirt at the Witches' feet, runes he had extracted and distilled, runes that would allow anyone to travel, regardless of the Sphere they attuned to. Just like those that led him to the Violet Sage, he traced a location amongst them, leading them straight to Outer Chicago.

He looked around at their camp. Mara stood at the front, Fire a low burn in her chest. He knew leaving her Clan felt like heresy, but that seemed to be the theme for everyone's life now.

The only way forward was through betrayal.

He forced himself not to look at Jarrett or Aidan. Forced himself to stay focused. He reached through Earth and twined it through the runes, felt as the others around him did so, as well. In a far corner of his mind, he knew the Dark Lady or any lower necromancer could storm in and use these runes to follow them straight back to the Guild. A veritable bread crumb trail.

But that was also the point.

Jarrett hadn't been exaggerating.

Outer Chicago was in chaos.

Tenn hadn't bothered teleporting outside the gates— according to Jarrett, the defenses had been down for hours, and the shield that protected Outer Chicago from the outside world had fallen as the mages that upheld it sought instead to put out the fires inside the city. There was no use protecting an ash heap.

Cassandra led the Witches into the Guild, introducing them to other Hunters and showing them their rooms—though it seemed unlikely those rooms would ever get used. Jarrett hung back, pulled Tenn to the side.

"I'm leaving him in your care," he said, nodding to Aidan.

"You aren't going to lock him up?" Tenn asked. "You still have that sigil."

Jarrett stared at Aidan and Kianna, doubt in his eyes.

"I'm going to trust you," he said. "Besides, locking you away didn't do anything, and I have a feeling he's wilier than you are."

He smiled. Tenn didn't know if he was trying to make a joke or an insult. The smile slipped.

"If we get out of this," Jarrett said, "I want... I want us to try again. Start over. Not as Tenn and Jarrett, but as ourselves. Not Hunters. Just humans. Would you...you want to try that?"

A few days ago, Tenn would have jumped on the offer. But now, he didn't know what he wanted, least of all from Jarrett.

"We'll talk when it's over."

Jarrett inhaled like he wanted to say more. Instead, he nodded and headed back into the Guild to rally the army.

Tenn watched him go. It felt like losing him all over again, but this time, it didn't hurt as much as he thought it should. *We'll talk when it's over.* He doubted it would ever be over. He doubted that was a future he could hope for.

Dreya's hand on his shoulder forced him back to reality. He turned. She and the others stood, silent, in the foyer of the Guild, waiting for him to make a move. Once more, he was in command. Once more, he was entirely unsuited for the job.

"Tenn," Dreya said. "We must hurry."

Outside, the storm clouds Tenn had thought were only above the Witches' camp had followed. Lightning streaked through the sky and winds howled, casting sprays of ashes up into the darkness from where the fires hadn't quite been put out. Tenn stared at the wide boulevard leading to the Guild. Only weeks ago, he had walked up there for the first time, past Caius and his converts and all those who wanted Hunters dead.

Now, this was where they would have the last stand.

Water quivered in his stomach; he felt the wrongness seep-

ing through the world, the plague of the Dark Lady strength-
ening and spreading. It wouldn't take long to reach here, and
they had to be ready when it did.

Tenn nodded.

"Let's go."

CHAPTER SIXTY-FOUR

TENN'S OLD ROOM WAS CRAMPED, BUT IT WAS THE MOST PRI-vate place he could think of, and the most secure. Nothing about it felt like home—not the worn bed or threadbare rug or stone walls, not the lantern light casting heavy shadows. And definitely not the four Hunters crammed in with him.

Aidan sat cross-legged on the bed, Kianna beside him with a hand on his shoulder. The twins stood against a wall. Which left Tenn by the door, watching them as they watched him.

"So." Great leader he was.

"So," Dreya replied. She took a step forward, her blue eyes glinting in the lantern light. "The Violet Sage...she taught you how to attune to Maya?"

Tenn nodded. His gaze flickered to Aidan. *Before we were interrupted.*

But whatever animosity he might have held was muted, dulled, drowned out by the pain Water dredged up. Aidan had only wanted to save his mother. Try as he might, Tenn couldn't hate him for that. Aidan seemed to catch the glance. He looked down to his hands. Or, what was left of them.

"It is dangerous," Dreya said.

"Yeah," Tenn replied. "She said that no one had achieved it before. At least…"

Not until the Dark Lady.

"What happens to those who fail?" Kianna asked.

"They die, I think."

"No," Aidan said. "They become the Prophets."

Everyone turned to him.

"You've seen the Prophets?" Tenn asked.

"I killed them." He hurried on, as it was clear his statement wasn't a welcome one. "I had to. The Dark Lady, she…well, she was persuasive. You don't want to end up like them, Tenn. Trust me. They were mad. Mumbling nonsense to themselves, locked in a cave in the dark. It was inhumane. I don't even think they knew I was there. I don't think they even knew they were being killed."

"At least you didn't say killing them was a humanitarian act," Kianna grumbled.

"Not much of anything I've done has been humanitarian."

"So how did she do it?" Dreya asked. "If none could attune, save her, what was her secret?"

"She said—she said that she had been close to death. That Maya wasn't a godlike Sphere, but a Sphere of the gods. And that she was already a goddess."

"None of us are gods," Devon said. "So what hope do we have?" He took a step forward. "Should we all just have a shot at it, then? See who goes mad and who becomes divine?"

"I don't think that's what any of us are saying," Dreya said.

"No," Tenn said. "It should be me. I'm the one the spirits picked out. If anyone has a chance, it's me."

"Conceited, much?" Kianna said.

"Did you want to try?"

"Nope. One Sphere is more than enough for me. Frankly, I'm hoping to return it once this is all over."

"Focus!" Dreya snapped. "We do not have time for light-heartedness. The Dark Lady will be here any moment. She has Maya. She has a Wight. We have nothing. One of us must attempt attuning." She looked to Tenn. "You are right. You are the one the elements bend toward. You are the one the spirits called to. And that is precisely why it must not be you who attunes. It is too risky. When the Dark Lady attacks, we will need our most powerful mages. And that is you."

Tenn's heart sank.

"Then who do you recommend?"

She opened her mouth, but it was Devon who answered.

"Me."

"What?"

"You said it yourself—we need the most powerful fighters when the Dark Lady comes. You, Dreya, are the fiercest fighter I know. Let me attune."

"I cannot—"

"It is not your place to decide," he said. He looked to Tenn. "Teach me the runes. Let me try."

"Devon, I can't—"

He shook his head.

Slowly, deliberately, he unwound the scarf from his face, looping it between his hands. Tenn had never seen Devon without the scarf. He'd expected to see the face of a grizzled warrior underneath, scarred and scruffy, but his jaw was smooth, unlined by war. Boyishly handsome.

"After our Clan died," he said, looking straight at Tenn, "we found this in the ashes. It had been our mother's. And I vowed, on that day, that every breath I took would be with the ashes of my family in my lungs, so I would know precisely what had been lost, and precisely what I was fighting for. You would honor me, and them, by allowing me this chance to avenge them. Let me attune. With Maya, we could wipe out the scourge forever."

Tenn wanted to say the runes didn't work like that. *Maya* didn't work like that. Devon was powerful, sure. But he wasn't a god.

None of them were.

Vibrations shook the floor, rattling the hurricane lamp.

"We don't have time to sit around and play spin the bottle to see who's going first," Kianna said. "He volunteered, and Dreya's right. We need you around." She looked at Devon. "No offense, mate, and best of luck."

Devon smiled. "None taken."

He sat on the rug in the center of the room.

"Okay then." He looked up to Tenn. "It's decided. Show me the runes."

Tenn glanced at Dreya, but she wasn't watching him. She stared at her brother as if she were about to lose him. Perhaps, in a way, she was.

Another rumble shook them. He had no idea if it was the Dark Lady or something else, but he knew it meant there was no more time to spare.

"Okay," he said. He opened to Earth and began darkening the pigments in the rug before Devon. "Let's just hope this works."

CHAPTER SIXTY-FIVE

AIDAN KNEW IT WASN'T GOING TO WORK THE MOMENT TENN started drawing the runes in the carpet. They weren't right. He couldn't place it, but they seemed incomplete.

He kept thinking about what the Dark Lady said, about her already being a goddess. That entire tirade had been convincing, but it also had the note of a lie. She had attuned to Maya without fear of failure. She was brave, but she wasn't stupid.

If there had been any chance her return would be thwarted, she wouldn't have done it. If Maya was so unreliable, she wouldn't have attempted attuning. She would have forced someone else to do it. She had spent too much time trying to become immortal. She wouldn't have risked death or madness the day she came back to life.

"Wait," he said.

Devon was already settling in, his eyes closed and his scarf draped over his lap. He opened an eye and glared at Aidan the moment the word left his mouth.

Aidan ignored him. He crept off the bed and onto the ground, peering at the runes intently.

"What?" Tenn asked.

This close, and Aidan couldn't deny that there was a pull to Tenn. Not an attraction, but a gravity. A power.

He'd underestimated Tenn. Had thought he himself was the strongest one here. Now, he was starting to realize Tenn was on par, even with Aidan's new runes. Aidan might have been fire and fury on the surface, but Tenn's power was still, deep and deadly. Just like water.

He almost rolled his eyes at how perfect it was.

"These aren't right," Aidan said.

"They're the ones she showed me."

"I know." *They're the ones I stole.*

The runes made sense. In a way. But as Aidan looked at them, he realized what seemed wrong. They felt like half an equation.

"The Dark Lady..." he said, but he didn't finish the sentence. *The Dark Lady spent four years half-dead, surrounded by the true dead gods, hearing voices we could only dream of. She had to have learned something.* "She wouldn't have spent four years floating around. She would have been trying to find Maya on her own—she wouldn't have just been waiting for someone else to do the dirty work. What if...what if that's why you were sent to find me?"

"I don't follow," Tenn said. Which was fine, because Aidan's thoughts were going so fast, *he* could barely follow them.

"You said the spirits told you to find me. And we know the Dark Lady serves different gods. What if Maya requires the language of both? The, I don't know, good ones and bad ones.

What if that's how she was able to attune so quickly, when the Violet Sage and all the Prophets never could? They were listening to only part of the story."

Tenn nodded along. Even Dreya looked at him like he might not be mad.

"What do you suggest?" Tenn asked.

Aidan didn't know. But he thought he had a way to find out. The spirits had always spoken to him through Fire, so he opened himself fully to the source, let the heat wash through him as his chest blossomed open. He let it burn through him, let himself succumb to the heat and the darkness. He let the flames speak.

And as it had earlier, at the Dark Lady's command, the words began to flow. Embers at first, then sparks and flame, whispers that grew to roars.

Behind his closed eyes, he saw the tendrils of fire appear, dancing before him in serpentine swirls. Runes from a darker language, from more devilish gods, harsh and cruel. And yet, somehow, necessary all the same.

He burned the runes into the carpet, filling in blanks, making small manipulations in the ones Tenn had left. Then the power left him, and Fire winked out in his chest. He sat back, suddenly exhausted, and stared at his handiwork.

Even though he could only truly read half of the runes, he knew this was correct.

"You're sure?" Devon asked. Not of Aidan, but of Tenn.

Tenn looked at Aidan. Aidan knew that glance—Tenn was trying to decide if they should trust him. Trust that he had fixed the runes, not sabotaged them. Aidan just stared back.

Either they trusted him or they didn't. There wasn't much he could do now to persuade them either way.

Eventually, Tenn looked back to the runes and nodded. "They seem right."

Devon took a deep breath. "All right, then. If I go mad, make sure to kill this one."

"Done," Dreya said, staring straight at Aidan.

Then Devon closed his eyes and fell silent.

Seconds passed, slow as blood, and Kianna shifted.

"Shouldn't you all attune to that shit? If that's the magic lottery ticket, wouldn't it make more sense to have everyone attuned to it?"

"It can take hours to attune," Tenn said. Aidan couldn't help but notice him glancing his way. "If it even works."

"Still—"

She didn't get to finish her sentence.

Aidan felt it right before the tremors ripped through the Guild. The sickness. The wave of disorientation, like a bad high. It didn't leave him as he rolled back against Kianna, as Dreya reached out to keep her brother from falling over, as well.

"It's too late," Aidan whispered. "She's here."

CHAPTER SIXTY-SIX

DREYA KNELT BEHIND DEVON, HER HANDS ON HIS SHOULDERS to keep him steady. Another earthquake rolled through the Guild. She felt it then. The acid that seemed to roil through the air, the faint ripple that twisted stone. Maya. Someone was using Maya, and that meant the Dark Lady had found them, just as Aidan had promised she would.

"What do we do?" Tenn asked. "We can't just leave him here."

Dreya's heart ached. She wanted to side with Tenn. But he hadn't heard Devon's final thoughts.

Avenge them, he had whispered to her. *And if necessary, avenge me.*

Devon would hate her if he woke up to find her still there, while the battle raged on outside. They had trained for this from day one. They had known their fight would separate them. She had just hoped it would be further in the future.

"We must." She pulled through Air, let it dry her eyes before tears could even form. She laid him back, placing his folded scarf behind his head. "The fight is out there, and he would see us there for it."

Tenn nodded. He gestured to the others, and Kianna and Aidan left the room. Kianna glanced back, once, and Dreya felt her heart soften. Tenn walked over and placed a hand on Dreya's shoulder.

"He can do this," he said. His voice wavered. "I know he can."

Dreya said nothing. She didn't have to ask for a moment alone; Tenn knew to give her the space. The door clicked shut behind him.

"You will not lose your mind to this," Dreya said to her brother. She stared down at his closed eyes, his gentle face. Her brother, her sweet, sweet brother, from whom the world had taken and asked for so much. "Nor will you lose your life. The fight continues. For both of us."

She kissed his forehead. Tried to memorize him in that moment. So peaceful, and yet, perhaps, fighting the most difficult battle of his life.

Thunder shook the room again. She stood, reached out with Air and snuffed the lamp.

Then, in darkness, she left her brother behind.

CHAPTER SIXTY-SEVEN

"COME OUT, COME OUT, WHEREVER YOU ARE."

The Dark Lady's voice echoed as Tenn and his companions stepped outside. Storm clouds hung heavy, pregnant and ready to break. Aside from that voice, all was silent. All was still.

It set Tenn's nerves on edge.

Above and around them, the magical shield surrounding Outer Chicago had been restored. It glittered in the darkening light, shimmering like moonlight on a lake. Beautiful, if not for its terrible duty.

Tenn glanced to the others. Then he shifted the dirt at their feet into travel runes and poured Earth into them, teleporting himself to the uppermost reaches of the wall.

The others appeared at his side in a swirl of dust, and together they stared out at what would be their doom.

Darkness spread as far they could see, stretching to the horizon like oncoming night. But these shadows weren't from the sun. Kravens and humans and humanoid Howls, hundreds of thousands of them, all spread out into the distance. Smoke hung low and heavy over the field, and it was then that Tenn realized what the earthquakes had been from. Not from attacks on Outer Chicago, but in the suburbs beyond.

The necromancers had razed the city, crumbled it to the ground. Making room for their army.

They had needed it.

"Shit," Kianna whispered. "That must be every Howl in existence."

Tenn nodded. The Dark Lady must have used the same travel runes he had. She hadn't just rallied, she'd gathered every last member of her army and brought them to his front door. The sight was enough to make bile rise in his throat and his legs wobble. He had never seen so many Howls before.

And at the front of the army was the Dark Lady herself, still in her deep purple dress, as though she were going to a ball. The Violet Sage—no, she was no longer the Violet Sage, she was now a monster, a puppet, a Wight—floated at her side, dull-eyed and rippling with power. Even from here, Tenn could see the nervous glances the other necromancers and higher-level Howls cast toward the creature.

A monster the world had never seen, and now it was the main weapon of the army.

The army stood only a few yards from the shield. Thousands of points of lights glowed from within the necromancers' Spheres. Tens of thousands of kravens bristled, starved for flesh. And the rest were Howls Tenn couldn't place, which made them even more dangerous. Breathless and incubi and bloodlings, able to freeze or asphyxiate the entire Guild in a heartbeat if they managed to get past the wall.

And of course they would get past the wall.

The Guild had maybe a hundred Hunters, two hundred at most. Even if every Hunter in existence magically showed up.

They didn't stand a chance.

They were going to die.

Even with the Witches and their reinforcements, even with all their knowledge and all their runes, it wasn't enough. It would never be enough. The Dark Lady had won. As, in the deepest pit of his heart, he'd known she would all along.

Tenn looked to his companions. To the Hunters beyond. Somewhere along the line, he knew, Jarrett stood just as grim. Tenn wasn't even going to get to see him before they died. Maybe he should go find him. Fight by his side as it should have been all along. Die next to his lover, rather than in the midst of a nameless horde. Then he looked at Aidan, and realized this was where he was meant to be, even if he didn't know why.

"Well," Aidan said. A thousand emotions warred over his face—despair and betrayal, but most of all, anger. A rage just waiting to be unleashed. Tenn knew Aidan had more to hate about the Dark Lady than perhaps any of them. She had promised him everything, had made him turn his back on everything he knew, before turning her back on him. "What are we waiting for? An invitation?"

Fire burned bright in his chest, flames flickering around him like fireflies. It made Tenn think of Devon, made him wonder if Devon had managed when so many others had failed.

Had the runes he placed been correct? Or had Tenn failed in that, too?

"Let's kill this bitch," Aidan growled.

Before Tenn could stop him, Aidan curled flame around his

fist, white-hot and bright as the sun, and hurled it straight at the Dark Lady's heart.

Everything seemed to pause in that moment. The fireball grew in brightness and size as it flew, until it burned like a comet, more destructive than a bomb.

Neither the Dark Lady nor the Wight moved, though a few of the lesser Howls and necromancers twitched or bolted away. The Dark Lady merely stood there, a slight smile on her lips as the fireball neared, and Tenn knew Aidan had wrapped so much hatred and fury into that sphere, it could wipe out a city. As he'd done before. He winced, readied himself for the explosion and rumble.

And then, five feet from the duo, the fireball exploded in a series of sparks that swirled around the Wight, spiraling around the crown of her head before vanishing, sucked inside the creature's forehead.

The Dark Lady laughed.

"How charming. I already told you, magic has no effect." She amplified her words, so they soared over the entire Guild. So everyone could hear how futile this defense was. "Anything you throw at her will only make her stronger. Here. Let me show you."

She snapped her fingers, and the Wight's vacant eyes snapped toward Aidan. It didn't move a limb. Instead, Fire flared in its chest, hotter than even Aidan's Sphere, and motes of light swirled in front of it, spiraling into a ball of fire that propelled itself toward Aidan. Tenn ducked on instinct.

The ball exploded against the shield surrounding the city, became a tidal flame that swept up and over them with a dull roar. Devouring the shield as it went.

"Shield down!" someone called out along the wall, which Tenn thought was a stupid thing to say. Not that it was a secret to the Howls beyond.

The moment the flame washed over them, the dark tide swept forward, and the war began.

CHAPTER SIXTY-EIGHT

DOUBT TWISTED IN AIDAN'S HEART FOR A SPLIT SECOND AS he watched his fireball sent back, as he watched it destroy the little defense they had. Then he pulled deeper through Fire and burned that doubt away.

"The Wight absorbs magic," he growled.

"No shit, Sherlock," Kianna replied.

"She's guarding the Dark Lady." He had to yell over the roar of the crowd racing toward them, over the thunder and lightning pulsing through the sky. Over the chaotic fervor of his own heartbeat. "We have to separate them. It's the only way to kill her."

"And how do you suggest we do that?"

It wasn't Kianna, but Dreya who asked.

"We need to distract the Wight. Draw it away."

Dreya watched the field, her three Spheres blazing, eyes locked on the Dark Lady. She looked otherworldly, her power enough to make his skin crawl. Even after all he'd seen, she had a radiance that was impossible to deny.

"The Dark Lady controls Maya." Her eyes were calculating, and it was clear she couldn't deduce an answer. "She could end us all in a heartbeat if she desired. Undo every last one of us. So why does she not fight?"

"She won't have to if we stay up here blabbing," Kianna said. She grabbed her pistol and unsheathed her sword, looked at Aidan. It was the same smile she'd given him before every other battle. Even here, facing the end of the world, it was a small comfort to know she hadn't changed. "Come on. Let's do what we do best and kill these fuckers."

He smiled.

This was what they had trained to do. What they were born to do.

"Always said we'd go out with a bang. Killing the Dark Lady and a Wight seem like the way to do it."

"Yeah," she said with a wink. "But let's not forget that you're the one who brought them about."

She opened to Earth and vanished, reappearing on the ground, just outside the perimeter wall. Right in harm's way. Despite her cockiness, seeing her down there, facing the oncoming tide of death, made his heart ache. A pain not even Fire could burn off.

This was the end.

This was *their* end.

Even though this was how they wanted to go out, it was still intimidating to realize that this, without question, was the moment they would die.

He turned to Dreya. "Protect her," he said.

She nodded, a dozen words unspoken between them. Then he pulled through Fire and teleported down to Kianna's side.

Just in time to see the cracked and misshapen faces of the Howls surrounding them.

Just in time to let Fire out to play.

CHAPTER SIXTY-NINE

TENN GROWLED AS KIANNA AND AIDAN DISAPPEARED FROM the battlements. They were the only two Hunters on the field, and the Howls swarmed around them like ants on fruit.

But the Hunters on the wall weren't waiting.

Above, the heavy sky broke apart with lightning and rain, and flames swept across the field—burning through foes but often deflected, or turned to fuel by some incubus.

Dreya closed her eyes and began to hum, a terrifying, melancholy noise that made the hairs on his neck stand on end. Air and Water and Fire blazed within her, and at her call, great tornadoes swirled down from the sky, flames billowing within and lightning flashing in tendrils. They scoured over the landscape, swallowing up Howls and burning them alive before tossing them like cannonballs amongst their kin.

Below them, by the wall, the earth rumbled and flames spiraled out, gunfire echoing amidst the chaos. Enough to let him know Kianna and Aidan were still alive.

For how long, he couldn't say. Judging by the tide of Howls, none of them had long at all.

He couldn't make out individuals in the dark mass anymore. But he could tell where the Dark Lady and her Wight wrought their magic—deep in the heart of the swarm, a circle seemed carved out, a place no magic would venture.

From it, the Wight cast her own magic, sent flames the size of tsunamis over the field, carved great swathes in the earth before her. Tenn could barely see the Wight through the blaze of her Spheres. But he saw the Dark Lady. She stood at the Wight's side, her eyes cold and calculating. Maya a constant halo around her, a mirage refusing to break. But she didn't seem to wield her own magic. Then again, why would she need to, when she had the Wight at her disposal?

He had to kill her. Had to. He'd been chosen, had runes the world had never seen and powers granted by the Ancients. This was his destiny. The thought was far from inspiring— with Water pulling at his heart, it was more a weight dragging through his veins.

He didn't have a choice, though. If he didn't act, they all died. And as Hunters took to the field, casting their magics and screaming battle cries and terror, he knew he didn't have long.

And so, he did what he had done before—he opened to Earth and drew the runes of hiding on his skin, wincing against the pain. Dreya glanced over as he winked from existence, but she didn't say a thing. Not that he would have been able to hear her over the roar of battle.

He felt guilty.

He should have said goodbye.

But he supposed, in a way, he'd already done so a dozen times before. They all had.

He visualized the runes of travel and vanished to the field below. He couldn't teleport to the Dark Lady's side, not when she might feel the magic of the runes. He had to rely on surprise. He had to do this the old-fashioned—and more dangerous—way.

This felt like suicide. He might be invisible, but that wouldn't save him from wayward magic, and he couldn't risk carving the Church's symbol into his flesh, not if it might negate the power of the runes. So he ran, Earth fueling his limbs, through the throbbing flesh of the undead horde, and tried not to vomit at the sight or the stench.

Kravens swarmed and gurgled all around him, some old, some freshly made—as was apparent by the amount of decay they'd suffered. He shoved through them. They couldn't see or smell him, and under normal circumstances an invisible force shoving them aside might have been enough to kick their dead minds into thinking something was there, but in the chaos and swarm of the undead tide, he was barely noticed. Not even when he had to cut down kravens who stood in his way with a lance of Earth. Only then, in the midst of death, he realized he no longer had his quarterstaff. He had a few daggers hidden in his coat, but they wouldn't go far.

Like the twins, he'd grown accustomed to relying on magic. He had to hope that was enough.

The ground exploded at his feet, tossing him and a handful of kravens to the side. One landed atop him, and he gripped its throat and pulsed Earth into its heart, ignoring the pain it sent through his own. With a terrible ringing in his ears, he rolled the kraven off and tried to stand.

His ankle gave out with a snap.

Shit. Broken.

He gritted his teeth and pulled deeper through Earth, his stomach rumbling at how much he'd drawn. He ignored it, and channeled the power into his foot, mending it with a sickening crunch as bone cracked into place. When he began moving again, his stomach roared and his body shook. Too much Earth. Too much. But he couldn't tire.

He knew he should utilize Water instead, but he couldn't risk drowning in it. Not now. Not here.

He continued pushing his way through the crowd, dodging swinging limbs and felling Howls, the tide unaware of the reaper in their midst.

And then, like crashing through a wave to the calm on the other side, he reached the Dark Lady and her Wight.

His heart broke to see the Violet Sage like this. Floating a foot in the air, her white robes limp and frayed, her skin dulled to nothing and her eyes pale. The only color on her seemed to come from her Spheres, which glowed with all the ferocity of the sun, a blinding rainbow.

The Dark Lady watched the battle unfold. Maya was a faint purple swirl above her, the shimmer of a thousand-petaled lotus, but Dreya was right—the Dark Lady could have unmade all of them the moment she arrived. Why hadn't she attacked? Why was she relying on the others to do her dirty work?

Now that he was here, he had no idea what to do. He stood on the edge of their perimeter and watched. The Dark Lady had already cheated death once, and that meant he had only one shot to kill her.

Maybe, if he cut her off from magic, she wouldn't be a threat.

The question was, how? He had to split her up from the Wight, and that wasn't going to happen on its own.

Then it clicked.

He knelt and pressed his hand to the frozen topsoil. He had to act fast.

He visualized the runes. And then, with a quick pulse of Earth, he furrowed them into the dirt, ringing them around both himself and the Dark Lady. In the same moment, he flooded the runes with power, and the war around them twisted away.

CHAPTER SEVENTY

DREYA COULD NOT SEE WHERE TENN HAD RUN, BUT SHE could feel the power as it flooded on the field, the twist of Earth that dragged him and the Dark Lady out of sight. She sensed for him, felt him not too far-off, perhaps a mile away.

Wise boy. He had dragged the Dark Lady off on his own accord. To face her alone.

They must work fast to kill the Wight. Before she returned. Before she killed him.

Dreya drew through Air and flew off the wall, floating down toward Kianna and Aidan like a goddess on high. She pulsed Air through the kravens surrounding them, sent the monsters sprawling. When her feet touched the ground, she looked to Kianna. Both she and Aidan were covered in black blood and slashes, but neither seemed to be tiring.

Indeed, it was the most alive Kianna had ever looked.

"Tenn has taken the Dark Lady," Dreya said. "They are perhaps a mile from here. We must act fast to destroy the Wight in her absence."

"But how?" Aidan said. "Magic doesn't work on her."

"See?" Without even looking, Kianna raised her gun and fired. A nearby bloodling fell to the earth in a spray of red. "That's your problem. You rely on magic too much." She looked to Dreya. That smile made Dreya's blood hot. "Lead me to her. I'll end the bitch. You—" she looked to Aidan "—go help Tenn. Gods know he'll need it."

"What about you?"

"I'll be fine. Or I'll die. Either way, there's not much you can do about it. Now go!"

Aidan looked between the two of them. Dreya nodded, remembering his previous words. *Keep her safe.* She would. On her life.

Aidan pulled through Fire and vanished.

Kianna reached out and touched Dreya's cheek. Gently. Her fingers left a streak of red.

"When this is over," she said, "I think we deserve a proper date." She smiled. Dreya's pulse doubled. "Shall we?"

Dreya nodded.

She drew deeper through Air, but for once, she didn't use it to wipe away emotion. She let her pulse race and her heart thrill. In a way, it made her feel even more powerful. Invincible.

With Kianna at her side, she reached deep into her Sphere and blasted a path before them, a lance of air that knocked all Howls and necromancers to the sides. A tunnel. Like parting the Red Sea.

An arrow pointing straight to the Wight.

"Let us end this," Dreya said. She took Kianna's hand. Together, they ran.

CHAPTER SEVENTY-ONE

"TRICKY, TRICKY," THE DARK LADY SAID. SHE DIDN'T SEEM fazed by Tenn's magic or his invisibility; in fact, she smiled. As though this were a game. As though it were finally getting fun. "But not clever enough I'm afraid."

Power rippled through the air, an undulation of a mirage, and Tenn staggered back as he felt Maya connect, as his skin burned, crawling with a million fire ants. He fell to his hands and knees, and when he staggered back up, the Dark Lady was smiling at him.

"There you are," she said.

He glanced to his hands. The runes hiding him were gone.

"Did you think you could save your friends by bringing me here? Did you think you would *spare* them? You merely delay the inevitable, Tenn. As you have always done."

She circled him. Once more, he wondered why she didn't attack, why she didn't rip him from existence with Maya's touch. Did she enjoy playing with them all so much?

Then, the question bounced back—why hadn't *he* attacked

her? After everything she'd done, why was he not on the offensive? Why was he letting her talk?

A voice inside whispered that he wanted to know. To know
why she had done it, why she cursed the world. But that wasn't
the truth. The truth was he still wanted to know why she had
set her sights on him in the first place.

"I've watched you from the very beginning," she said, reading
his darkest thought. "I've watched your struggles and your tears.
I've watched you run from my minions, watched you wrestle
with your fledgling power, with the idea that you might be the
Chosen One. But you are not, Tenn. You are merely another
fighter, another pawn on my chessboard to move as I desire.
Every step you have taken has been by my design. Do you not
see? I needed you to discover the runes that had been hidden
from me, the secrets of the Ancients and the Violet Sage, the
powers that they tried so hard to keep from my hands. And
you gave them to me."

She stepped closer.

"Everything you have fought for has been in vain. Even
now, the lover you went to the ends of the earth to bring
back fights his last fight. Soon, he will die, and he will be
back in my arms once more. Just like your parents." She tilted
her head, a movement that reminded him all too strongly of
Tomás. "Your fight had been in vain then as well, was it not?
Ten days it took you to reach them. And by then, you were
far too late." Her smile chilled his blood as much as her words
did. "But you have served me well, child. Even if you did not
intend to. And I always reward those who serve me."

The world around them rippled.

"Creation is mine to bend. Past and present, they are merely words on a page, words I may at any point rearrange, should I so desire."

He blinked. And there, standing to either side of her, were the two people he had convinced himself he would never see again. At least, not in this lifetime.

"Mom?" Tears filled his eyes. "Dad?"

They looked at him with all the love in the world in their eyes. They were happy. Whole. Not like the corpses he'd found torn apart in the garden shed. Not like the memory that years and violence had bloodied beyond distinction.

He nearly fell to his knees.

The Dark Lady smiled. "They are here. As they have always been, in my arms, from the moment they left this world. I am the Goddess of Death, Tenn. If you were to serve me, I could bring them back to you. I have use of your knowledge. The language of your gods is still largely forgotten. Together, we could bring it back. The power of the old gods, and the new."

When she stroked his cheek, he didn't even have the resolve to slap her hand away. Her words struck too many chords. He could barely even focus on her. He wanted to run over and hug his parents, but he knew that the moment he moved the vision would fade.

He didn't want it to fade.

He reached up, gently took the Dark Lady's wrist, her fingers still light on his cheek.

"You'd bring them back?" His parents might be illusions, but the tears choking his words were all too real. They were here. They were *here*.

"Of course, my child," she cooed. "I could give you everything you desired. The family you lost. And the family you so desperately want to have."

Another ripple, and the world around them changed. His parents vanished, replaced by another vision, one that hit him even harder.

They were no longer outside, but in a kitchen. The walls bare wood, the counters granite, the room crowded with cabinets and hanging pots and the scent of soup. Outside, rain streamed down, filling the room with its incessant patter.

And humming. Someone was humming. He knew the sound...

Jarrett appeared behind the Dark Lady, stepping over to the large pot simmering on the stove. He was older, his long blond hair streaked with gray. But he was more handsome than ever. Tenn watched with a fist around his heart as Jarrett stirred the soup. He was wearing a wedding ring.

Something thudded farther in the house. Jarrett looked up as a great big golden retriever covered in mud scampered in, trailing filth all over the tile floor. Jarrett let out a yelp, and then Tenn appeared in the picture. Older as well, not in the Hunter's garb but a rain jacket and rubber boots, all covered in mud and sopping wet.

Jarrett burst out into laughter as the shadow Tenn tried to reign in the excited dog, making the kitchen even messier in the process.

"This could be yours, Tenn," the Dark Lady whispered, breaking through the illusion. "All of it. You have already proven your love to the gods when you brought the boy back. Do you not deserve a future together? Happiness?"

The vision wavered, but it didn't fade. It was then that he realized he was crying.

He tightened his grip on her wrist. She was so close, he could still smell the grave dirt and perfume clinging to her dress.

"I don't deserve this," Tenn said.

"But you do. You do."

"No." He looked back at her. "The only thing I deserve is your death."

He lashed out, a lance of Earth to her flesh. Just like he'd done to Tomás, but this time, he drew a different rune over her heart.

The sigil of the Church.

The Dark Lady howled and staggered back, her hands to her chest. The illusion faded.

They were back in the field, back in the rain, with Outer Chicago's war still raging in the distance.

He took a step back and readied himself, opened deeper to Earth and Water.

Then the Dark Lady's yell turned to laughter. It made Tenn's skin go cold.

"Not as gullible as the other one, then. But still not very intelligent. What did you do?" She traced her hand over her chest, the smile not slipping. "You didn't try to kill me. No. Ahh, I see. I know that mark."

Her smile widened. Above and behind her, the air rippled with power. Maya. It didn't work. *It didn't work.*

"Did you truly think that some mortal symbol would have power over the Sphere of the gods? You're going to have to try much better than that to stop me."

"That's why I'm here," came a voice.

Tenn looked over, and despite everything, the sight made hope flutter in his chest.

Aidan.

CHAPTER SEVENTY-TWO

AIDAN HAD WATCHED THE TWO OF THEM. THEY LOOKED LIKE they were about to make out, what with the way the Dark Lady stroked Tenn's cheek and he held her wrist. Except for the blank expression on Tenn's face, the tears that spilled out unchecked. And the smile on the Dark Lady's lips that made her look like a panther ready to devour.

Aidan was too far away to hear them. But when he felt the flash of power and the Dark Lady stagger away, he thought perhaps Tenn had done it. She *looked* surprised. What had it been? A lance of power to the heart? Stopping the blood in her veins? Aidan couldn't imagine Tenn would draw out the Dark Lady's death. Not like Aidan would have. Not like she deserved.

Then she laughed, and Aidan knew whatever Tenn had done was nothing more than a scratch.

When she opened to Maya, he knew Tenn had tried cutting her off from magic—his forearm twinged with the memory of that cursed sigil—and failed miserably.

He stepped forward and made his grand entrance.

He still had no idea how the hell they were supposed to kill her.

Tenn looked relieved to see him, and Aidan for his part felt a small surge of pride in that. Until the Dark Lady started laughing.

"Ah, together at last. Let me guess—you believe that your powers combined can defeat me? Because some cultists in the woods told you so?"

"Something like that," Tenn growled.

"Well, then, shall we see how wrong they were?"

She reached out, clawing her fists at both of their hearts. Pain shot through Aidan from his head to his toes, his heart twisting and burning. He fell to his knees. Heard Tenn thump down beside him.

Fire winked out in a breath. A breath that wouldn't return.

He felt himself falling. Falling.

In the darkness, he heard his mother scream.

CHAPTER SEVENTY-THREE

SCREAMING.

In the darkness, he heard screaming.

The screams of his family as they ran from the necro-mancers. The screams of his friends as they ran from his flames. The screams of his enemies as they paid for their sins.

In the darkness, Devon heard only screaming.

Amongst the screams were his own.

Offerings on the altar.

Atonements.

I am not worthy.

I am sorry.

I must end this.

I must avenge you.

He reached through the darkness, toward the glowing white door.

It opened on silent hinges.

Silent hinges.
Light flooded.
Screaming stopped.

CHAPTER SEVENTY-FOUR

KIANNA RAN AT DREYA'S SIDE, SWORD FLASHING IN THE HALF-light. The Wight floated before them as if confused without her master next to her. Confused, but not without purpose. She opened to Earth, and behind them, half of Outer Chicago fell with a disastrous roar, a rumble that nearly toppled Kianna and Dreya to their knees.

Dreya glanced back. To see the great plume of dust. The fires that billowed up to the sky.

A hundred innocent lives snuffed out in a heartbeat.

Not for the first time, she doubted they stood a chance.

Then the Wight took notice of them, and Dreya's emotion vanished as a great burst of flame swept toward them.

She yelped, tossing Air ahead of her and forming a hasty shield. The Wight's fire roared off it, searing the ends of Dreya's hair, crisping her fingertips. It had been close. Too close; if she let herself get distracted, they would surely fail. They kept running.

The Wight wasn't finished; the ground crumbled away, disappearing in a chasm that yawned down to infinity. Kianna yelled out as she leaped to the other edge. Dreya hoisted herself up with Air. And still, they ran, Howls on either side of them straining against Dreya's shield.

She ran, and her breath came out in gasps. Not from the exhaustion, but the magic used to keep the other monsters at bay, and the one before them from killing them on the spot. Her mind swam, a blur from the haze of Air spiraling in her throat. She kept her eyes on the Wight. With that in sight, even the backlash of Air could not sway her from her true purpose.

Kianna fired her gun, a single shot, but the Wight was fast. Too fast. The bullet exploded in a tiny burst of Fire inches from the creature's face. Kianna growled.

"Distract her!" she yelled.

Dreya did what she could.

They were closer now, only a few yards away, close enough to feel the wrongness emanating from the Wight like a disease. Dreya called down lightning, striking not the Wight but the ground beside her, sending up chunks of earth that sent the Wight reeling to the side.

Dreya didn't let up. If magic wouldn't affect the creature, she would harm it with the environment.

She opened to Water and froze the rain spiraling from the sky, sending it down like daggers onto the Wight. Only a few shards made it through the creature's shield, but it was enough to disorient it.

Enough to divert its attention solely to Dreya.

Flames burst around Dreya as the Wight struck. Another quick shield, this one thinner than the first. Just enough, barely enough. Dreya struck back, a bolt of lightning that nearly blinded her.

"Oy! Watch it!" Kianna yelled.

Dreya bit back the panic, her stray thoughts reeling. She was flinging magic around without a care. What if she hit Kianna?

Another burst of flame shot the thought from her mind.

No time for precision. No time.

She was so close to the Wight that she could see her pallid features, the unique markings on her skin. The dark runes scratched over every inch of exposed flesh—the Dark Lady's workings, no doubt. Runes to bend the girl to her will.

The pity returned, just for a moment, until the Wight struck out again, a pulse of Air that knocked Dreya backward. The air didn't let up. It pinned her to the ground, and as she tried to right herself the earth itself wrapped around her ankles and wrists, binding her down.

The Wight hovered over her.

And for the first time since she watched her family burn, Dreya was afraid.

She tried to open to Air, but the Sphere eluded her. Her breath caught.

She stared up into the Wight's pale eyes and began her internal prayer, a hymn for her own death. Around her, the shield she struggled to uphold faded. The monsters were starting to break through. She would die. She would die.

A gunshot.

A hole burst through the Wight's forehead.

And the Wight crumpled to the ground at Dreya's feet, a marionette loosed from its strings.

Silence fell. A breath after a storm. Dreya's own breath. Her lungs burning.

Even the Howls went silent.

Kianna stepped to Dreya's side, reached out a hand.

"Looks like you owe me a date."

Even surrounded by monsters, Dreya smiled and took her hand. Let Kianna pull her up.

"The war isn't over quite yet," Dreya said, her voice breathy.

Kianna smiled and let go, turning to face the Howls that had begun crawling forward, seeking fresh meat.

"Consider this the foreplay, then."

Dreya giggled. Opened to Water and Fire.

Then she heard her brother's voice within her mind: *You two are disgusting.*

CHAPTER SEVENTY-FIVE

POWER FLOODED THROUGH HIM, ELECTRIC AND HOT, AND sent flames over his skin and through his veins and he felt alive, *alive*, his senses, synapses and the light everywhere, everywhere, *everywhere* as he awoke from the dream or the meditation or maybe he had awoken *to* the dream, because when he opened his eyes he was in darkness; he knew he mustn't be in darkness, knew there was a fight, a light, and he willed himself to be there—

and he was.

floating above the Guild with fire in his veins and he could see them, the thousands of Howls stretching to the horizon and the thousands of threads stretching even further, the threads that connected the Howls to each other and the Howls to the Hunters and the Howls to the Everlasting that lay beyond and behind and within them—he felt them, he saw them, and he saw the smaller threads, the ones connecting stone and grass and wind, and he knew how he could manipulate tug stretch pull snap them, and he knew to do so would have its own equal and opposite effect on him, as that was the way of the world—he could kill.

and he would be killed.

because that was the balance, that was the way, but there was another thread, a darker thread, one that pulsed on the horizon with shadows and raven wings and he knew *that* thread should not be, had lasted far beyond its time; that thread was wrong, and it was worth dying for, but as he floated and watched the threads and the flames he saw the threads snapping off, cutting apart, as life after life was lost—Howl or human, they made no difference, the threads were all the same—and although he couldn't give his life to use Maya for those lesser threads, Maya was not the only power in his veins.

he had a fire within him, one he had snuffed and stuffed deep within with meditation and mantra, and he had burned himself from the inside out to contain it, had let it burn away his words and burn away his hopes and burn away his everything until he was just a shell for the flame, a vessel for the anger, and now he was something new, something more, but that flame still burned and that anger still raged and he still had to find a way to let it out—

he let it out—

fire from his hands and from his fingertips.

fire from the sky and fire from the ground.

and the world was the sun and the sun a darkness compared, and he roared with anger and ecstasy as he finally released the flame, as he finally became the flame, as flames licked his skin and seared his flesh and charred his clothes and burned his hair and even his scarf trailed to the ground, a smoldering flag, a burning offering, floating to the fires that raced across the countryside below, burning through threads and snuffing lives as he himself had snuffed out his, and in the flames he felt his sister, heard her voice.

her love.

her eternal love for him, her faith that he was not a monster, even though he *was* a monster, even though he now let the world see it; he didn't burn her, nor the woman that stood beside her—Dreya deserved a better life, a life only he could give her, a life his death would ensure,

and as the flames scouring the Howls spread, as the screams lessened until the only sound was the roar of flame, he turned his sights to that darker thread, that pitch-black strand that wound itself from decay and back again, and he willed himself there.

and he was.

facing the woman that should not be.

and the boys who thought it was their destiny to destroy her, the boys who writhed in agony on the earth;

she faced him.

she knew him.

just as he knew her, the thread that bound both of them, the shears they both wielded, the act they could each only do but once;

You are the Goddess of Death, he said without speaking, *and now it is time for you to die*—

and he struck, reached out and grabbed the thread that bound her to life, that one immortal cord—

she didn't have time to scream or respond—

he severed her thread.

and in turn severed his—

CHAPTER SEVENTY-SIX

TENN STOOD IN SILENCE, AIDAN AT HIS SIDE, STARING AT THE place Devon and the Dark Lady had been.

Seconds had turned to minutes, and he still wasn't certain what he'd seen.

Fire on the horizon, brilliant and bright.

And then, Devon before them, the air around him rippling like water on a lake. Staring down the Dark Lady. Before—

"Are they dead?" Aidan asked.

"I don't know."

One moment the Dark Lady and Devon had been standing there. The next, they were gone. Only space and silence.

He and Aidan didn't move. Moving felt like it would shatter a dream. Only Tenn couldn't decide if it was a dream or a nightmare. The Dark Lady was gone, but so was his friend.

Dreya and Kianna appeared later in a swirl of magic.

They were holding hands.

"Did he—?" Dreya asked.

"He undid her," Tenn replied. "They both vanished."

"Of course," Dreya whispered. She paused and looked at the emptiness. "All Spheres have a price. A blowback for their use. Maya's must have been one of balance. Any act would require an equal and opposite payment. That is why the Dark Lady did not kill with Maya. To do so would have destroyed herself. She had the greatest power in existence, but could not herself wield it to kill." She sniffed. A single tear traced her cheek. "Devon gave his life to end hers."

Light and power flared above Outer Chicago, and moments later, Jarrett stood in their midst.

"Is it over?" His face was bloodied and scratched, and despite everything, Tenn wanted nothing more than to reach out and heal those cuts. "The Dark Lady and the Wight—"

"They're gone," Tenn said. "Along with Devon. He...he was the one who destroyed the Dark Lady."

"And I," Kianna said, stepping forward with a bow, "killed the Wight." She winked at Aidan. "May not be the first person in history to kill a Kin, but I'm definitely the first to shoot a Wight between the eyes. Suck on *that*."

Aidan rolled his eyes.

Jarrett took a step closer to Tenn. He opened his mouth as if to speak, but there was nothing to say.

It felt like this should have been a triumph. Surely, somewhere, other Hunters were celebrating.

But here, in this circle, they bowed their heads, paying tribute to the one who gave his life to save all of theirs.

"I don't get it," Aidan said.

They sat alone in one of the remaining rooms. The others

had all gone off on their own. Dreya and Kianna, still holding hands. And Jarrett, to find Cassandra and deliver the news.

The Dark Lady was gone.

The threat was over. For good.

"What don't you get?" Tenn asked.

"I thought…" Aidan flicked a small flame around his fingertips. "I thought that it was supposed to be us. Or one of us. You know. Who killed her."

Tenn nodded.

"Me, too. But I guess… When I was with the Violet Sage, she told me it wasn't about being the Chosen One. It was about choosing to take up the call. It was about all of us. I guess it didn't matter who decided to attune to Maya. It just mattered that someone did."

"Yeah, but. That still doesn't explain why you were sent to find me."

It made Tenn think about what Jarrett had said. Or, a variation of it. "Some people think they know what the gods want. But I don't think it's possible. We worked together to find the runes to truly attune to Maya. If we hadn't found each other, we never would have been able to do that. Maybe that was why—we needed to see the light and the dark in order to end things."

"Maybe," Aidan said. He watched the flames dance. Tenn thought maybe that was the last of their conversation. He found it strange that he'd spent so much time around this guy, and this was the first time they'd truly talked. At least, as equals, and not as enemies. "Do you miss him?"

"Who?" He knew.

"Tomás."

Tenn sighed. He tried not to think of the Kin. After all, Tomás was gone, and there was no changing the past—besides, he was a monster. Even if the monster had treated him like a prince. He had Jarrett; Jarrett, who had apologized, who had asked to start over. He'd also lied to and imprisoned Tenn. Tenn still wasn't certain what that meant for the two of them. With Tomás, he had always been the prey, had always been the one toyed with. At least with Tomás he always knew where he stood.

He hated to admit it, but there would always be a part of him in love with Tomás. Or, at least, in lust. Tomás was the embodiment of all his darkest desires, the ones even Tenn hadn't known he'd harbored. It was hard to ignore just how powerful that was, even when it had been used against him.

"I do," Tenn said. "He made me feel—"

"Alive."

"Yeah. Alive. Do you?"

"Bastard tried to kill me," Aidan said. Emotions flickered over his face. Not one of them was anger. "But yeah. I do. I probably shouldn't have, you know, killed him like that."

"I don't know. It was dramatic. I think he would have appreciated that at the very least."

Aidan watched the flame a bit longer, sighed, and let the sparks die.

"What happens now?" he asked. "I doubt that was all the Howls in existence, and you heard Kianna—so long as we have magic, there will be people out there who will abuse it. Before long, another Dark Lady or, I don't know, Dark Lord, will show up, and it will be hell all over again."

"You almost sound sad about that. I thought you liked killing?"

"It just means none of us are out of a job yet. Besides, there's still the Church to contend with. I don't think they're going to be happy to learn their little secret's out. Can't imagine they'll have many followers when the world realizes the Dark Lady was one of them. And that they'd made a deal with the Kin."

A knock on the door. Tenn knew who it was even before he opened his senses to the runes that bound them. He opened the door with a pulse of Earth, and Jarrett stepped in.

Jarrett paused when he realized it was the two of them. He looked younger then, awkward. The cuts on his face had been cleaned up and healed. With a pang, Tenn realized he was jealous he hadn't been the one to do it.

"Sorry." Jarrett looked to his feet. He actually seemed sorry. "Didn't mean to interrupt."

"You weren't," Aidan said. He stretched and took a step to the door. "I was just leaving."

"Leaving?" Tenn asked. His heart fell. They were finally on good terms. Could finally start pooling their knowledge.

When he saw the resolve in Aidan's eyes, however, he knew better than to push. There was still a gravity between them. Aidan could go to the ends of the earth, and they would still find themselves back within each other's orbit.

"I'm back in America. I can finally go find my family. Or, you know—"

"Yeah," Tenn said, remembering his own parents, trying to remember them as they would want, and not as corpses or toys of the Dark Lady. "I know."

"Do you think Kianna will go with you?" Tenn asked.

"Nah. I think she's finally found a reason to stick around."

"And you?"

"I don't stick around." He grinned. "But I'll be back. Haven't you realized? We're the chosen ones. We're bound to be together."

He patted Jarrett on the shoulder and walked out the door.

Jarrett watched him go. Tenn didn't know what to expect from his former lover. But then Jarrett chuckled.

"I can't pretend I'm sad to see him go," he said when Aidan was out of earshot.

"I heard that!" Aidan yelled from down the hall.

Well, almost out of earshot.

Tenn laughed.

"I don't think that's the last we'll see of him."

"Of course not. I wouldn't be so lucky."

Jarrett went silent. An awkward, heavy silence that hung between them.

Jarrett had asked if they could start over. This felt like starting over. It felt like they had never seen each other before. And maybe they hadn't. Tenn had always been the chosen one in Jarrett's eyes. Now, he was just another human. Just like Jarrett.

"Can I sit down?" Jarrett asked.

Tenn scooted over on the bed and patted the cover. Jarrett sat awkwardly.

Neither of them spoke. Tenn had no idea what to say.

It was Jarrett who broke the silence.

"You may have gotten your wish."

"What do you mean?"

"It's over. We can have a normal life now."

"This will never be over." Tenn's voice was more bitter than he meant it to be. He tried to soften it. "And we'll never be normal."

Jarrett nodded.

"But I'm okay with that. It will keep things interesting."

"That it will," Jarrett said. He put his hand on top of Tenn's. "That it will."

Despite the last few days, Tenn didn't flinch away. Jarrett's hand was heavy and warm on his. Comfortable. Tenn leaned his head on Jarrett's shoulder. Closed his eyes. Tried to imagine a new future. And then, when he realized it was futile, he let the thought go.

They sat in silence, listening to each other's breath, letting the future unfold on its own.

For once, that was enough.

That was enough.

CHAPTER SEVENTY-SEVEN

AIDAN PAUSED OUTSIDE THE GATE TO OUTER CHICAGO.

He'd considered seeking out Kianna. Telling her his plan. Giving her the choice to join him. But he didn't want to tempt her, didn't want to give her any reason to leave this place. They'd known from the beginning they'd part ways. That had always been the endgame. He was just following through, and letting her do her thing guilt free.

Not that he really thought she had it in her to feel guilty. Did he?

He stared out at the ashes. Sun was beginning to peek through the clouds, illuminating the reds and the blacks, the embers and sparks, all of it billowing slightly in a breeze. He felt it, that siren's call, but it was muted.

Fire was no longer as angry.

Without that heat, he thought he'd feel empty. Without the Dark Lady whispering in his heart, he thought he'd feel aimless. He'd killed all the Kin. He'd saved the world. Well, mostly him, anyway.

Did it redeem him? For everyone he'd killed?

He looked down to his arm, to the Church's brand and his mangled fingers. He'd never believed in redemption. And if he did, he'd already paid in blood. At the end of the day, it evened out.

At least, that's what he told himself.

He also realized that, if he found his family, he might leave a few details of his claim to fame out of the narrative.

He knew he was lingering. Drawing this out.

If he was honest with himself, he was scared. Not of any monster, but of what he might never find. But that was no reason to stay.

He'd spent his life seeking out reasons to kill.

Now, it was time to find a reason to live.

He looked back one more time. Hoping to see Kianna standing in a window, waving him on. Giving him her blessing. Behind him, there were only shadows. He looked forward.

Looked ahead.

He opened to Fire and, like a spark in the sun, vanished into the light.

CHAPTER SEVENTY-EIGHT

DREYA LAY BACK IN HER BED, IN THE ROOM SHE HAD ONCE shared with her brother, stroking Kianna's hair as the woman rested her head in Dreya's lap. The room should have felt emptier, and perhaps in a way it did. But with Kianna there, the emptiness was almost bearable. It was a comfort that would not last—she knew this in every rational cell in her body. Soon, she would turn to take her brother's hand, or speak his name in her thoughts, and she would find only silence. The thought brought tears to her eyes. And she let this happen. Let the room waver in the firelight. Let her tears fall atop Kianna's head.

If Kianna noticed, she said nothing. A small grace.

At least, right now, she did not feel alone in her pain. And that pain did not make her feel small. Or powerless. It made her feel human.

Her thoughts shifted when she felt Aidan leave, and she opened her mouth to tell Kianna this. But when she looked down, she found Kianna sleeping.

Peaceful.

Dreya did not want to disturb that peace. They would each battle their own emptiness soon enough. For now, let them be together.

So she sat there, and she breathed, and she closed her eyes, letting herself feel the pain of her brother's loss. The absence.

I am sorry, she called out. *I just hope… I want you to know…*

And perhaps it was her imagination. Perhaps it was her need.

But there, in the darkness, she felt his hand on her cheek, wiping away her tears, and she knew he wasn't gone—not truly. He was with the Ancients now. He was ever with her.

Perhaps they were her own words curling through her head, and not the spirits. But they carried his voice, and she heard them all the same.

I know, Andrea. And I will always love you, too.

What do I do now? she asked.

You live, he responded. *This is our story. All of our stories. And it is up to you to write it.*

* * * * *